ANOTHER TIME, ANOTHER LOVE

Other Scholastic books you will enjoy:

Winter Love, Winter Wishes
by Jane Claypool Miner

A Winter Love Story
by Jane Claypool Miner

Forbidden
by Caroline B. Cooney

Unforgettable
by Caroline B. Cooney

Malibu Summer
by Jane Claypool Miner

ANOTHER TIME, ANOTHER LOVE

Vivian Schurfranz

SCHOLASTIC INC.
New York Toronto London Auckland Sydney

No part of this publication may be reproduced in whole or in part, or stored in a retrieval system, or transmitted in any form or by any means, electronic, mechanical, photocopying, recording, or otherwise, without written permission of the publisher. For information regarding permission, write to Scholastic Inc., 555 Broadway, New York, NY 10012.

ISBN 0-590-50966-7

12 11 10 9 8 7 6 5 4 3 2 1   5 6 7 8 9/9 0/0

Printed in the U.S.A.   01

First Scholastic printing, November 1995

Chapter 1

Cathy threw down her napkin, glaring at her mother. "You just want to get rid of me!"

Sara O'Brien reached over and placed a hand over Cathy's. "Now, you know that's not true. Until you decided to accept Aunt Hannah's invitation, Zack had planned to buy four tickets for the Shaw play. One for you, for Johnny, for me, and for him."

Cathy pushed back her thick red hair and sniffed. "I wouldn't want to interfere with you and Zack anyway!"

"I'd love to have you stay in Chicago," Sara said in a soft tone. "And so would Zack. He thinks you're a special young woman."

Zack! Zack! She was sick of hearing his name. "Forget it! I'll be in Princeton and glad of it!" she snapped. As soon as the words were out of her mouth, she regretted them. She glanced into her mom's reproachful eyes.

"Sorry," she murmured. She wouldn't hurt her for the world.

When her dad died three years before, she and her mother had drawn together. After their home was sold, they hunted for a place to buy. They trudged to every model apartment and went to one open house after another. They consulted Johnny, her younger brother, and Dylan, her older brother, every step of the way, as they checked out condominiums and townhouses. Johnny, only five, was asked what he wanted in a room.

Finally, they located just the right townhouse on Lake Michigan.

A year later, her mom began to date, but no one man for any length of time. For the last few months, however, she'd only been interested in Zack Preston. Clearly, this romance was serious. Why, Cathy thought bitterly, did he have to enter their lives? And now he'd spoil the Christmas holidays, too! But not for Dylan, away at college. And not for Johnny. He liked Zack. Or maybe it was the Cubs baseball games Zack took him to last summer. Or now the Bears football games.

She had to admit, though, that she'd never seen her mother so happy. After all, if she, Cathy, had Mike Novak, why wasn't her mother entitled to have someone? But Mom was forty-six years old, for pete's sake! Cathy pushed back from the kitchen table and re-heated her coffee in the microwave.

She should be glad that she had somewhere to go. Aunt Hannah and Uncle Frank had coaxed her to visit and since she'd never been East to see them, she'd agreed. She'd miss Mike and even though she didn't say it aloud, she'd miss Mom and Johnny, too. She hated to be away from home but she'd never admit it. After all, she had turned sixteen last month! Old enough to be independent.

"You'll have fun with Aunt Hannah," her mother said, her pretty face breaking into a smile. "You can help out in her antique shop." She cleared the dishes, putting them in the dishwasher. "I'll be working most of the time."

Cathy loaded her coffee with sugar and cream. "Since you were elected city clerk, all you do is work," she complained. A black and white cat entwined itself around her leg. She reached down and scratched his ear. "No food, Phineas. You've been fed." The cat stalked away, his tail raised high like a plume.

"I need to be the best city clerk Chicago's ever had," Sara said, "so I'll be reelected."

Cathy sighed. Everyone was a workaholic. Sure, she studied hard. If she intended to go to college, she had to stay on the honor roll.

That wasn't easy with volleyball practice and being captain of the swim team. Also, writing for Pulaski's school paper, *The Write Stuff*, took lots of time. But at least she was home *some* of the time.

Cathy knew she was feeling sorry for herself, but no one had time for her over the holidays. Her two best friends, Liz and Dana, would be gone. Liz Majeski was off to Mexico with her family, and Dana Greene was going skiing in Ironwood, Michigan. But worst of all, Mike Novak, the boy who put stars in her eyes, was *again* helping his father, Bill Novak. Obviously, Mike wanted to be a politician just like his father, who was an important alderman on the city council. Plus last September Mike had enrolled at DePaul University. Being a freshman in political science, Mike needed to study. He was *always* busy!

Cathy wished she could be as focused on *her* future. Right now she didn't have a clue as to what she wanted to do. At present she needed to concentrate on her junior year at Pulaski High.

"In a few days you'll be on vacation," Sara said. "I think a couple of weeks of play is exactly what you need. You'll be able to do that at my sister's."

"I suppose so," Cathy murmured. Only a few more days to be with Mike. This afternoon they planned to walk by the lake, then pig out on pizza, and tonight take in a Dracula movie. Because she hadn't seen Mike for three days, she couldn't wait to be with him!

"Would you like to go with me to St. Luke's Hospital to see Ruth Erickson?" Sara asked.

"What happened to her?" Cathy inquired.

"A car hit her while she was biking along Fullerton Avenue. Poor Ruth! She has a broken arm and leg!"

"Tough break," Cathy replied, without thinking. Then smiled at her pun. So did Sara. "Mike will be here at two," Cathy continued. "Otherwise I'd go with you." She paused, giving her mother a sidelong glance. "Isn't Zack coming over?"

Sara O'Brien shook her head. "Not today. His architectural firm is drawing up blueprints for the new civic center. He'll be working until midnight."

Well, Cathy thought, standing up, that was one less day she had to face Zack. "Mike and I will be home by ten," she said. Her heart picked up a beat. To think she'd be with Mike a whole afternoon and evening! What reason did she have to be glum?

" 'Mornin'." Johnny bounded into the room, shook cereal into a bowl, added milk, and plunged in with his spoon.

"You certainly slept late," Cathy commented, smiling at how his orange-red hair, more fiery than hers, spiked out around his freckled face.

He shrugged. "Why not? Sundays are great for sleep!" He reached for a cinnamon roll. "Mom," he asked, between mouthfuls, "can I stay overnight at Ronny Michelini's tonight? He's got a new computer hockey game."

"Yes, if it's okay with his parents. Will you go to school with him in the morning?"

"Sure."

"Don't you have a project to turn in?" Sara asked. "You don't want to forget it." She reached over and turned down his turtleneck sweater. "I hope your assignment is finished before you play any games."

"Ronnie and I are working on our reports first thing. Mine is going to be the best animal report and drawing in the whole class!" He grinned at his mother and puffed out his chest.

"Such ego!" Sara said with a smile. Johnny could be an irresistible imp! "What animal did you research?" she asked.

"The skunk," he replied. "I wish I could bring a real one to class."

"I don't think Ms. Dreblow would like that," Cathy said.

Johnny hooted with laughter. "It'd be fun, though! Everyone would rush outside!" He faced his mother, and said hopefully, "Is Zack coming soon? He promised to play Hockey on Ice with me."

Cathy gave him a resigned look. How easily little kids could be won over! "You and those games, Johnny," she said in an annoyed tone. "It's a wonder your brain hasn't mushified!"

Playfully, the young boy jabbed her shoulder. "Just 'cause I beat you every time."

Cathy nodded, trying to suppress a smile. "I hate to admit it, but you're the best."

"Outside of Zack," Johnny hastened to add.

With a pang, Cathy realized how much Johnny liked Zack, and how much she hated him. Why did this tall stranger have to invade their lives?

"I've got to run," Sara said, slipping into a checked jacket. Her Levi's and sweater emphasized her trim figure, and her short blonde hair, framing an oval face, gave her a youthful air. "I'll be back around five. Then tonight I plan to soak in a hot tub and read the latest Michael Crichton book. Have fun, you two."

As soon as her mother closed the front door, Johnny crammed his books and papers into a backpack. "See you tomorrow after school's out, Cath!" he shouted, scampering out.

Cathy glanced out the window at the bare trees and the blue lake just beyond. She enjoyed the quiet. Going upstairs she tried to decide what to wear. Something special. For Mike.

Phineas, sprawled across the bed, yawned and stretched at her approach. Cathy sat next to her lazy cat and stroked under his chin. Phineas lifted his head and rumbled a low purr of pleasure. "You're a silly cat, Phineas," Cathy said, rolling him over and rubbing his stomach.

Standing, she straightened the duvet cover and placed the stuffed penguin at the head of her bed. She smiled, remembering how her penguin collection started. In sixth grade Ms. Barkley had asked each student what they collected. In a panic she hadn't known what to say. She didn't collect anything! When her eyes fastened on a poster of Antarctica with penguins on the ice, she relaxed, knowing what to answer.

"Cathy?" Ms. Barkley asked. "Do you have a hobby?"

"I collect penguins," she blurted out.

"How unusual," Ms. Barkley commented. "Good for you."

She had breathed a sigh of relief, and from that date penguins began to accumulate. Every birthday and every holiday brought a new penguin. It was surprising how many penguins were manufactured in all shapes and forms. Clay, wood, glass, cloth, and paper ones. Her bookshelves overflowed with the black and white creatures!

The phone shrilled, interrupting her memories.

"Hello," Cathy said.

"Hi, Cathy, this is Zack," he said in a cheerful voice. "How are you?"

"Fine, thank you," she responded coolly.

"Is your mother home?"

"No, she's out."

"Do you know when she'll be back?"

"No, I don't." And she didn't know *exactly*, but she should have volunteered the approximate time.

"Okay, Cathy, would you have her call me? I'll be in and out all day, but she has my car phone number."

"Okay," she answered, hanging up. She felt guilty not telling him her mother was at the hospital, but she didn't care if he ever called again.

She'd just replaced the receiver when the phone rang again.

"Hi, Cathy."

This was the voice she loved. "Hi, Mike, I thought you'd be on your way." She clutched the phone tighter, willing him to be late and *not* to say he couldn't come.

But her worst fears were realized when he said, "Sorry, Cathy." His words were halting. "I wanted to be with you, but I can't today. Could we postpone it until tomorrow?"

For a second she remained quiet, too crestfallen to speak. She should say she had plans, but time was too precious. Besides, she longed to be with him too much to play games. "Tomorrow is okay," she said in a choked voice. "Why couldn't you come today?"

"There's an important vote coming up tomorrow in the city council," Mike said in his deep resonant voice, "and my dad is preparing a report. We need two more reading centers in the forty-ninth ward. I'm drawing the graphics for the meeting."

"Oh," she said, unable to hide her disappointment. "Then I'll see you tomorrow." Abruptly, she hung up and threw herself on the bed. Phineas nuzzled her hair and she reached back pulling the cat against her. "Phineas," she cried into his neck fur, "it's going to be another lonesome night." Tears burned her eyes and she found it difficult to swallow.

When the phone rang again, she almost didn't answer but was happy she did. Dana wanted to meet her at the mall and go ice-skating. She didn't hesitate. Wiping her eyes, she jumped off the bed and raced downstairs. Why should she mope here alone?

Struggling into her down jacket and tossing her skates over her shoulders, she hurried to the Skate on State rink at the State Street Mall.

"Hi, Dana," she said breathlessly, sliding onto the bench beside her good friend. "I'm glad you called." She hoped her face wasn't all blotchy and red, but Dana didn't seem to notice.

Pulling on her shoe skates, Dana stood, skating up and down in front of Cathy.

"I had to get out of the house," Dana explained. "The twins were driving me crazy!" She rolled her eyes, wrinkled her nose, and twisted her mouth. "What's more I almost had to take them with me!"

"What saved you?" Cathy said with a smile. Dana always had crises, and her face always reflected them.

"Dad. He promised Terri and Tony ice cream. While they ate, I sneaked out the front door before they could miss me." Dana, her plump figure clad in bright blue tights, a Pulaski

High School jacket in black and gold, and a red stocking cap, didn't notice the crowd's good-natured waves. She leaned back, arms high overhead, and twirled in an easy lay-back.

The brisk air, the laughing skaters, and the rush of a cold breeze across her face as she raced around the ice, erased Mike from Cathy's mind. When "Rudolph, the Red-Nosed Reindeer" blared from the loudspeakers, Dana grabbed her hand.

"Come on, Cathy, I'll lead the way. Put your arms around my waist. Hey, everybody!" she shouted, speeding up. "Let's have some fun and snake around the rink."

A tall boy hugged Cathy's waist, followed by two girls. Then many skaters fastened on, weaving to and fro around the circle to the rhythm of the music. Faster and faster Dana flew, her powerful legs pumping. "Crack the whip!" she yelled. Others tried to join the long line but couldn't latch onto the last skater.

At last the line of skaters peeled off, and Cathy dropped onto a bench, exhausted. Dana skated a few more laps and joined her.

"Ready for a Coke?" Cathy asked, removing her skates.

"Sure, let's head for Mustard's Last Stand," Dana replied, not even winded.

Once they ordered, Cathy wished she could

match Dana's high spirits, but when she remembered Mike and their lost day, her heart sank.

Dana chattered on, her round cheeks and snub nose as red as Rudolph's. "Tomorrow after school, Mom and I will pick up Felix at the Cat Tree House."

"Oh, Felix, the cat with a sneeze?" Cathy asked. "I hope he's well so you can adopt him."

"We called. He's fine." Dana lifted her brows and grinned. "You should see Felix. I knew he was for me when he leaped onto my lap and made himself right at home."

"Felix sounds almost as perfect as Phineas," teased Cathy.

"Oh, he is!" Dana said, nodding positively. "What a place, Cathy! The Cat Tree House is an orphanage for cats." She chuckled, drawing on her straw. "I just want to take every cat home. But Mom said I could have *one* cat, not *one hundred*!" Finishing her Coke, she pushed it aside.

She snapped her fingers. "Why didn't I think of it. Why don't you come with us? You'll adore Felix."

"Sorry, Dana, but tomorrow Mike and I are going out." Cathy bit her lip. It would be their last time together. Tuesday was a half day of school because of Christmas Eve, and Mike's family was driving to Des Moines, Iowa, to visit his grandparents. Early Wednesday morning she'd leave for Princeton.

"So, why so gloomy?" Dana questioned. "You want to see Mike, don't you? Be glad you've got a boyfriend. I'll be lucky if I get asked to the junior-senior prom!"

"Oh, since Mike started college, he's either studying, or helping his father, or volunteering at the reading center." Cathy toyed with her straw. "I want to be part of his life, not just someone he sees occasionally." She took a deep breath, remembering last summer. "In August we saw each other a lot."

"I know," Dana said. "Remember I asked you up to our cabin in Wisconsin, but you couldn't go 'cause you and Mike were making posters for the Howard Street Community House and the reading program." She puckered up her mouth and gave Cathy a wink. "You're pretty busy yourself, you know."

"I always have time for Mike, though!"

Dana pushed herself out of the booth. "If only I had a Mike. He's tall, dark, and handsome, just like the hero in *Love's Tender Embrace*, the romance novel I'm reading. Mike Novak is serious, but when he smiles, his whole face lights up. Yup, I'm not the only girl who's drooling after such a hunk!"

"I know I'm lucky. Mike's a sweet guy."

"Of course, Cathy, you're not so bad your-self. I wish I had your thick hair instead of these wisps growing out of my scalp." She blew upward and a thin strand flew off her forehead. "And that color! Women who color their hair in fancy salons would kill for that deep shade of red. And your bod! And those green eyes!"

"Stop, already!" Cathy laughed. "You make me sound like a model!"

"You could be a model!" Dana countered, zipping up her jacket. "Another Cindy Craw-ford!"

Cathy touched her good friend's arm. "You always make me feel better, Dana. But it still hurts when Mike cancels out. And on one of our last days together, too!"

"If you don't want to wait around for Mike, you could choose a dozen other guys!"

"I wouldn't choose anyone but Mike!" Cathy said, following Dana outside. "He's the one for me!" Their boots crunched on the snow as they walked by the animated store windows of Fields, depicting the Pinocchio tale. "And," she continued, "you have to admire him for volunteering in Chicago's reading program. I just wish he'd volunteer a little more time for me!"

That night, Cathy snuggled deep beneath the covers. She had hoped Mike might have left a message on the answering machine, but he hadn't. Why should she be surprised?

With a pang, she sat up. Zack's call! She hadn't told her mom. Had she deliberately forgotten? Maybe subconsciously she wished to sabotage their friendship. She sank back on her pillow and firmly closed her eyes. But sleep wouldn't come. Relationships! Some days you could do without them!

Chapter 2

Monday morning Cathy awoke, relishing the day ahead. School would be a "write-off," and at three o'clock Mike would pick her up. Humming, she pulled on a bulky sweater, stirrup pants, and ankle boots. She checked herself in the mirror, lightheartedly flipping back the thick hair that fanned out over her shoulders. Her glowing complexion needed no makeup, but she outlined her lips in wine-rose. Stepping back, she was pleased how her green sweater brought an emerald sparkle to her eyes. Could it also be the anticipation of seeing Mike?

Going into the kitchen, Cathy poured a small glass of orange juice, glancing at her watch. Eight o'clock. She had plenty of time. Liz wouldn't be here until eight-thirty.

"Good morning," her mother said, taking a slice of bread and dropping it into the toaster.

Cathy admired her mom's silk blouse and

slim-tailored black skirt. A perfect look for her!

" 'Morning, Mom," Cathy replied, sipping her orange juice. "Is Johnny still at Ronny's?"

"Yes, they'll go right to school from his house, remember?" Sara answered, taking an envelope from her pocket. "We heard from Dylan."

"Great, read it, will you?" Cathy said, nibbling an English muffin.

Sara poured a cup of coffee and sat down.

Oxford, England
December 5, 1995

Dear Mom and Cat,

Oxford is great. My room overlooks the Thames River and I like Clive Chatman more and more. It's nice to have an English roommate who explains the meaning of: "tube" = subway; "lift" = elevator; "bonnet" = car hood; "boot" = trunk; "lorry" = truck; "bumbershoot" = umbrella; "petrol" = gas, etc.

I learned the meaning of food terms in a hurry. So, Mom, when I come home and ask for these, you'll know what I mean:

"rasher" = bacon

"bangers and mash" = sausage and potatoes

"bubble and squeak" = cabbage and potatoes

"chips" = french fries

The campus is full of huge old trees and Gothic arches. The countryside is just like every English film I've ever seen. Clive is a good chap (see, I'm even talking like the British) and knows his way around. Yesterday we walked the length of High Street, stopping in the Lion Pub. We ate fish and chips washed down by a pint of ale.

Cat, I understand you're visiting Aunt Hannah and Uncle Frank. When you see Princeton, you'll get a good picture of where I'm living. Bertrand Russell once said, "Princeton is as much like Oxford as monkeys can make it."

Clive and I are going into London for the weekend. We'll stay with his friends. Hope to take in the theatre and gawk at London Bridge and the Tower of London.

Pip-pip and cheerio to you both and Johnny and happy holidays!

Dylan

"Sounds like big brother is having a good time," Cathy said.

Sara smiled. "It does, doesn't it?"

All at once Cathy felt a stab of guilt. She bit her lip, unable to eat another bite. She finally stammered, "Zack called last night. I — I forgot to tell you."

"He did?" Sara said, her brows lifting. "How could you forget when there's a pad and pencil by each phone?"

With no excuse, Cathy couldn't reply.

Sara poured a second cup, turning her back on Cathy, and said in a low voice, "You know, Zack and I are very fond of each other. I'm sorry that every time he calls or comes by, you're miserable." She faced Cathy. "I want to continue seeing Zack, but not at the expense of losing my daughter."

Cathy lowered her eyes. What could she say? Zack made her feel rotten! No one could take Dad's place. Finally, she whispered, "I'm sorry." She rose. "Liz will be here any minute. We'll talk about Zack later. I promise."

The toot of a car horn saved her. "There's Liz," she said, grabbing her sheepskin jacket and rushing outdoors. The air cooled her burning cheeks.

As she climbed in the front seat of Liz's Blazer, Steve Billingsley, Liz's latest, slid to the middle. "Hi-ho!" he chortled, "Happy hollydays to you!" The gangly tall boy peered at her over his glasses.

She smiled. "And you, too, Steve." She liked him.

"Hi, Cathy," Liz said. "You look sensational."

"Thanks, Liz." Cathy smiled at her close friend. Liz's long blonde hair, pink complexion, and big blue eyes gave her a baby doll exterior, but underneath there was grit and determination.

Putting her mother and Zack out of her mind, Cathy turned to the back of the car and greeted Dana, Danielle Tobin, and Jonah Allen. Dana gave her a high five. "Only half a day left!" Dana sang.

"Amen!" Jonah shouted.

"Amen!" Everyone echoed.

Their high spirits continued all the way to the student parking lot.

School was as much fun as she thought it would be. In French they sang French carols. History class passed quickly. A panel of four dramatized a meeting of Freud, Hillary Clinton, George Washington, and Joan of Arc. Jonah, who portrayed Freud, affected a gutteral accent and was marvelous. The only bummer was period three, English. After a spirited discussion of *David Copperfield*, horror of horrors, Ms. Schmidt announced a test on the Dickens novel the next day. With her arms folded, she waited patiently for the groans and protests to die down. She explained firmly how much easier it would be to take the exam now, rather than wait until they returned.

Right, Ms. Grinchness, Cathy thought. Well, she didn't intend to study Charles Dickens tonight. She had better things to do! She looked at Dana, who twisted her face into a terrible grimace.

Journalism, loose and informal, fared much better than English.

Mr. Kyropoulos greeted her. "A Merry Christmas to you, Cathy." He indicated a row of computers. "Before you leave today, will you finish your article on the volleyball tourney?"

"Sure, Mr. K.," Cathy said brightly. "No problem." Her happiness, which had dimmed in English, again bubbled to the surface.

Cathy worked fast, writing up the Pulaski Kits' loss to the East Leyden Eagles. She concluded the piece on an upbeat note, writing how strong the 1995–96 season would be with so many returning seniors.

Someone placed their hands on Cathy's

shoulders. "This is farewell, my lovely." He twirled her swivel chair around.

A short boy with twinkly eyes grinned at her. Cathy's eyes widened. "Eric Chapell! I thought you had left."

Grinning, the jaunty boy leaned over, dangling a sprig of mistletoe above her head. "Pucker up, Cathy." And before she could protest he swiftly bent down and kissed her cheek. "Hmmm. Delicious!" He smacked his lips. "Our bus whisks us to the airport in an hour!"

"Christmas in Japan!" Cathy beamed at him. "You'll have tales to tell. How many students is Ms. Nickels taking?"

"Fifteen. Our first stop is Osaka, our sister city. Most of our time, though, will be in Toyko." His grin widened. "By the way, Mara Dusalt is going." He waggled his brows in a leer.

"Now's your chance to get better acquainted," Cathy said. "Just don't come on too strong." She remembered his attempted romance with Traci Wilkes. He'd followed her everywhere — sat next to her in the cafeteria, set up his easel next to hers in art class, trailed her home after school, and generally made a nuisance of himself.

"Oh, I'll be subtle," Eric promised. "I learned my lesson with Traci. But," he added in a teasing voice, "since you're taken, Cathy, I need to find a new heartthrob."

Cathy laughed, standing and looking down at Eric. "Oh, Eric, you're loco. I guess that's what I like about you!"

"Sure, *now* you tell me!" His smile vanished. "Oh, Cathy," he said, a warm look crossing his puckish face, "Mara is perfect. She's nice, she's cute, and she's short!"

Cathy boosted herself up on a table, swinging her legs. "Enjoy Japan, Eric, and give me an interview when you get back."

"Sure thing!" Waving the mistletoe high overhead like a lasso, Eric called over his shoulder, "With this, my flight will be quite jolly! Sayonara, Cathy."

A husky tall boy, Eric's opposite, came by. "Got your story for the sports section, Cathy?" Lance Bigelow asked. The editor of *The Write Stuff* was always on top of each story. Lance, efficient and meticulous, drove the staff berserk. But not today, Cathy thought. Nothing could upset her today.

"I'll print it out, Lance," Cathy answered cheerfully, jumping down from the table. In a few seconds she handed him the copy. "It's finished!"

Removing a pencil from behind his ear, he checked it over. "It's fine." He glanced at her through heavy horn-rimmed glasses. Then a small smile creased his frown. "Cathy, have a great holiday. But," he added, "as soon as we return in January, I want a sensational piece on the Flipper swim team, okay?"

"You got it," she said.

When three o'clock came, Cathy dashed down the steps and outside.

"Cathy!" Mike shouted. "Over here."

A familiar red convertible inched around a long line of cars with a dark-haired boy sitting behind the wheel.

"Hi, Mike," Cathy said, buckling her seat belt and nestling comfortably in the crook of his arm.

He drove carefully around the parked cars and headed toward Lincoln Park and Lake Michigan. It was a beautiful December day. Sunny and bright with a light coating of snow.

Waves, glistening in the sunlight, rolled up onto the shore. Gulls dipped and sailed high overhead, while ducks waddled along the shore. Mike and Cathy got out and strolled arm in arm by the lake. It was their favorite place.

Mike brushed Cathy's hair with his lips. "I missed you yesterday."

"Not half as much as I missed you," she said, remembering her tears and talk with Dana.

Mike, a head taller than Cathy, looked down at her, his dark eyes sober. "I wish you were going to be here over vacation."

"But you'll be in Iowa."

"Only for a few days. We come back on Sunday." The wind picked up and he raised the collar of his leather jacket. His hair ruffled in the breeze. They walked to the lighthouse and back.

Once in the car, Cathy asked, "How did the presentation go?"

"Very well. Dad has enough votes to set up two more reading centers in his district," he said, clearly pleased.

"You're such a do-gooder," Cathy teased with a smile.

He chuckled. "You've helped me lots of times. You can't fool me, Cathy. You care as much about people as I do."

"But the Howard Street Community House isn't my whole life," she protested.

As they left the park, Mike drove to the shopping mall and parked. He helped her out and they hurried into the Olive Garden Cafe, sitting in a back booth. "Cathy," he said, "you should see the look on my foreign students' faces when there's a breakthrough. Teaching them to read English is one of the most rewarding things I've ever done!" He stopped to give the waitress their order. "Last week," he went on, "one girl stumbled through a few words from a primer. Today she read whole paragraphs from the *Tribune*." He smiled. "Her whole face lit up!"

"Like yours now," Cathy bantered, drinking her Coke and gazing at him. "I know it's wonderful, Mike, but you're spreading yourself too thin."

He held her hand and smiled at her. She could drown in those soft brown eyes. "I stay busy, sure," Mike said. "But my grades are high. Besides, Dad needs my help."

"I need you, too," she stated in a quiet tone, an ache touching her heart.

His hand tightened on hers. "You're the love of my life. Please understand, Cathy, that I want to be with you all the time, but I do have other commitments."

"I understand," she responded, squeezing his hand. "Truly, I do."

They ate a spaghetti dinner and they caught the seven o'clock movie. Afterward they sipped an espresso, then Mike took her home.

Standing on the front stoop of the townhouse, Mike said, "Tomorrow school is out at noon, isn't it?" He bent and touched her cheek.

"Yes, but I'm through at eleven. No Journalism."

"We're not leaving for Iowa until two," Mike said. "Why don't we go for a quick lunch. We'll say good-bye then."

"I'd love that," she said. "And, Mike, I'll be back before you know it. It's less than two weeks."

He wrapped her in his arms and kissed her.

His arms were secure and loving. If only they could stay like this forever! Cathy thought.

"You're the only girl for me," he said in a husky voice. He backed away. "I'll pick you up at eleven, okay?"

"I can't wait," she whispered, looking into his eyes.

"In the moonlight your eyes sparkle like the stars," he said smiling warmly.

"See you tomorrow," Cathy said, her heart racing. "I love you, Mike."

He blew her a kiss. "And I love you!"

Opening the door, she felt like the luckiest girl in the world. As she hung up her coat, she heard the buzz of voices.

Johnny's laughter erupted from the kitchen.

Cathy moved forward, but froze when she heard Zack laugh. She listened, not moving a muscle. "Over the holidays we'll take in a Blackhawks hockey game," he promised. "Would you like that, Johnny?"

"Would I!" Johnny whooped.

"I understand you're quite a hockey player, yourself, Johnny," Zack said.

"Oh, he is," Sara chimed in.

"You should see me, Zack!" Johnny shouted. "I can outskate some fifth graders!"

Cathy moved forward, peeking in the kitchen. Her mother, Johnny, and Zack were smiling and eating chocolate cake and ice cream. Sara and Zack drank coffee and Johnny's mouth, ringed with white, obviously had milk.

"Cathy?" Sara called. "Is that you?"

Reluctantly she entered the kitchen. "Hi," she said, placing a hand on Johnny's shoulder.

"We're eating chocolate cake," Johnny said. "Want some?"

"I'll cut a piece for you," Sara offered, rising.

"No, thanks," Cathy said hastily, backing up.

"Did you have fun tonight?" Zack asked, his eyes crinkling in his lean leathery face when he smiled.

"Yes," Cathy answered shortly. "No cake, Mom. I'm tired." She turned. "Good night, everybody."

With leaden feet, she climbed the stairs. Apparently Zack had won over Johnny, but he'd have a more difficult time with her!

She undressed; she wished Zack would go away, but as she slipped between the sheets, she somehow knew he was here to stay! She turned out the light, her heart heavy. How could Mom forget Dad so easily?

Chapter 3

At school the next morning, Cathy's classes were almost empty, since many students had started their vacation a day early. Cathy wrote her English exam and thought her essay rated at least a B. Not bad for not studying. Her last class sent an elated tingle up her spine. She'd be seeing Mike in fifteen minutes.

She walked toward her locker quickly.

Dana rushed toward Cathy, wisps of hair flying. "I'm leaving, Cathy. Dad is out front waiting for me."

Cathy gave Dana a hug. "Have fun, and don't break a leg on the slopes!"

Dana chortled. "Hey, why not! The ski group I'm going with has lots of beauty queens. If I sit in the lodge with my broken leg propped up, maybe the boys will notice me!"

"They'll notice you without a broken leg!" Cathy said, smiling.

"And you, Cathy," Dana said, narrowing her eyes. "Don't you dare go out with those Princeton college boys! You might forget Mike!"

"No chance!" Cathy laughed. "I'll never forget Mike!"

Just as Dana turned to leave, Liz flew down the hall, hailing them. "Wait, you two!" Breathless, she stopped. "I hoped you hadn't left!" She embraced first Dana, then Cathy.

"Yep, I'm off for schussing and sloshing," Dana quipped, a wide grin creasing her features, and her eyes crinkling into tiny slits.

Cathy glanced from Dana to Liz. How different her two friends appeared. Dana, short and plump, with thin brown hair ringing a round face. In contrast, Liz, tall and slender, had long golden hair. Cathy loved them both.

Dana wagged her head in agreement. "I've got to run!" She pursed her lips, blew them a kiss with her fingertips, and spun about. Soon, she was out of sight, lost among the many students in the corridors.

Liz smiled at Cathy. "How about you? Will you see Mike before your flight?"

"Yes," Cathy said. "We had a wonderful time yesterday, and today he's picking me up for lunch."

"Cool," Liz said, hugging her books to her

chest. "In ten hours I'll be basking on the beaches of Puerto Vallarta. While you'll be having a Princeton holiday, I'll be having a Mexican one!" A slight frown clouded her blue eyes. "I'll miss Steve, though." Her face brightened. "But I'll be with my whole family! Dad is footing the bill, just so everyone can be together!"

"That's great," Cathy said. "Your older sister and who else?"

"Well, my older sister, Elise," Liz repeated, "along with her husband, Walt, and their three kids."

"Wow! Quite a family reunion!" Cathy smiled.

Liz grabbed Cathy's arm, steering her down the hall and stopping at her own locker. "Mom and I have been buying bathing suits and shorts like crazy." Her laugh was low and soft. "You should see Mother! She's about to jump out of her skin with excitement!"

"You, of course, are calm and collected," Cathy bantered.

Liz smiled. "I can't wait to get on the plane. I wish Steve were going."

"I know he'll miss you, Liz. Wouldn't anyone?" Cathy said, catching a glimpse of a tall boy leaning against Liz's locker. "Speaking of you-know-who!"

"Steve!" Liz called out.

"Liz! I've been waiting for hours!" Steve Billingsley said, standing up straight. But behind those glasses, he smiled warmly at Liz and held her books as she twirled combination numbers.

"Hi, Cathy," Steve said, giving her a side glance. "Going away for the holidays?"

She answered, although clearly his mind and eyes were riveted on Liz. "Yes, I'm off to Princeton."

The tall boy stared at her. Now, she had his full attention. "Princeton! That's one of the best! Are you planning on enrolling there after you graduate?"

Cathy shook her head. He sounded like Mr. Ober, her guidance counselor. Counselors wanted juniors to visit colleges and make decisions, but she wasn't ready to think about college. Steve had set his sights on Stanford when he was a sophomore and expected others to be just as efficient and farsighted. Who knows, she thought. Maybe she'd work a year before she went away or maybe she'd stay right here in Chicago. She could choose from loads of good colleges and universities in her hometown.

"No, Steve," she answered. "I'm not checking out the university. I'm visiting my aunt and uncle. Uncle Frank is a history professor at Princeton."

"Oh," he said, losing interest and turning back to Liz. "Enjoy yourself, Cathy." His casual tone dismissed her, but she didn't mind. He was too wrapped up in Liz.

"Mike is out front, waiting for me," she said, moving away. "Have a merry Christmas and happy New Year."

Liz squeezed her hand. "You, too. Tell Mike hi."

Cathy walked away until she reached the Gothic main doors.

After a few minutes, she checked her watch. Mike should be here by now. She craned her neck, but no familiar red convertible appeared. Students rushed by her, eager to begin their holiday.

"Cathy O'Brien?" a boy named José Cardova hurried to her side. "I look for you. Sorry. I take you a message."

"Hello, José," she said pleasantly. She had met this boy in one of Mike's night classes at the center. Tilting her head, she waited for his message.

"We beg Mike to learn us one lesson. One more." José flashed a smile and his dark face lit up. "He go away. We ask for one more lesson."

Cathy forced a smile. "And Mike agreed to tutor you, of course!"

"Yes, yes, how you know?"

I know Mike better than you think, she thought. She glanced at José with a touch of bitterness.

"Mike say you understand." He scooted past her. "*Felíz Navidad*," he called and disappeared down the street.

"And *Felíz Navidad* to you, too, José," she murmured, going down the steps. She kicked at the mushy snow as she walked along the deserted sidewalk. Happy shouts and laughter that had filled the halls had faded. Joyful students and teachers had long since left the building. Cathy reached up and hit a branch, showering wet snow over her hair and shoulders. A van drove by, its loudspeakers electrifying the air with strains of "Joy to the World."

"But there is no joy in Mudville," she whispered, "Mighty Casey has struck out!"

Going into the house, she heavily climbed the stairs. Tonight was Christmas Eve. Mom, Johnny, and she would have a lovely dinner and open their gifts. She should be thankful.

Phineas sat on her bed, gazing at her like the Sphinx. "I know," she said, talking to her enigmatic cat. "I mustn't take it out on Mike.

A missed lunch isn't a disaster."

Phineas yawned.

"But we didn't even have a proper good-bye," she protested.

Phineas jumped off the bed and meowed.

"It's too early for your dinner, Phineas!"

Phineas rolled over on his back, his sea-green eyes observing her face.

"You think I'm crazy, don't you?"

Phineas sat up, licking his paws then rubbing his ears and whiskers.

Cathy changed into sweats. "A run is what I need."

And before Phineas could meow again, she was down the stairs and out the door.

Jogging to the lake and along the shore, Cathy relished the cold rain that pelted her face. She ran north to Touhy Beach and back again. By the time she returned, she had shaken off her self-pity.

"Hi, Cathy," Mom called. "Want to help Johnny and me bake gingerbread men?"

Winded, Cathy paused in the doorway and smiled at her brother. "I can see you're a big help, Johnny!"

"I *am* a big help!" he said, grinning. A smudge of flour dotted his snub nose. "I'm licking the bowl!"

"Ugh, raw cookie dough," Cathy said, wrinkling her nose. "You two are doing such a good job, I'll go up and shower and change."

Sara said, "We're almost ready for tonight."

After showering, she dressed. As she put on her red plaid skirt, navy sweater, and navy tights, the image of her father filled her thoughts. Thick snow-white hair topped a youthful face. His turned-up nose and jaunty walk matched his personality. Everyone liked Sean O'Brien! And how her dad loved the holidays! He was a fine tenor, being a member of a barbershop quartet. She loved to hear him sing the old Irish songs.

A lump formed in her throat at the memory of his funeral. She had bit back her tears for Johnny's sake, but when the pallbearers carried Dad's casket down the aisle, and sang "When Irish Eyes Are Smiling," uncontrolled tears rolled down her cheeks.

"Cathy," Sara called. "Will you make the salad?"

"Sure, Mom." She hurried downstairs, grateful for her mother and Johnny. Christmas, though, would never be the same.

Chapter 4

Christmas Eve was a magic time of trimmed trees, twinkling lights up and down the streets, and pine wreaths decorating doors. Along the lakefront stood a giant menorah, reminding everyone what the season represented — peace and brotherhood.

The O'Briens' tree, decorated with golden balls and topped with a golden angel, stood in the window. In addition, a cranberry garland scalloped along the banister, a velvet Santa Claus perched on the end table, and red and green candles were everywhere.

In the kitchen, Cathy arranged the cranberry mold on salad plates, and helped her mother remove the crispy brown turkey from the oven. Johnny poured water into crystal goblets. Tall candles cast soft flickering lights over the sparkling silver and china.

After giving thanks, they heaped their plates

with turkey, mashed potatoes and gravy, dressing, and scalloped corn. Cathy wondered where Zack was tonight, but was grateful he wasn't here. Mom respected the time she had with her son and daughter.

Cathy glanced at Johnny. "What did you do this afternoon besides lick cookie dough?" she asked.

"Melissa came over and we played outdoors." Johnny's eyes shone with excitement. "Look in the front yard and you'll see what we did."

"I'll do that," Cathy said, smiling. She felt warm and happy, and hoped Mike felt that way, too. In Iowa, he'd eat a late dinner, similar to this one. Well, she thought, smiling, not quite. Grandmother Frances Novak always served sauerkraut, roast goose, and Polish sausage plus the customary turkey.

"Did Dylan eat a dinner as good as this?" Johnny asked, slumping back in his chair and clasping his hands across his stomach.

"I'm sure he did," Mrs. O'Brien said. "Instead of turkey, he probably had Yorkshire pudding and roast beef. I hope he's enjoying himself."

"We know from his letter that he loves England," Cathy said, finishing her salad. "Clive is really showing him London."

"Does anyone have room for dessert?" Sara asked, a small smile playing about her lips.

"I do!" Johnny said in a loud voice, an infectious grin spreading across his freckled face.

"I thought so," Sara said, chuckling. She left the room and returned with pumpkin pie and whipped cream.

"Coffee, Cathy?" Sara asked, filling her own cup.

"No, thanks," Cathy said, tasting her pie. "Hmmm. Yummy."

"Time to open presents?" Johnny sang out.

"Almost," Cathy said, pushing back her chair and helping her mom clear the table. Johnny, using the candlesnuffer, doused the candle flames.

Cathy came into the den, drying her hands on a dish towel. "Before we open our gifts, let's see what mischief you and Melissa cooked up this afternoon."

"No mischief!" Johnny gleefully ran to the window, drawing back the drapes.

Cathy peered out. In the moonlight stood a snowman. No, wait. It was a snowwoman! The rounded figure wore an apron, a yellow wig, slightly askew, a red hat, and she had a red purse. The kids had stuck in plums for eyes, strips of red pepper for lips, and from the wig dangled carrot earrings. "What a sweet little woman!" Cathy purred in a soft voice. "You tied an apron on the little dear."

"That was Melissa's idea," Johnny said, his bright blue eyes direct.

"Sure, Johnny," Cathy said, laughing. "Your snowwoman is gorgeous."

"Gift time," Sara called.

Sitting cross-legged around the brightly lit tree and near the fireplace, Cathy handed Johnny a package.

Untying the fancy bow, Johnny lifted out a complicated computer football game. "Yes!" He pumped the air with his arm.

Cathy unwrapped a long box. "What can this be!"

"As if you didn't know," laughed Sara.

Cathy lifted out a pair of shiny skis. "Oh, Mom," she said, warmly, "how did you guess what I wanted?"

"I have my ways," replied Sara, pleased that Cathy liked her gift.

Sara opened her present from Johnny and held up a large wool scarf. Leaning over, she squeezed his arm in delight. Next, she opened a smaller box from Cathy. Nestled in the tissue lay a silver frame containing a picture of Johnny, Dylan, and Cathy. Holding it at arm's length, Sara exclaimed. "It's beautiful. My three babies!"

"Babies!" Johnny snorted.

"We sat for a photographer last summer," Cathy explained.

"What a perfect gift!" Sara's eyes became suspiciously moist.

They were about to open smaller presents when the doorbell rang.

Sara jumped up. "I'll answer it."

Cathy sank back on her heels, wondering who could be calling on Christmas Eve.

Her back stiffened, though, when she heard the familiar deep voice. Zack! Why did he have to show up!

Johnny ran to the door! "Zack!" He danced around the tall man who had shed his overcoat and gloves. "Come in."

A smile creased Zack's craggy features as he strode into the room, blowing on his hands. "Temperature's dropping!" he exclaimed.

Sara slipped an arm through his and gazed at him warmly. "Sit by the fire," she said, indicating a wingback chair. She sat on the floor beside him, hugging her knees to her chest.

Cathy rose, her stomach clenched tight, and dropped into a chair across the room. She examined Zack from a distance. He wasn't particularly handsome. He wore glasses, had long legs, a prominent nose, and graying-brown hair. Age lines, too, furrowed his forehead. His eyes, though, showed self-assurance and intelligence and when he looked at Sara his eyes brimmed with love. Cathy had a glimmer of why her mother was infatuated with him. That's all it was . . . infatuation, Cathy thought.

But he'd never win Cathy O'Brien over. Not in a million years! She resented the way Johnny sat on the floor beside him. Both her mother and her brother fawned at his feet. Not her! Not ever!

Zack reached in his pocket and handed Johnny a gift, then held out a small box to her. It was beautifully wrapped, tied with a red bow surrounded by red satin roses. "For you, Cathy," Zack said. "I hope you like it!" His expression was kind but wary. He appeared to say, Cathy, why do you dislike me?

Reluctantly, Cathy accepted the gift. She hated to owe Zack anything!

First Johnny opened his box, his mouth forming a large O. "Whoa! Look at this!" He held up a large-faced sports watch. "Thanks, Zack!" Immediately, he strapped it on his wrist.

Cathy opened her box as fast as she could.

Might as well get it over with! In a small velvet box shone a pair of silver hoop earrings. "Thank you," she said, trying to keep her voice cordial. The earrings were lovely, but she doubted if she'd wear them.

"You're welcome, Cathy," Zack said, quietly searching her face. "I hope you have a wonderful holiday in Princeton."

"Oh! Speaking of Princeton," she exclaimed, leaping up and moving toward the stairs. "I'm not packed yet. Will you excuse me?"

A slight frown settled between Sara's brows, but her tone was light. "Of course, dear. I'll see you later."

As Cathy climbed the stairs, she glanced back. Zack gave Sara a gift wrapped in gold and tied with a gold ribbon. Her heart plummeted. What if he'd given her mom an engagement ring? She entered her room and flung her bag on the bed. She couldn't bear Zack for a stepfather. If they married, maybe she'd stay in Princeton and never return! Maybe she'd run away from home! Her thoughts raced along with each item she packed: Pajamas, robe, slippers, sweaters, jeans, panties, bras, and blouses. Obviously, Zack Preston's gift to her mom was very expensive. She was sure of it. And the package, just the right size, might contain a diamond ring!

A terrible loneliness descended over her. Her mother was always occupied with Zack, and Mike was always plain occupied. Left out in the cold, she wondered where she belonged. Sometimes she felt alienated from everyone and everything!

Chapter 5

On the ride to the airport, Sara drove. Cathy sat in front and Johnny sat in back. As unobtrusively as possible, Cathy glanced at her mother's left hand. She almost gave an audible sigh. No diamond ring.

Sara said, "You went upstairs too early, Cathy. You missed the exciting gift that Zack gave me."

"Oh?" Cathy replied, feigning disinterest. "What was it?"

"This!" Sara said in a light happy tone, pushing up her sleeve.

Cathy's eyes grew big. She didn't want to gush, but she exclaimed, "It's beautiful!" And it was. The gold bangle bracelet, at least an inch wide, sparkled in the morning sun.

"Yes, I couldn't believe such an elaborate present," Sara said, moving her wrist so that the heavy gold circle glittered and shimmered.

"Architects must do very well," Cathy commented drily.

Sara laughed. "Yes, Zack is quite well-off, but he works hard for his money, too."

"His condo is cool!" Johnny piped up. "You should see it!"

"When were you there?" Cathy asked, turning and looking at Johnny.

"Last week," Johnny replied. "He invited Mom and me for supper before the Blackhawks game."

"Oh, I remember," Cathy said.

"Wait until you see Zack's place!" Johnny grinned, his blue eyes crinkling into slits. "He owns a pool table!"

Cathy said nothing. She didn't care if she ever saw Zack's condo. As they rode by motels and cafes, she dismissed Zack from her mind.

Going through the toll booth leading into O'Hare Airport, Cathy breathed easier. At least now she didn't need to worry about her mother marrying. Of course, Zack could present her with a ring anytime. It was sort of like waiting for the guillotine blade to fall.

Large planes circled the tarmac. One taxied directly overhead, on a runway crossing the highway.

"Look at that jet!" Johnny shouted, twisting his head to get a better look.

"That's the kind of plane you'll be on, isn't it, Cathy?" Sara asked.

"Yes, it's a jumbo jet that flies into New York's La Guardia Airport."

"While you were in the shower this morning," Sara said, "Aunt Hannah called. She and Uncle Frank will meet you at the gate."

"Good." Cathy shuddered to think what would happen if no one met her. Being lost in New York would be scary. Sure, she was a city girl, but she still didn't want to be left alone in a *strange* city.

Sara easily maneuvered her van around double-parkers, taxis, and limos, stopping before a United Departure entrance.

"Call me tonight," Sara said. "I hate us being apart on Christmas Day."

"Zack is taking us to a Japanese restaurant, Mom," Johnny interrupted. "Did you forget? He said it would be a very different kind of Christmas."

"Cathy will be in Princeton before we leave for Kyotos," Sara said.

"We're going to eat raw fish!" Johnny said, pleased with himself.

"Sushi," Cathy corrected.

"Why are you shushing me?" Johnny asked in an indignant voice.

"No, I'm not shushing you," Cathy said with

a laugh. "Raw fish is called sushi."

"Sushi?" Johnny repeated, liking the sound of it. "Sushi."

"And when you come back, Cathy," Sara said, "Zack has promised to take us to a new restaurant."

"That's nice," Cathy said, "but chances are, I'll be going out with Mike."

"Zack enjoys talking to Mike," Sara said. "He'd like Mike to join us."

Cathy leaned over and kissed her mom. "We'll see," she murmured. "Two weeks is a long way off.

" 'Bye, Johnny. Merry Christmas," Cathy said, giving him a bright smile. She'd miss him, but would he miss her? Not with Zack keeping him occupied. "Don't eat too much raw fish!" she teased.

"Sushi," he retorted, pleased with his new word.

"Do you want me to come inside with you, Cathy?" Sara asked.

"No, Mom. You don't need a ticket. The way the police shag cars out of here, you don't dare leave for a second."

Cathy hugged her mother. "Merry Christmas."

"You, too," Sara answered, kissing Cathy.

Cathy scrambled out of the car, grabbed her bag, and hurried into the terminal. She hated good-byes and didn't intend to prolong hers any longer than necessary.

Checking her bag, Cathy walked through the metal detector and stopped to buy a Coke. Before she'd finished her drink, her flight was called.

Seated by the window, she fastened her seat belt and leaned back. She adjusted her earphones and tuned her radio, ready to turn it on when they were in flight.

Once in the air, surrounded by clouds, her thoughts drifted to Mike. Did he miss her as much as she missed him? She had the uneasy feeling that the only one who'd miss her would be Phineas, and she wasn't so sure about her cat.

The flight attendant poured an orange juice, handing it to Cathy. Adjusting her radio to dreamy music, she closed her eyes, remembering a day last August. She'd dubbed Mike's convertible "the roadster." They'd picked up Liz, Steve, Dana, Nick, and Tony, who Mike laughingly named "the chums."

They drove to Oak Street Beach for a swim. The sun-splashed day had been filled with laughter and a wild game of volleyball. Later, when the moonbeams shone over the lake, they'd grilled hot dogs and brats.

When they were alone, Mike had taken her in his arms. She smiled at the memory. Mike, tan and lean, tenderly gazed at her, whispering against her hair that he'd never met a girl like her. She'd been so happy and his kiss had caused her pulse to race. How she had longed to stay in his arms forever!

Dear serious Mike. He'd told her he planned to enter politics like his father. Maybe that way he could contribute something to this world, even if he only made a small dent. She'd nestled in the crook of his arm, content to listen and feel safe and secure.

That summer night they'd fallen in love. And every day her love for this sweet interesting boy had deepened. Even though he was a "take charge" person, he was vulnerable, too.

The pilot broke in on her thoughts, "In fifteen minutes we'll be landing at La Guardia." She removed her earphones when the fasten seat belt sign flashed on.

Cathy gazed out at New York City's magnificent skyscrapers looming along the horizon. As the plane dipped lower, a complex of apartments, factories, and shoreline came into view.

Deplaning, Cathy walked into the United Airlines waiting room.

"Cathy!" Aunt Hannah waved, from behind a roped off area.

Cathy moved toward her aunt and uncle, kissing first Aunt Hannah, then embracing Uncle Frank.

"Merry Christmas. It's good to see you, Cathy," Uncle Frank said. "Let me look at you." He held her at arm's length, admiring her. "You've grown into a beautiful young lady." He beamed at her, and Cathy smiled, too. How much he looked like the typical professor. His bald head, with tufts of gray jutting over his ears, glasses, beard, tweed jacket, and vest pulled tight over his big stomach, all gave him a jaunty air.

Aunt Hannah hugged her again. "Come along, Cathy. We want to show you Princeton before the sun goes down and it's over an hour's drive from New York."

"I'm ready," Cathy said, squeezing her aunt's hand. Hannah, short and plump, didn't look anything like Sara, her sister. Her short straight hair and bangs surrounded a round smiling face. Her too tight jeans and too big sweater were visible proof that clothes weren't her first priority.

"I'd love to see Princeton," Cathy said, walking between the two of them. Maybe Mom was right. This vacation might be just what she needed. Her aunt and uncle appeared genuinely glad to see her.

Chapter 6

Arriving in Princeton, Uncle Frank drove down Nassau Street, the main street, passing the college campus and into a charming neighborhood lined with maple trees. Frank parked before a two-story frame house, painted yellow and trimmed in white with black shutters. Nearby houses were painted the same shade. "What a pretty house," Cathy said.

"You might call it 'Princeton yellow,' " Uncle Frank said. "Many houses in town are this color."

"Let's get your bag," Aunt Hannah said, "and go in."

Once inside, Cathy glanced around. If Aunt Hannah owned one antique shop, this house could be a second. The small living room had a fireplace with an Early American eagle hanging above it. Two curved loveseats were placed on either side and upholstered in a Colonial print. The red design with tiny blue and yellow flowers looked wonderful against the pale yellow walls.

"You'll get the tour later," Aunt Hannah said with a smile. "Come upstairs, and I'll show you your room."

Cathy loved her back bedroom, decorated in lavender and white.

"I'll leave so you can unpack, Cathy," Aunt Hannah said in a cheerful voice. "Then come down and we'll have tea." She grabbed Cathy's hand. "I'm glad you're here. We'll have a good time."

Cathy returned her smile. "I know we will." And as she put away her clothes, she hoped she would have a good time, but she'd be away from home, in a strange place that she knew nothing about. She'd be without Mike, without her friends, and without her family. She stared at the quilt with squares of American and British soldiers of the Revolutionary War. How could she have a good time? She drew in a deep breath. She'd try to make the best of her holiday.

After brushing her hair, Cathy joined Hannah and Frank in the living room. She sat in a loveseat across from them, admiring a porcelain tea set displayed on the coffee table. A small tree decorated with miniature antique toys and Santa Clauses stood before the bay window, white lights twinkling. Beneath, a wooden train circled the tree.

"I'm eager to show you my antique shop, the Blue Tiger," Hannah said, handing Cathy a pink teacup.

Uncle Frank chuckled. "You know everything in Princeton has to do with tigers since that's the name of our football team."

Carefully, Cathy lifted the cup to her lips. The gold-rimmed teacup must be a real antique, she thought, fearing it might break for it was as fragile as an eggshell. "When will I see your shop? I'd love to help out." She set the cup down, not wanting to handle it any more than necessary.

"Oh, Cathy!" Aunt Hannah said. "I'd love it if you'd help. We're taking inventory tomorrow."

"We?" Cathy questioned, glancing at Uncle Frank. He looked rather ludicrous holding the delicate teacup with his little finger extended. "Are you helping, too, Uncle Frank?"

"Me?" he guffawed, setting down his cup and adding more sugar. "Not on your life. I'm researching a book on the Revolutionary War. You won't see much of me. I'll either be working in my office or at the library."

"You're writing a book?" Cathy said, impressed.

"My second," Frank said proudly, draining his tea. "My first was called *The Summer of 1776*. My new one will be *The Valley Forge Winter of 1776*."

"I'm sorry," Hannah said, "that you're too late to see Washington crossing the Delaware!"

Puzzled, Cathy repeated, "Washington crossing the Delaware?"

Uncle Frank smiled broadly, unbuttoning his jacket to free his ample stomach. "No, no. Every Christmas morning they reinact Washington and his Continental Army crossing the icy river. That's the day he actually rowed across the Delaware, you know."

"It's very thrilling," Hannah said. "The men are dressed in tattered Revolutionary uniforms."

"I'm sorry I missed it, too," Cathy said, thinking of her camera. That scene would have given her some great shots.

Hannah removed the quilted cover from the teapot. The cozy top was in the shape of a rabbit. She poured more tea. "Frank rarely comes to my shop." She smiled at her husband, then facing Cathy, she said, "But I have a fine part-time employee, Susan Gorman. You'll like her, Cathy. Like you, she's a junior in high school."

"I've had enough tea!" boomed Frank, rising. "How about a spin around the old town, Cathy? Would you like that?"

"Would I!" Cathy said, gently setting her cup of unfinished tea on the table.

"You and Frank go ahead," Hannah said. "I have a few things to do around the house."

Once in the car, Uncle Frank drove through the campus, winding in and out among the buildings.

"There's Whig and Clio halls." He pointed to two Greek-style buildings. "And that ivy-covered one over there is Nassau Hall, the oldest building on campus. Prince Town was settled in 1724." Cathy, though, scarcely heard, being too enthralled at the sight of tree arbors and Gothic arches.

"I teach on the second floor of that building," Uncle Frank said, indicating an old brick building. You're going to hear more about Princeton's history than you ever wanted to know." He laughed. "I teach a course in the Revolutionary War, you know."

"History's my favorite subject," Cathy said.

Frank stared at her. "You're serious, aren't you?"

Cathy laughed. "Is that so odd?"

"When I tell people what I teach," Frank said, smoothing his luxuriant beard, "I'm usually met with a terrible grimace. It's a pleasure to find someone who truly likes history."

Cathy smiled. She liked her aunt and uncle.

Turning onto Nassau Street, Frank said, "This street separates the university from the town. Washington marched down here."

He drove slowly so Cathy could absorb the sights. Not many students were evident, most being home for the holidays.

"Now we're on Mercer Street." He stopped before a marble sculpture. "This commemorates Washington's victory over the British at Princeton."

Cathy peered out the car window. The monument had a scene carved in relief.

"That depicts Washington leading his men, and the fallen soldier is the mortally stabbed American general Hugh Mercer. He died at the hands of the redcoats."

Cathy wished she knew more about the Battle of Princeton. "Do you have any books on the Revolutionary War, Uncle Frank?"

The stocky man threw back his head and laughed. "About six shelves is all!"

Cathy smiled. "Do you mind if I read more about the history of this area?"

"Help yourself, Cathy. You'll find all the tomes you want in my den."

"One more stop, then home," Frank said, driving along Quaker Road until he reached a park. "That's the Princeton Battlefield and over there is Stony Brook Meeting House."

"What's the stone wall?" Cathy asked.

"It surrounds a cemetery." Frank stopped. "Do you want to get out and stretch your legs? It's such a nice day, who would believe it's December."

Cathy opened the car door. "Shall we go for a walk?"

"Not me," Frank said, stepping out and stretching. "I'm allergic to walks, but you go ahead. I'll wait here."

Cathy walked along a narrow path, pausing to shade her eyes and survey the large park. What was the battle like that took place on this very spot? A few patches of snow spotted the ground. She halted before a pyramid of cannonballs and a huge oak tree. Reading the plaque she learned this was where General Mercer had died.

She moved on, walking faster when she neared the stone-walled cemetery. The area was well-kept except for one weed-choked corner. Several tombstones, half-hidden by dead leaves and debris, were chipped and cracked.

Bending over an isolated marker, she brushed aside dead leaves and twigs. She read the engraved words on the broken stone, surprised a British soldier lay here.

EDWARD MARSH
1757–1777
British Fourth Regiment
Killed at Battle of Princeton
January 3, 1777

"How young you were, Edward Marsh," Cathy murmured. "I wonder what you were like? Did you have dreams for a future?"

The sun disappeared and the bright day suddenly darkened. A small wind picked up, swirling a dusting of snow across the grave. Cathy turned up her jacket collar and turned to leave.

She glanced over her shoulder. Strange. The breeze had slackened, but the snow still whirled above the tomb.

Chapter 7

The next day at Aunt Hannah's shop, Cathy set to work taking inventory of small porcelain boxes and snuffboxes. She examined each lovely box, admiring its workmanship. A few were Russian designed but most were French.

Hannah, who had been working in the back, entered the front two rooms. Peeking over Cathy's shoulder, she said, "Cathy, you've done marvels!" She wiped her hands on her apron. "You've saved Susan and me a ton of work."

"I'm having fun," Cathy said. "These hand-painted boxes are exquisite."

"Aren't they?" Hannah agreed. "They sell exceedingly well, too."

"Your shop is cozy," Cathy said, glancing at the two attractive rooms. From the wooden rocking horses to the fine china, each piece was artfully displayed. "You have a decorator's touch."

"Thank you, Cathy. I try to arrange things to attract buyers," Hannah said, smiling. Clearly, she was pleased that Cathy liked the Blue Tiger. "I enrolled in a correspondence course in decorating and a few evening classes. Plus I study magazine articles and consult with other antique dealers."

Cathy ran her hand over a brightly painted carousel horse, thinking of her aunt's words. I guess if you wanted to get anywhere you really had to be motivated and work at it. Maybe someday she'd find her niche, too.

"Lots of new merchandise has come in, but I'm leaving it in the back room until all this is inventoried." Hannah waved a hand at a collection of antique dolls.

It would be a big job to itemize all the Bohemian glassware, pottery, toys, jewelry, miniatures, portraits, furniture, and quilts. But Cathy was glad to be busy. Time would go faster. Then, too, she found her mind drifting to thoughts of yesterday and the grave of the young soldier she'd seen. She felt herself drawn back for a return visit.

The overhead bell on the front door tinkled. "Here's Susan now," Hannah said.

A tall girl breezed in, rosy cheeked and

windblown. "Thanks for letting me be two hours late, Hannah," she said, pulling her heavy-knit sweater over her head and throwing it on a chair. "I was able to say good-bye to Grandmother before she took off for Atlanta." She smiled at Cathy. "This must be your niece." She held out her hand. "Hannah has been talking about you for weeks and couldn't wait until you arrived."

"Really?" Cathy replied, pleased that her aunt was eager for her visit. At least she wouldn't be a burden.

"Susan, meet Cathy O'Brien from Chicago," Hannah said, hugging Cathy's waist. "And Cathy, this is my A-one helper, Susan Gorman."

"Hi," Susan said. "So you're from Chicago, the windy city."

Cathy laughed, looking up at Susan. "It's windy, all right, but Chicago earned the nickname 'windy' for her loudmouthed politicians."

"Really?" Susan's brows lifted. "I hadn't heard that one." She took long strides to the front door where several packages were stacked. "Hannah, shall I unpack these boxes from England?"

"Yes, would you, please?" Hannah shrugged into her multicolored coat. "I'm meeting a salesman for an early lunch." She hesitated.

"Cathy, would you help Susan?"

"Sure thing," replied Cathy.

"Good." Hannah opened the door. "I'll be back in an hour, then you two can go to lunch."

Cathy and Susan worked well together. Cathy asked her loads of questions about Princeton. Susan laughingly told her about the running battle between "town and gown," the townspeople and the college students.

Susan asked about Chicago and soon they were chattering away as if they'd always known each other.

"Are you involved with anyone?" Susan asked bluntly, cutting open a box and removing a jade vase.

"Yes," Cathy answered, helping Susan pick up the scattered popcorn packing. "His name is Mike Novak and he's studying at DePaul University." She really didn't want to go into her feelings about Mike just yet. Opening a package from England, she asked, "How about you, Susan?"

Laughingly, Susan flipped back her long ponytail. "Oh, no one in particular. I used to think I had to find someone at least six feet tall, but no longer. I don't care how tall he is. When I was teased about my height in grade school, I'd become all red and flustered. But no longer." She grinned at Cathy. "I guess

I've accepted myself. Naturally, I shine on the basketball court. At least in high school, most of the boys have caught up with me and my altitude isn't an issue."

"You carry yourself so well," Cathy said. "You're so straight and . . ."

"Tall?" Susan finished. "Yes, I guess I over-compensate by holding my chin up and my shoulders squared. It doesn't bother me any longer when someone makes a remark about 'the amazon.' I'm five feet ten, and I'm comfortable with that. I don't shop in the petite department, that's for sure."

Cathy hadn't mentioned Susan's height, but was relieved when Susan brought it up herself. Now that they'd gotten that out of the way, she could take her height for granted, too.

Susan's eyes flicked over Cathy. "How tall are you? About five six?"

"Exactly," Cathy said, amazed how Susan could be so accurate.

"Hi, I'm back," Hannah called. "Time for you to go to lunch." She inspected what they'd unpacked. "Hmmm, lovely things." Carefully, she placed a soup tureen on a shelf. "I have a buyer for this."

Susan slipped on her sweater. "Come on, Cathy. We'll go to the Tiger's Den."

Cathy was pleased to have a new friend.

* * *

Once they were settled in a booth, Susan gazed at Cathy with big brown eyes. "So," she said in her brusque voice, "tell me about Mike Novak. You didn't sound too high on him. Is he a boyfriend or just a friend?"

Mike just a friend? Cathy hid a smile. He was much more than that. She would usually be reticent in discussing Mike with a stranger but Susan didn't seem like a stranger. She was one of the easiest persons to talk to she'd ever met.

Their burgers and fries arrived and before Cathy took a bite of her sandwich, she thought of how to answer Susan's question. "Mike and I are close and I adore him, but at times I'm furious with him. He has time for everyone else, but doesn't save enough time for me."

"Oh?" Susan asked, demolishing her fries. "Is there someone else?"

Cathy gave a low laugh. Maybe she could cope with another girl. "Not really, Susan. His studies and volunteer work at the reading center come first."

"I could think of worse rivals," Susan said in her throaty voice. "Mike sounds okay to me. I wish a little of his dedication would rub off on my brother."

"You have a brother?"

Susan nodded. "Bryan's two years older than me and a freshman at Princeton. You'll meet him later today when he picks me up at the shop." She gazed at the ceiling, rolling her eyes. "Bryan would rather go dancing or take in a movie than crack a book. It doesn't bother him if he's behind in a course. I guess we Gormans aren't easily intimidated. I'm at ease with my height and Bryan has more self-confidence than any lowly college freshman has a right to." Her eyes twinkled. "Cathy, watch out. Bryan might sweep you off your feet. He does have a 'way' with girls."

Cathy chuckled, drawing up on her straw. "I can take care of myself."

Susan picked up the check, figuring her half of the bill. "We'll see," she said in a light tone.

The afternoon flew by and at five o'clock Susan's brother dashed in. Cathy knew instantly this was Bryan. It wasn't just his height, it was his manner. He wore cowboy boots, jeans, a fringed leather jacket, and a Stetson hat cocked over one eye. For a moment he stood, arms crossed, leaning against the doorjamb and gazing at Cathy.

He could be straight off a Montana ranch, Cathy thought.

"Well, well, what do we have here?" He said with a lopsided grin.

"Bryan," Susan cautioned. "Your antenna is twitching. This is Cathy O'Brien. She's Hannah's niece and is visiting." She added drily, "I've already warned her about you, so she's on her guard."

"All the more challenging," Bryan said, lifting an eyebrow.

"Let's go home, Bryan," Susan urged.

"Not so fast. I'd like to talk to this girl." Bryan moved to Cathy's side. "I always was attracted to redheads!" He helped Cathy on with her jacket. "Cathy, would you like to take in a movie tonight?" He breathed against her hair. "Smells good," he said, emitting a sigh of pleasure.

Cathy stepped back. "Sorry, I'm staying with my aunt and uncle. I'll be eating with them tonight."

Bryan swept off his hat, revealing chestnut curly hair. His dark eyes flashed with an amused glint. "If not tonight, how about tomorrow? You're old enough to go out, aren't you, Cathy?"

Cathy bristled. "Certainly I am!" she snapped.

He tilted his head, studying her. "You're not *afraid* to go out with me, are you?"

"No, I'm not afraid," Cathy said, testily.

"Then, give me a chance?" His smile radiated charm.

"All right," Cathy said. "Tomorrow night."

"I told you to watch out," Susan said under her breath. In a louder voice, she said, pulling on Bryan's sleeve, "Hurry up, Brother. I'm starved. Let's go home."

Bryan tipped his hat in Cathy's direction and was gone before she had time to reconsider her acceptance. Well, why not? It would be something new. She hadn't dated anyone except Mike for months but they'd never promised not to see other people. Nonetheless, doubts about tomorrow assailed her.

Hannah locked up the shop and they left to meet Uncle Frank at the Mexican Village Cafe.

Uncle Frank, already seated at a table tiled in Mexican squares, motioned them forward. He stood until they were seated. "How are my two favorite women?" he asked, white teeth showing against a dark beard.

"Fine, Frank," Hannah said. "I'm hungry. Did you order an appetizer?"

"On its way even as we speak," Frank said, as a waitress arrived in a frilly lace top and full skirt. She set guacamole, fritos, and salsa, before them.

"I don't cook much," Hannah explained, dipping a chip into the hot salsa sauce. "Frank and I know every dining spot in the area."

"This one couldn't be better," Cathy said. "I love Mexican food."

After ordering chili rellenos, refried beans, and rice, Cathy said, "I accepted a date with Bryan Gorman tomorrow night. I hope that's okay."

"Of course, Cathy. We want you to enjoy yourself while you're here," Hannah said. "I know Bryan. Beneath that brash exterior, breathes a nice fellow." She chuckled. "He's Susan's brother and is more reliable than he lets on."

After finishing their coffee and a dessert of flan, Frank rose. "I'm headed for Firestone Library. Want to come along, Cathy?"

Cathy glanced inquiringly at Hannah.

"Go ahead, dear. I intend to put my feet up and watch a program on Mozart."

"Well, I could use your books at home, Uncle Frank, but I'd like to see the library."

"Then come along," Frank said jovially, fitting on his knitted black and orange cap, in Princeton's colors. "I'll bring you a book on the Battle of Princeton and you'll be comfortable in the reading room. I only need to check a few references so we'll be home by nine o'clock."

Going through the magnificent library doors with her uncle, Cathy again wondered if Mike would be upset knowing that she was going out with Bryan. After all, it was only a movie. And maybe Bryan could make her forget her loneliness in being without Mike. But Bryan's devil-may-care attitude unnerved her a little.

"Here's the reading room," Uncle Frank said. "I'll bring you a few books in a minute."

Cathy strolled into the huge room marveling at the burnished wood walls, tables, and tall Gothic windows.

She opened one of the history books Uncle Frank brought to her, turning to a chapter on the Battle of Princeton. All thoughts of Bryan evaporated.

Avidly, she read about Washington's route into the city. He'd surprised the British force there, and although they'd fought well, they were hopelessly outnumbered and most of the redcoats were either killed or captured. Many of the wounded British troops had been cared for in Nassau Hall.

Cathy closed the book and stared at a window, but her unseeing eyes didn't notice the stained glass. Instead, an image of a forlorn grave and the dead soldier lying there, haunted her. Edward Marsh. Had he been one of the wounded cared for in Nassau Hall? Or had he died on the battlefield? Poor Edward.

Chapter 8

Arriving home from the library, Cathy went to her bedroom. The welcoming room with its wonderful four-poster bed, quilted bedspread and curtains, armoire and private bath comforted her. After reading about the Battle of Princeton, she needed to be alone to reflect on what she'd discovered.

Undressing, she slipped on her flannel nightgown and brushed her hair. One, two, three strokes. Her first full day in Princeton had been filled with new people and places at every turn. But the Battle of Princeton, fresh in her mind, was all she could think of. It wasn't fair Edward Marsh had to give his life for his country. He was too young. Had the dead soldier lived in London? Had he been rich? Poor? What was life like in eighteenth-century England?

Her thoughts wandered as she brushed her hair. What was Mike doing? It was ten o'clock here in New Jersey, but only nine in Chicago. Mike and his father were probably working on a new campaign for funds by cranking out handouts for additional reading centers, or maybe another homeless shelter. Maybe he was studying the history of political parties for his course. She smiled. She didn't need to worry that he'd be seeing another girl.

The light from her dressing-table lamp cast a shimmering glow over her thick hair, giving it garnet highlights. Her green eyes and high cheekbones with just a smattering of freckles over her small nose didn't look too bad. She nodded in approval. She could look worse! What was it Dana had said? Oh, yes, that she could be a model. She gave a snort of disgust and threw down her brush. Why was she admiring herself like this?

She climbed the three-step footstool into her bed, snuggling beneath the flannel sheets. Mike couldn't expect her to sit home with her aunt and uncle every night. On her holiday she wanted to have a good time. Yet, nagging guilt pricked at her conscience. Damn Mike! Sometimes she didn't think he was human. He was too idealistic! He didn't know *how* to have a good time.

From the end table, she chose one of the three mysteries she'd brought along. Propping up the book on her knees, she left it unopened. Mike *did* know how to have a good time. Could she ever forget the wonderful times they'd spent together?

In October Bill Novak had taken a business trip to Mexico and invited her to come along to Cozumel.

She and Mike rode horses, and went scuba diving. They swam and dove like two seals. How delicious it had been cutting through the crystal clear waters of the Caribbean Sea. A fairyland of coral reefs and a bottom spread with white sand opened before them. They swam with graceful turquoise, emerald-green, and sapphire-blue fish. Darting in and out of rocky precipices, they had played and splashed like two otters. When they came together underwater, Mike embraced her. Later, they searched for shells and ate under a moonlit sky. She flung open her book. Why did she make herself feel more guilty, thinking about Mike?

She read for an hour, becoming engrossed in *The Mystery of the Chattering Teeth*. There was something to be said for reading. It put you in another world. And for a time she forgot about Mike, Bryan, and Edward Marsh!

* * *

The next morning, dressing in black tights, an oversized plaid shirt, and short denim vest, her thoughts returned to Edward Marsh. Pulling on her boots and lacing them, she glanced in the mirror and gave her hair a quick comb. She went downstairs and into the kitchen. Uncle Frank had left for the day, but Hannah sat reading *The New York Times*.

" 'Morning, Cathy." Hannah looked up, giving her a bright smile. She poured a cup of steaming coffee and placed it before Cathy. "Do you want toast or an English muffin?"

"Neither, thanks." She didn't feel hungry. A sudden strange sensation swept over her and she knew what she had to do. She had to return to Edward Marsh's grave.

"Now, Cathy," Hannah said, standing, "you do as you please today. Don't think you need to come to the shop and keep the hours I do."

Cathy smiled. "Thanks, I'll come in later, then."

"Fine." Hannah patted her shoulder. "I'll see you when I see you."

After Hannah had left, Cathy zipped up her jacket and hurried to the graveyard, only six blocks away.

Crossing the stone bridge, she glimpsed the neglected area of overgrown weeds.

Bowing her head, she stood before Edward Marsh's tomb. He'd been killed January 3, 1777. Had he been a hero? Was he tall, short, a blond, or dark-haired? Had he been afraid in battle? As she stared at the grave, a cloud hid the sun. She shivered.

All at once she felt someone standing behind her. She spun about. Nothing. No one was there. Confused, she walked to a stand of elms, glancing in all directions. "Is anyone here?" she called out. The only answer was the sighing of the wind through the tree branches. Alone, she turned back. Her imagination played a trick on her. No! She'd definitely felt a presence next to her. She was positive.

Walking with her hands in her pockets, she headed for the Blue Tiger. An eerie sensation still surrounded her. Something or someone had been at the cemetery with her.

Relieved to be back in the shop, Cathy found Susan using a feather duster. Life was back to normal. "Hi, Susan," she said. "I see you're hard at work."

Susan gave her a wide smile. "I'm not killing myself. Hannah has gone to an antique fair over in South Brunswick. Not one customer has come in." She'd no sooner gotten the words out of her mouth, when the bell tinkled and a lady entered, dressed in purple from her hat to her stockings.

"May I help you?" Susan said. Then she smiled. "Oh, hello, Ms. Wassom. I didn't recognize you with your hat brim pulled down."

"Hello, Susan." Ms. Wassom glanced in Cathy's direction, but immediately turned back to Susan, giving her her full attention. "I'm looking for an eighteenth-century grandfather's clock. What do you have?"

"Well, I have a beauty over here," Susan said in a low pleasant voice, walking to a corner. "Let me show it to you."

She led Ms. Wassom to a towering clock in light wood with a large face. "This was made during the time of Paul Revere. Isn't it spectacular? As you know these clocks are exceedingly rare. This is the only one we have."

Ms. Wassom took off her glasses and drew closer to the clock, examining it from top to bottom. "This is a beautiful specimen. I've looked elsewhere but this one is the most attractive."

"It was designed by Gawen Brown in 1749 in nis Boston workshop," Susan explained. "Would you like to hear it chime?"

"Oh, yes," Ms. Wassom said, giving Susan a warm look.

There was no doubt about Susan's ability to deal with customers. No wonder Hannah said she was lucky to have her as a helper.

The clock chimed, a thin tinny sound, but Ms. Wassom, clasping her hands to her chest, was enchanted. "I'll take it." Removing a checkbook from an expensive leather bag, she said, "You have my address, don't you?"

"We do, Ms. Wassom." Susan said, leading her customer to a desk. "That will be sixty-five hundred dollars."

Cathy gulped — $6500! The huge amount, however, didn't faze Ms. Wassom, who quickly wrote out the check and handed it to Susan.

After Ms. Wassom was gone, Cathy stared at Susan. "You were marvelous. You knew just how to handle her."

Susan laughed. "She's an old customer and has bought loads from us. But Hannah will be pleased that I made the sale. If we don't sell another thing all day, the clock will more than make up for it."

Susan gave a sidelong glance at Cathy. "Have you written or called Mike?"

"I haven't had time," Cathy replied. "Besides, I gave him my aunt's address and phone number. He can call me, too." She picked up the feather duster and flicked it over a set of silver spoons. "It works both ways, you know."

Susan's throaty voice sounded amused. "If Mike is as busy as you say, I'll bet he'd love to hear from you."

"Maybe," Cathy said lightly, moving over to a portrait of a little boy, who was a miniature of a full-grown man.

Cathy dropped into a chair and asked suddenly, "Don't you think I should go out with your brother?"

Susan shrugged her shoulders. "Sure, you should! It's just a vacation date. You'll enjoy yourself, Cathy, I guarantee it."

"Doesn't Bryan have a girl?" Cathy asked as casually as possible. She couldn't believe "Mr. Personality" didn't have a girlfriend.

Susan paused before replying. "I don't know if he'd want me to say . . . well, maybe he wouldn't care, but yes, he did have a girl. They broke up three weeks ago. Bryan acted as if he didn't care, but underneath, I think he was pretty upset."

Cathy knew Bryan wouldn't have been without a girl too long. But now at least she knew she wouldn't be stepping on anyone's toes.

At five o'clock Cathy went home with her aunt. She dashed upstairs to shower and dress.

An hour later Bryan rang the doorbell and Cathy greeted him. "Hi, Bryan."

"Hello, there!" Bryan said. He gave her a broad smile. "You look even prettier than I remember," he said.

Cathy laughed. "You know what we Irish call that? A bit of the old blarney." Secretly she was pleased he found her attractive. She was glad she'd worn her red sweater, jeans, and navy blazer.

She reached for her down jacket on the hall tree, but Bryan was too quick for her. He held it while she slipped into the sleeves and zipped it up.

"Your carriage awaits, m'dam," Bryan swept his hand before him and led her to his two-seater sports car.

"Very nice," Cathy said, but getting into the luxurious car, she wished it were Mike's "roadster" instead.

She glanced at Bryan as he wheeled deftly around a corner. She sank back against the plush leather. To afford such a car he must be wealthy.

"Like my wheels?" he asked.

"Hmm, nice," Cathy said.

"Dad bought it for me for a graduation present and for getting into Princeton. He's an old alum of Princeton himself." Bryan chuckled.

"I guess he would have been crushed if his only son entered Yale or Stanford."

As if leading a charmed life, Bryan swung around into the lot, tires squealing, and parked directly in front of the theater.

"What about Susan?" Cathy asked. "Does your dad want her to go to Princeton, too?"

"Oh, sure! My sister's different, though. Who knows where she'll go to school. She's even working part-time when she doesn't have to."

"I take it your family is wealthy." Cathy was beginning to think Bryan was just a spoiled rich boy.

Bryan opened her car door, taking her hand. "Mr. Bryan Gorman is a well-known trial lawyer in these parts," he said lightly. "I'm Bryan Gorman II." Laughing, he shook his finger under her nose. "And don't forget my title! On the other hand, you may call me Bryan." He gave her a crooked grin as he linked her arm through his. Laughing, they went into the movie.

Buying popcorn and super-giant Cokes, Bryan handed Cathy her drink. Still laughing, they found their seats.

The movie was silly, with lots of high-tech tricks, perfect for their lighthearted moods. Even when Bryan held her hand, Cathy didn't mind. It seemed like the natural thing to do.

Bryan's attentiveness didn't stop after the movie. His charm and humor continued when they went to a Japanese restaurant in an outlying area of Princeton.

It wasn't until Cathy read sushi on the menu that she recalled Johnny and his first experience with raw fish. Did Johnny and her mother have a good time with Zack at the Japanese place? Her face clouded at the thought of Zack Preston, wondering what new tactic he was using to win over her mother. Evidently, though, from the stars in her eyes, he'd already won the battle. Both her mom and Johnny loved Zack. It would be nice if Johnny grew up with a father. A boy of nine needed guidance. Although she hated to admit it, Zack had been a good influence.

Bryan reached over, tilting her chin up and looking in her eyes. "No thinking allowed," he said in a light tone, "unless, of course, it's of me."

She gazed at Bryan and batted her eyelashes. "Is this better?" she teased, smiling.

"Much better." Amused, Bryan nodded with approval. Then his smile vanished. "Susan tells me you're seeing someone back in Chicago. Could I persuade you to forget about him? At least while you're with me?"

Cathy shook her head. "No, Bryan. I'll be your friend, but I won't forget Mike." Silently she wondered why Susan had told Bryan about Mike, but maybe he'd asked. After all, she'd asked Susan about Bryan's girl, hadn't she?

When Bryan paid the bill, Cathy was glad it was time to leave. She wanted to be home. Now that Bryan knew about Mike, things could get awkward. What was the sense of prolonging their evening?

Bryan, however, talked about his studies in pre-law and asked about her future plans. Obviously, he didn't care if she were seeing someone else.

Arriving at her aunt's, Bryan put his arm around her, but made no further moves on her. He even asked if he could see her the next night.

Surprised, she glanced at him. If he didn't mind about Mike, why shouldn't she go out with him? As long as Bryan didn't expect a romantic relationship, they could still see each other.

After telling Bryan good night, she went inside. Aunt Hannah had thoughtfully left a light on. She hadn't realized it was midnight already.

For a time she sat in a rocker, looking out at the moonlit trees. Had she done the right thing? Mike wouldn't think of going out with anyone. Bryan, though, had been sweet and hadn't even tried to kiss her. Tomorrow he was taking her ice-skating along with Susan and her date. She turned off the lamp and climbed the stairs. After such a nice evening, why did she have such a heavy heart?

Chapter 9

On Saturday morning, Cathy still wondered if she'd done the right thing in going out with Bryan. As she buttoned her sweater vest, she thought about whether she'd tell Mike. Would he understand? He'd never dictated to her what she should or shouldn't do. She must be honest with him. They had built their love on trust. She smiled. Mike would kiss away her guilt. She loved Mike. And yet she was going out with Bryan again.

When she came down for breakfast, Aunt Hannah set a plate of French toast before her.

"Hmmm, I thought you didn't cook," Cathy said.

"Once in awhile," Hannah said with a smile. "By the way, did you have a good time last night?"

"Yes, I did," Cathy replied. Hannah treated going out with Bryan as the most natural thing in the world. She felt her guilty feelings disappear.

"Where did you go?" Hannah asked, "if it's any of my business."

Cathy drank her juice and laughed. "Of course you can know, Aunt Hannah. We saw *The Dizzy World of Diane*, and ate dinner at a Japanese restaurant."

"I knew you'd like Bryan," Aunt Hannah said, drizzling syrup over her toast. "Everyone who knows him thinks he's the nicest person they've ever met."

Then she must be careful not to get too interested in him, Cathy resolved.

After they'd eaten she cleared away the dishes while her aunt filled the dishwasher. "Cathy, what's on your agenda today?" Hannah inquired.

Cathy suddenly knew the first thing would be visiting the cemetery, but her answer was evasive, "I — I'm not sure." She could never tell Hannah about Edward Marsh. "I'll come into the shop late, and help Susan finish inventory."

"Now, you know you don't need to come into the shop everyday, Cathy," Hannah said, turning the knob to start the dishwasher.

"Let's have our coffee by the fireplace." Hannah poured two cups. "I'm not going into the shop until this afternoon." She settled herself in a wingback chair across from Cathy. The blaze crackled and a log shifted. In her denim skirt, Irish knit sweater, navy pantyhose, and loafers, her aunt looked like a young girl, Cathy thought.

"It's foggy today," Cathy said, looking out and seeing the tops of trees poking through the thick grayness.

"Yes, and I have to drive to Middlesex to see a client," Hannah said, two frown marks creasing her eyebrows.

"It should be lifting soon," Cathy reassured her. Drinking her hot coffee, she finally said what had been on her mind. "I'm going out with Bryan again tonight."

"You are?" Hannah said with a smile. "I knew you two would hit it off. Bryan's quite a self-assured young man, isn't he?"

"Yes, he is," Cathy replied. "We had a good time. Tonight Susan and a friend are coming along."

"I'm glad you're going out," Hannah said. "You don't want to sit home with Frank and me every night."

"I love being with you and Frank," Cathy replied honestly. "I feel I'm deserting you."

"Nonsense! You're in Princeton on vacation. We don't expect you to be with us constantly,"

Hannah said. "I'm glad you've found someone your own age to be with."

"Bryan and Susan come from a well-to-do family, don't they?" Cathy asked in a casual tone.

"Indeed they do. Bryan Gorman Senior is a prominent community leader. He's earned a fortune in defending celebrities and wealthy people. His reputation is known throughout the country." Hannah leaned back in her chair. "Everyone knows he wants Bryan to be his partner when Bryan finishes law school." She chuckled. "But I don't think Bryan is in any hurry to finish school. He's loving every minute of university life.

"Time to meet my client." Hannah rose, dousing the fire. "By the way, if you find any paperweights missing at the shop, don't be alarmed. They're in the car." She went to the hall and put on her misshapen hat. "Ms. Esther Brock is in a wheelchair and asked me to bring the antique glass paperweights to her home. I know she'll buy at least four or five. I'm glad to do it. Esther is always a cheery person."

"You have an interesting career, Aunt Hannah," Cathy said. "Nice clients and you can drive to customers' homes or go to antique fairs. Your work isn't monotonous."

"As long as I have Susan, I can drive here

and there," Hannah said, wrapping a scarf around her neck. "Once her vacation ends, though, she'll only come in after school."

"What do her parents think about Susan's job?"

Hannah slipped on her jacket. "Susan's mother is constantly on the society pages." Hannah switched to a high-pitched snooty tone. "Mrs. Beatrice Gorman, chairperson of the annual Hospital Auxiliary Ball, announced her committee." Hannah tittered. "But I have to hand it to Beatrice Gorman. She cares about her family and also keeps up with her charity work. I think she and her husband are proud of Susan for doing as she pleases."

"Are they proud of Bryan?" Cathy questioned, picking up the cups.

"Oh, my, yes. Bryan can do no wrong." Hannah opened the door. "Must run. See you later, Cathy."

" 'Bye, Aunt Hannah," Cathy said. Thoughtfully, she carried the cups into the kitchen. The Gormans sounded like an ideal family. Could anyone be that perfect? Surely they had some flaws. She hoped Bryan, the perfect son, didn't have clay feet.

After rinsing the cups, she put on her jacket and hurried out. She knew exactly where she was going. On the way to the cemetery, she stopped at a florist and bought a single red rose.

As Cathy arrived at the quiet park, the sun peeked through the clouds, bathing trees in a silvery glow. She was glad that a white gazebo in one area of the park was empty, and no tourists were poking about the battlefield.

Cathy stopped before the Battle Monument, gazing up at General George Washington. His square jaw had a determined set. He must have been a brilliant leader, she speculated, to convince his ragtag army to follow him on a cold winter night and attack the Hessians. The German soldiers, or Hessians, the British had hired were known for their fighting skill. But Washington believed in surprise offensives, which certainly had won the day. And to think after his Trenton victory, he'd turned around and fought the British force on this very spot. Cathy gazed about trying to picture the redcoats facing the Colonials. What a battle that must have been. Where had Edward been in this clash of arms?

Cathy walked to the cemetery and when she came to Edward Marsh's tomb, she gently placed the rose on the granite slab. "Edward Marsh," she whispered, "I wish I'd known you."

With her head down, she stayed silent and contemplative.

"Caaa — thy," her name echoed hollowly on the wind.

Her spine went rigid. She couldn't move a muscle.

Finally, she swiveled slowly and glanced behind her. The cemetery remained quiet and peaceful. Had someone uttered her name or was it her imagination? "Who is calling me?" she asked in a shaky voice.

No answer. Only the wind in the trees. Cathy should have been afraid. Here she was alone in a graveyard and she'd heard her name called as clear as if someone had been standing next to her, but she was calm. "Who's there? Please, answer me," she begged.

Gazing at Edward's grave, she was confused. She knew her name hadn't risen from the tomb. But who called to her? She was the only one in the cemetery. She sank down next to the stone marker, not knowing how long she waited. Yet, no one appeared and her name wasn't called again. The only sound was the moving, scraping branches.

Chapter 10

Eventually, Cathy glanced one last time at the red rose atop Edward Marsh's broken tombstone. She wished the aching cry of her name would be repeated, but the quiet solitude of the park remained unbroken.

She walked across the frozen ground toward the white gazebo. The graceful dome of the pavillion lined with benches inside looked inviting. She should return to the shop, but for some reason she couldn't pull herself away from the cemetery. The fog had lifted and bright sunlight flooded the park.

Cathy entered the gazebo and sat down. Frosty air nipped at her cheeks, as she thought of her experience at Edward's tomb. After some time, however, she shook herself free of her reverie. She should be helping Susan.

But not quite yet. She was held here, puzzling over her strange morning. Each time she visited the cemetery a new sensation had enveloped her. Yesterday, she'd felt someone near her. Today her name had floated on the crisp air. Was someone trying to reach her?

A cracking branch underfoot startled her. She stared into the dazzling sun. A figure walked in her direction. She jumped to her feet, shading her eyes. Her heart pounded. She couldn't quite make out who approached her. Sunbeams danced around a man who appeared to step out of the light and move forward. He held out a gloved hand.

Her breath caught in her throat. The young man, in white trousers, a red jacket and black boots, wore the uniform of a British soldier! She'd read enough about the Revolutionary War to recognize an eighteenth-century British Regular.

As he drew closer, her pulse quickened. The fair-haired soldier, straight and tall, smiled. In a low well-modulated voice, he said only one word, "Cathy."

"Y-yes," she stammered. "Are you . . ." she hesitated. Could she say it? "It can't be! But . . . are you Edward Marsh?"

He nodded. His clean-shaven face radiated pleasure as she touched his outstretched hand. The cross straps across his chest were sparkling white. His eyes were as blue as the sky.

She was confused. What did you say to a ghost?

Edward gazed longingly at her face. "You're as lovely as I knew you'd be." He walked to a bench and seated himself, stretching out his legs and crossing his feet before him. "Thank you for the rose, Cathy."

"You're welcome," she gasped. Edward had known about the rose she had placed on his grave. With her hands in her pockets, she stood on the other side of the pavillion. Although she was unsure of herself, she was unafraid.

"Tell me who you are, Cathy," the young soldier said, motioning her to come and sit next to him.

Gingerly, she seated herself, not believing this was happening. "I'm Cathy O'Brien," she said, attempting to keep her voice from trembling. "I live in Chicago, Illinois, with my mother, Sara, and younger brother, Johnny."

"Chicago." He tested the word on his tongue. "A place I've never heard of."

"Fort Dearborn, the first settlement of Chicago was founded in 1773," Cathy explained.

"Ah." He nodded in understanding. "And your father?"

"He died of a heart attack three years ago."

"That is too bad. Do you have any other brothers or sisters?" he asked.

"Dylan, my older brother, goes to Oxford."

"Oxford," Edward repeated, still gazing at Cathy. "I wished to attend Oxford, but the war interrupted that."

"Tell me about *your* family," Cathy urged. "Did you live in London?" She wanted to know more about this young man . . . this ghost.

"Yes, I lived with my mother and father and older brother, James." He continued in a calm tone, "My father came from a long line of military men. He enlisted in the Royal Guard of King George the third. My brother served in Bengal, India, where he protected the East India Company. Our family was devastated when we learned he had been killed in a skirmish with Indian tribesmen."

"How sad," Cathy commented.

"Yes, but we were brave," Edward said sardonically. "If one comes from a military family then wounds and death are to be expected."

Her heart went out to this young man. "Your poor mother," she said. "To lose two sons in such faraway places."

Edward nodded. "Because of my death and James's, she pined away. My father continued to serve in the Royal Guard, but took to drink.

At the age of fifty he died of too much rum."

"The fighting in America must have been terrible," Cathy murmured. "You were so young."

"I thought fighting the Colonials would be a matter of days and I'd be back in London before the year 1777 was out." His quick smile was soon replaced by a rueful expression. "We found the ill-equipped Americans were courageous fighters. Although we redcoats won several battles at the beginning of the war, the battles of Trenton and Princeton demoralized our army." He shook his head. "I, of course, didn't live to see the British surrender by General Cornwallis at Yorktown."

Cathy had always read about the Americans and their brave fight for freedom, but now suddenly she was confronted with an enemy soldier who had been brave, too, and her heart went out to him.

"Edward, did you always want to be a soldier?" she asked.

"No," and his blue eyes took on a steely quality. "My course was set by my father. I yearned to be an artist as a youngster." His face broke into a smile again. "I listened to the lectures of Thomas Gainsborough. His greatness as a landscape and portrait artist was known throughout England."

Cathy nodded, "Yes, I've seen some of his paintings in a Chicago museum."

"I sketched, too, but hid them when my father came home."

"I know you would have been a fine artist," Cathy murmured, admiring Edward's handsome features.

"If I had had a model like you, Cathy, I would have painted a beautiful portrait." He lifted his hand as if to touch her cheek but dropped it onto his lap. "Your green eyes, rich red hair, and high cheekbones would have rivaled any of Gainsborough's works."

"But you were forced into the army instead," Cathy felt a deep sense of loss. What would Edward's life have been like if he hadn't become a soldier?

"Cathy, what are your ambitions?"

How could she admit to Edward that she didn't know what she planned to do. She stared at her hands. "I-I'm not sure." She looked into his intent blue eyes. "Maybe I'll decide next year when I'm a senior." It sounded so silly . . . so young. "When I'm a senior."

"Or maybe you'll wed," he added.

Wed? Didn't he know she was too young to be a wife? But most girls in the eighteenth century married in their teens. "Before I marry, I intend to graduate from college," her voice trailed off, "then I'm not sure."

His golden brows lifted. "You will go to college? But you're a girl," he said.

She laughed at his astonishment. "Lots of girls go to college these days," she explained.

He laughed, too. "I forget this is a new country and a new age."

Their gazes locked and Cathy seemed mesmerized. Edward Marsh was everything she'd envisioned. A sensitive and caring young man. He looked more knowing than his twenty years, but his face had a boyish quality. If only they could stay this way longer.

But it wasn't to be. Gently, Edward lifted her hand to his lips. "I must go."

Stricken, she spoke in a low urgent voice, "Must you? Will I see you again?"

"I promise I will come to you again." His amused smile delighted her. "How could I resist you, Cathy O'Brien," he added, rising to his feet.

Before she could protest further, he had walked away. She stared after him until he had disappeared beyond the stone wall.

All the way home she thought of what she'd just witnessed. She longed to turn around and run back to his grave. Would he really show himself again? When?

Tomorrow, she vowed, she'd return at the same time and same place and wait for him. If only she could share Edward with someone. But who would believe her? No, she'd keep her secret close to her heart.

Arriving at her aunt and uncle's, she went into the empty house. She was glad no one was home. She didn't care to see anyone at this time.

On the table, propped against a vase of flowers, was a letter addressed to her. For a time she held the letter in her hand, staring out the window at the bare tree limbs. Glancing at the envelope, she jolted to attention. She recognized Mike's handwriting immediately. Ordinarily, she would have opened his letter at once, but it was as if she were still under a spell.

The ringing of the phone brought her back to reality.

"Hi, Cathy, this is Susan. Are you coming to the shop?"

"Yes, I'll be there within an hour," she replied in a mechanical tone, too numb to do otherwise. Susan, she thought, if only you knew the encounter I just had.

"Well, it's almost time for lunch," Susan said, "why don't you meet me at Pete's Place?"

Cathy glanced at her watch. "Fine. Is twelve o'clock okay?"

"Yes," Susan replied. "See you then. 'Bye."

Cathy hung up and hastily opened Mike's letter. An image of his dark handsome face flashed before her. He was real and he loved her. Happy he'd written, she began to read his words:

Wednesday.
Christmas afternoon

Dear Cathy,

Yesterday we arrived safe and sound in Iowa. Good weather all the way. I drove most of the distance.

Today is Christmas and we did the usual. Opened presents and ate one of Grandmother's sumptuous feasts. Roast goose, perogi, potatoes and gravy, and all the trimmings. Everyone laughed and talked and ate too much. Grandfather gave me the usual "Mike, how you've grown! What are you studying?"

After dinner everyone crashed, so this is a good time to write to you. I hope you're enjoying New Jersey. But not too much. I don't want you suddenly deciding to go off to Princeton to school.

I was sorry to cancel out on our lunch on Tuesday, but I'll make it up to you when you return. I was glad I'd helped José. What a breakthrough! You should hear him read passages from *A Christmas Carol*. (And Dickens has a dickens of a vocabulary.) José did very well, reading difficult words and phrases, not stumbling once.

We leave early Sunday morning and I promised José I'd meet with him and several others in the group that evening. Hope we don't run into a blizzard.

Exams in Poly Sci are in two weeks, then we can have more time together, Cathy. There's a student dance on January 20th. Say you're free that night!

I miss you and
I love you!

Yours, always,

Mike

Cathy read the letter twice. She *knew* she loved Mike, but a young man in a British army uniform kept creeping into her mind.

* * *

When Cathy met Susan for lunch, she was glad that her friend had had a busy morning. Susan related her sale of an expensive pewter pitcher and mug set to an elegant gentleman. She chattered on, content with Cathy's interspersed one-syllable comments.

Returning to the shop, Cathy tallied a number of porcelain cups and saucers. In this way she didn't need to make conversation with either Aunt Hannah or Susan.

Later in the afternoon she polished a silver tea set, but as she rubbed the silver surface until it gleamed, she thought of Edward. The morning had been like a dream. And then she thought of Mike and what he meant to her. Yet, here she was going out with Bryan tonight. Suddenly her vacation had turned into a confusion of these three men. Why was she going out with Bryan? Last night she had happily anticipated seeing him again. But now, since Edward's appearance and Mike's letter, she wasn't so certain. Her mind was so muddled.

Scrubbing the tea server with more ferocity, she contemplated getting on the next plane and flying home before her emotions became hopelessly entangled.

Chapter 11

Dressing for her evening with Bryan, Cathy buttoned the one dress she'd packed. The red plaid wool with black velvet collar and cuffs fitted her well. Black tights and shoes completed her outfit.

As for jewelry, she hesitated, staring at the silver hoop earrings Zack had given her. How could she have forgotten she'd thrown these in her bag? Especially when she'd sworn never to wear them. Still she picked them up, holding one hoop to her ear lobe. What was the difference if she did wear them? With a deft motion she fastened them in her ears. Maybe Zack wasn't the ogre she'd fancied. If her mother went out with him he couldn't be all bad. On the other hand, just because she wore his earrings, didn't mean she found him so charming.

When the doorbell rang, she quickly outlined her lips in a natural shade of lipstick and went downstairs. She heard Uncle Frank's rumbling voice and Bryan's quick laugh in reply.

As she came downstairs, Bryan eyed her from top to bottom, smiling with pleasure at seeing her. He looked very handsome, himself, in a tweed jacket, dark trousers, and shirt.

After they said good night to her aunt and uncle, Cathy took Bryan's offered arm. He leaned over. "You not only look good, you smell good, too. What are you wearing, Enticement?"

She gave him a playful side glance. "No, it's called Temptation," she answered.

"Hmmm," Bryan said, opening the door for her, "I was close, and temptation is a wonderful name."

Cathy walked toward a long black car. "A Cadillac?" she asked in a questioning tone. "Yours?"

Bryan chuckled, seating himself next to her and starting the engine. "No way! Dad loaned it to me tonight, since there are four of us."

Cathy turned around. "Hi, Susan."

Bryan checked the rearview mirror and the car purred onto Witherspoon Street. "That tall guy next to Susan is Phil Bronstein," he said. "Phil is the one that gave us the tickets for tonight's play."

"Hi, Cathy," Phil said, his long face creasing into a smile. "I can see why Bryan was so anxious for me to meet you."

Cathy felt relieved that no one could see her blush in the semidarkness.

Susan laughed. "Phil is a senior at my school and he gave me a few compliments, too. I think both these guys are . . ."

". . . full of blarney," Cathy finished. "Bryan told me that your dad has one of the leads in tonight's play, Phil."

"Yes," Phil replied. "Dad acts in lots of community plays." His narrow face matched his grasshopper legs which poked up in front of him. "He's been in several off-Broadway shows, too." His lips twitched. "Even around the house he's a ham."

Susan gave him a teasing jab in the ribs. "Louis Bronstein is an excellent actor. I saw him last year in a revival of *Dial M For Murder*. His portrayal of an evil husband had me squirming."

"That's right," Phil said. "We went to that mystery together." His voice had a wistful sound, as if he wished to see Susan more often.

Bryan pulled into a parking space. "We're just in time. Curtain time is seven-thirty."

Cathy looked up at the marquee of McCarter Theater. The title *She Stoops to Conquer* blazed in bright lights. Underneath was the name Louis Bronstein.

Once seated, Cathy opened her program and saw that the playwright, Oliver Goldsmith, had lived in the eighteenth century. He'd written *She Stoops to Conquer* in 1773. Her heart jumped. Had Edward seen this same play in London? He would have been sixteen years old.

When the curtain rose, Phil's dad was one of the first to appear on stage. A marvelous tall actor, Louis Bronstein acted the role of Marlowe's father, speaking in a deep mellow voice. His lines resounded clearly throughout the theater.

Enchanted, Cathy hung on every word. She scarcely answered Bryan's whisper when he commented on the actress who played Mrs. Hardcastle. Intent, she listened, attempting to absorb every gesture and every word. She studied the costumes and powdered wigs. So, she thought, this was the kind of comedy that Londoners enjoyed in 1773. Did Edward laugh and applaud just as they were doing?

After the play, Bryan drove to a steak house.

"Phil, your dad made the play come alive," Cathy said.

"Yes, he's not bad," Phil replied, folding himself in a booth next to Susan.

Lost in thought, Cathy caught only a few snatches from everyone's conversation.

"Cathy!" Bryan said in a loud voice. "Are you with us?"

"You look pale," Susan said. "Are you feeling okay?"

"You do look pale, Cathy." Solicitously, Bryan leaned toward her. "You look as if you've seen a ghost."

A ghost! Startled, Cathy's fork slipped from her fingers and clattered to the floor. Phil reached down with a long arm and plucked it off the tile. Her face warmed and reddened. Phil shot her a strange look. Cathy twisted and retwisted the napkin in her lap, trying to calm herself.

The waitress, who had heard the noise, brought Cathy a clean fork.

"What's with you tonight?" Bryan asked with a tilt of his head, as they ate dinner.

"Sorry," she said with a half-smile. "I guess my stomach is a little queasy." This was an easy out. How could she explain that she'd *really* seen a ghost today? Who would understand such crazy talk? Yes, they'd believe she was sick, all right.

After dessert, Phil glanced at his watch. "It's time to get home. But this has been fun." He gazed at Susan. "Let's get together again before Cathy leaves."

"I'd like that," Cathy said, flashing everyone a smile.

After they dropped Phil off, Susan rode with them as Bryan drove Cathy home. After all, she and Bryan would return to their parents' house.

Bryan walked Cathy to the front door where Aunt Hannah had left the outside light burning. "How about a movie tomorrow night?" he asked.

She looked into his dark eyes. "I guess so," she said, automatically.

"Eight o'clock?" he said, with a warm grin on his face.

"All right," she replied, frankly admiring the bold outline of his face. She was glad that he wanted to take her out. It helped distract her a little. She smiled at him, but when he bent down, she blew him a kiss and went inside.

Once in the house, with her back against the door, she took a deep breath. The remark about seeing a ghost had unnerved her. Hanging up her coat, she climbed the stairs while the clock struck midnight. Her aunt and uncle were in bed.

She undressed and brushed her hair. Tomorrow, she promised, she'd return to Edward's grave. She must see him again.

Before going to bed, she tiptoed into Uncle Frank's study and looked over his history collection. Before long she found a book entitled: *English Men and Manners in the Eighteenth Century*. She yearned to learn more about Edward's time.

Scanning the contents she sighed. Fashion, drama, artists, authors, the bluestockings, the middle class, soldiers, admirals, and music were covered. Perfect! Tucking the book under her arm, she returned to her bedroom.

In bed, she read until the clock struck two. Yawning, she switched off the light.

The next morning, before her Uncle Frank or Aunt Hannah were up, she rose and dressed.

Silently she went into the kitchen and hastily opened a package of cinnamon buns and poured a glass of milk.

Finishing her hasty breakfast, she slipped on her boots and jacket, and opened the front door, carefully closing it after her.

On her way to the cemetery she thought of Edward and what she'd read about eighteenth-century Englishmen and their manners. She needed to ask him a hundred questions.

Arriving at Edward's tomb, she quietly stood with bowed head. A light snow began to fall, wetting her face. "Edward," she whispered. "Are you near?"

A slight noise alerted her and she wheeled about. Disappointed, she saw only a squirrel scurrying along a branch.

Of course, she thought, what a ninny I am. Edward would come to her where she'd last seen him . . . in the gazebo! Maybe, even now, he waited for her there.

With a light step she quickly moved to the lacy structure in the north end of the park. The rapidly falling snow obstructed her view. Edward might disappear if she didn't hurry. She broke into a run.

When she reached the gazebo, however, she was alone under the domed roof. Shaking off the snow, she dropped onto a bench, and caught her breath. For an hour she waited, but Edward didn't appear. No matter how much she strained her eyes against the swirling flakes, trying to see every angle in the park, no one came into view. Had it all been her imagination? Was there no Edward Marsh?

"Edward!" she cried.

Silence.

"Edward Marsh!" she called, her voice breaking miserably.

The scolding of a squirrel was the only sound.

With a painful knot in her stomach and with her head down, Cathy walked away, leaving the cemetery behind her.

What a fool I've been, she thought, chasing after a dead man.

Chapter 12

At the Blue Tiger Cathy kept busy, which was her only consolation as she thought of Edward. She dusted every curio on a corner shelf, but the hurt of Edward not appearing crept into her mind. Why didn't he come to her? She would never see him again.

The bell over the door tinkled and a woman entered the shop. Hannah came from the back where she and Susan unpacked new merchandise.

"Hello," Hannah said pleasantly. "May I help you?"

The woman, dressed in a black leather coat and boots, glanced around. "What a darling shop!" she exclaimed.

Cathy removed a porcelain rabbit from the shelf and dusted its ears.

"What I'm hunting for is a unique present for my husband's den," she said, picking up a pewter candlestick. "Something Early American," she added.

"Would he like those candlesticks?" Hannah asked.

"Oh, dear, no. Something more masculine."

"Where would this be placed in his study?" questioned Hannah.

"Above the fireplace." The woman shrugged. "A portrait or landscape, perhaps."

"How about an Early American rifle?" Hannah pointed to a highly polished gun, over five feet in length, hanging above a small desk. "This is an eighteenth-century rifle."

Cathy's head jerked up and she almost dropped the fragile porcelain rabbit. She couldn't control her gasp of surprise. Was this a gun that one of Washington's men had carried?

The woman frowned at Cathy, then turned back to peer at the gun, pushing her glasses up on her nose.

Hannah continued, lifting the gun off its rack, "The cherry stock has been rubbed or 'browned' with soot and oil. Notice the metal mountings and on the left side is a small star where the marksman's cheek rests."

"Is that a Kentucky flintlock rifle?" Cathy blurted out.

"Why, yes, it is, Cathy," Hannah said in

astonishment. "How do you know so much about Revolutionary War weapons?"

Tongue-tied, Cathy merely stared at the gun. Was this the type of weapon that had killed Edward? Oh, she'd like to smash it into a million pieces.

The woman asked a question and she and Hannah conversed in low tones. Gingerly the lady lifted the gun. "Why, it's so light," she said.

"That's one of the characteristics of this rifle," Hannah said, giving Cathy a questioning look.

"I'll take it," the woman said, obviously happy with her choice. She handed Hannah a credit card. "Herbert will be ever so pleased."

Hannah rang up the sale, then broke down the gun into parts and gift wrapped it in a box.

All the while, Cathy couldn't take her eyes away from the gun. That awful weapon of destruction.

When the woman left, Hannah didn't utter a word, busily jotting figures in a ledger, but Cathy knew she was waiting for an explanation.

Cathy gave an anxious cough and said, "I was reading one of Uncle Frank's books last night and it contained a chapter on weapons."

Hannah looked up and smiled at her warmly.

"I was beginning to think I had an antique expert right under my nose and didn't know it."

"No, no," Cathy said with a wave of her hand. How could she tell Aunt Hannah her fears about a rifle that could have caused Edward's death?

Susan came from the back. "It's two o'clock," she said.

"Closing time already?" Hannah said. For Cathy's benefit she added, "We close at two on Sundays. You girls run along. I have a few loose ends to finish up."

Arm in arm Cathy and Susan went outside. When they were halfway down the block, Susan suddenly turned to Cathy. "Do you bowl?"

"A little," Cathy said. "But I'm no ace."

"I'm meeting Phil at the bowling alley for a couple of games." Susan said. "He twisted my arm last night so I agreed to it. I wish you'd come. At times Phil gets too serious, but if you were there it would keep things light." She flipped her ponytail over a shoulder. "Phil is special, but I don't want to go out with him exclusively."

Cathy's boots crunched along on the snow. Maybe she felt the same way. In Chicago Mike had been her one love and now here in Princeton she was going out with Susan's brother and hoping to meet Edward once more.

The noisy bowling alley and Phil's good-natured greeting were just what she needed. After bowling two games in which she lagged behind both Phil and Susan, she unlaced her bowling shoes and pulled on her boots.

"I have to go, but you two stay and see who can out-bowl the other," Cathy urged.

"I wish you'd bowl one more game," Susan said, glancing at Phil who hefted one bowling ball after the other for the right weight.

"I'd like to, but I really need to go."

Susan blew a few loose tendrils off her forehead. "Okay, Cathy. You and Bryan have fun tonight. Just remember, Bryan's a heartbreaker."

Cathy laughed, but once outdoors, she sobered. If Bryan was a heartbreaker, what was she? But neither of them were serious, so who was breaking who's heart? But it was Edward who haunted her every thought. She wished she could run to the cemetery right this minute. Maybe he'd be waiting. But she'd promised Aunt Hannah she'd eat an early dinner with her and Uncle Frank.

When she came into the house, Hannah called out, "Cathy, we need to hurry if we're going to get a booth at Sabatino's. I hope you like pasta."

"Love it," Cathy responded, dashing up the stairs. "Give me five minutes to wash up," she called.

Soon she was ready and met her waiting aunt and uncle downstairs.

The Italian cafe, decorated with candles set in wine bottles, and murals of Florence, was filled with music played by a musician with a concertina, who wove in and out of the tables.

"This is great," Cathy said, settling into a booth beside Hannah. Uncle Frank spread himself out opposite them.

Uncle Frank grinned at her. "The big portions here are delicious." He brushed away a few snowflakes clinging to his beard.

Once they had ordered, Hannah turned to Cathy. "How are you and Bryan getting along, if you don't mind talking about it?"

"We're getting along fine, Aunt Hannah. He's really very nice, but we're just passing a little time together."

Cathy knew they knew about Bryan's girl. "I wouldn't be surprised if Bryan went back to his girlfriend."

Hannah nodded. "Yes, they were very close and I was surprised they agreed to go out with others."

Cathy was curious about Bryan's girl but

hesitated to ask. "Well, in a little over a week, I'll be gone," she said, "and perhaps they'll get back together."

"I understand you're reading some of my books." Uncle Frank tucked his napkin into his shirt collar. "If you have any questions you can always ask me. I'm glad you're interested in my field of expertise, the Revolutionary War."

"I do have a question," Cathy said, twirling her spaghetti around her fork. "Was George Washington as wonderful as all the history books indicate?"

Uncle Frank ate a forkful of veal, relishing every bite. "You bet he was, Cathy. Without Washington's military leadership during the first stages of the war, we'd probably not even have a United States. George was a gambler, too. Most great military men are. But in 1776 if Washington hadn't retreated from the British in New York and crossed the icy Delaware River, the British would have surely captured him."

"That was the awful winter at Valley Forge?" Cathy interjected.

"Yes, the bitter cold was more than most men could stand. Washington's soldiers were sick, poorly clothed and fed. Some even picked up their guns and sneaked away." Uncle Frank frowned. "Yet Washington rallied his troops to follow him in an attack on the British."

"Then," Cathy said, triumphantly holding up a breadstick, "his men crossed the river, surprised the Hessians at Trenton, and won a great victory!"

Uncle Frank threw back his head in a hearty laugh. "You're right, Cathy. With sleet and snow blinding them, the Continental Army attacked the German garrison at Trenton and captured one thousand Hessians!"

Uncle Frank paused for dramatic effect, then went on, "But the British under General Cornwallis rushed to attack Washington." He leaned forward, his eyes narrowing. "And this is how clever Washington was. He kept his campfires burning all night, so the redcoats believed he was still in camp. Meanwhile his men, under cover of darkness, slipped silently away and moved inland."

"Is this where they attacked Princeton?" Cathy wanted to know every detail of the battle. Maybe then she would understand how Edward Marsh had been killed.

"Oh, Frank," Hannah said with a smile. "How you love to go on when you have a captive audience."

"Look at Cathy! She's thirsting for knowledge!"

"Please go on, Uncle Frank," Cathy begged.

"I do want to know more about Washington. Did he march to Princeton, then?"

Uncle Frank's bushy brows shot up. "You do know a little history." Clearing his throat he continued, "General Washington marched on Princeton where one of his generals, Hugh Mercer, was killed when he unexpectedly came upon a small British force. Washington now cut up three British regiments at Princeton. One regiment barricaded themselves in Nassau Hall, but soon surrendered when the Americans fired cannonballs at them."

Cathy groaned inwardly, pitying the trapped British soldiers.

"Washington had now ruined all chances of the British General Howe to end the war," Frank said. "Washington was a master strategist. A master!"

Three regiments! Cathy thought. Which one had Edward Marsh been in? Cutting up a force sounded so bloodthirsty. She knew both Americans and British used bayonets and she shut her eyes against such a horror.

"That's enough, Frank!" Hannah scolded. "Don't you see Cathy is tired of this history lesson?"

"No, I'm not really," Cathy protested.

"We'll have more discussions later," Frank

promised, adding a tip to the check.

"I found it fascinating, Uncle Frank," Cathy said, slipping out of the booth. "If you don't mind, I'll quiz you later."

"Delighted, Cathy, delighted." His eyes twinkled as he helped her on with her jacket.

She was full of questions later that evening when she went out with Bryan, too. But she didn't have an opportunity to ask any. After the movie, Bryan drove her to Battlefield Park.

Cathy's throat closed when she saw the park. Her heart pounded wildly. This was Edward Marsh's domain. Why was Bryan taking her here?

As if she'd said the question aloud, Bryan said, "I thought a walk in the snow would be fun. Carnegie Lake should be beautiful in the moonlight."

"I-I'd rather not go walking," she replied in a shaky voice.

"Tired?" Bryan gave her an astonished look. "Not you, Cathy. You're always so full of energy. I'm the one who should be tired. I was cross-country skiing all day."

She tried to smile, but all she saw was the wide expanse of snow covering Battlefield

Park and the gazebo outlined against a silvery sky. "If you don't mind, Bryan, would you take me home?"

He shrugged. "Sure, if that's what you want." Making a U-turn, he headed back to Cathy's.

Once parked in front of her aunt and uncle's house, Bryan pushed a radio button and soft music wafted throughout the convertible. Bryan moved closer, slipping his arm around her. With his fingertips, Bryan turned Cathy's face toward him and tilted up her chin. He dipped his head, finding her lips.

Cathy's eyes closed. His kiss was sweet and lingering. Her pulse began to race, and any thoughts of Mike . . . or Edward were far away.

"I've wanted to do that from the day I first met you," Bryan said, releasing a sharp breath. "You're a lovely girl, Cathy . . . bright and pretty." His voice was husky, as he pushed back a curl on her forehead. He smiled and his handsome face glowed with pleasure and his dark eyes shone like black satin.

"That fresh lemony scent you wear would drive anyone crazy," Bryan said, a mischievous glint invading his eyes.

"Are you saying *you're* crazy?" she teased.

"Crazy over you," he whispered against her soft hair.

For a moment she remembered the questions she had intended to ask Bryan about his girl, but instead, she sat next to him quietly. For a time they said nothing, enjoying the music and each other.

Bryan could sway any girl with his charm, she thought, moving slightly away. Well, I won't be another one, she vowed. With her hand on the door handle, she said, "I'd better go in, Bryan."

"So soon," he murmured, kissing her neck.

She felt heady and wanted to stay in his arms, but she stated firmly, "Yes, Bryan. I need to go in!"

"Okay," he said good-naturedly, helping her out. "But will I see you tomorrow?"

"I-I'm not sure," she said in a hesitant voice. Too much of Bryan could be dangerous. "I should spend some time with my aunt and uncle."

"Hey! You can visit with them during the day," he protested. They stood facing one another in the snow. Bryan tucked her scarf around her neck. "Your nights belong to me!"

"Whoa!" she laughed. "You're awfully sure of yourself." She unlocked the front door. "Call me. I'll let you know."

"I'll call you first thing in the morning!"

She couldn't hide her amusement. "Will that be after twelve o'clock?"

"About then," he said in a light tone.

She went inside, still smiling when she undressed and pulled her nightgown over her head. With a pang she remembered Mike. She hadn't thought about him today. Not once. She dropped in a chair, sitting very still. How could she forget Mike? Reaching for his letter, she read and reread his words. The image of his rugged profile danced before her eyes. Dear Mike, she thought, pressing his letter to her lips, I *do* love you.

She slipped into bed, pulling the covers up to her chin, visualizing Mike's grave smile. All at once Bryan's face floated in front of Mike's. She squeezed her eyes shut. Damn! She *was* mixed up! Plumping up her pillow, she didn't wish to think of either one of them.

When she slept, she didn't dream of either Mike or Bryan. Instead, she dreamed of a soldier in a red uniform who took her riding in a carriage pulled by two white horses. Gazing into his face, her heart soared. Edward Marsh held the reins!

Chapter 13

Early Monday morning, Cathy again stole out of the house and hurried to the cemetery.

"Please, Edward, come to me," she whispered. But even as she uttered the words, she was afraid she'd never see him again.

Arriving at Battlefield Park, she moved to the gazebo, pulling her parka around her head against the frigid cold.

A red sun peeped above the horizon, breaking the gray dawn. She sat in the gazebo, her frosty breath coming in white small puffs. She waited. As the minutes passed, however, she was afraid her time was wasted. She swallowed with difficulty. If only she could see him one last time.

In the distance a jogger ran along the edge of the park and disappeared beyond the trees.

"Edward," she whispered, "please."

But the park remained silent and cold.

Reluctantly she left, cutting across the park and plodding through deep snow until she reached the cleared walk of Quaker Road.

She didn't know how long she walked, but when she passed a street of shops, she stopped. Ahead, she noticed a sign, "The Grenadier's Cafe." A hot drink would thaw her out.

Peeking through the cafe's frosty window, strung with red lights, she could see a few early risers eating breakfast.

Entering the narrow cafe, no larger than Aunt Hannah's living room, she removed her jacket. The heat tingled on her cold skin. Sitting in a back booth, her chilled feet soon warmed.

The waitress ambled over. "Your cheeks are as red as those decorations in the window," she said, observing Cathy. "The temperature is seventeen degrees."

"Hot chocolate, please," Cathy ordered, not wanting to discuss the weather.

"Is that all, Sugar?"

"Yes," Cathy said, removing her gloves.

When the waitress set the steaming mug before her, Cathy wrapped her hands around it. How wonderful it felt. She took a small sip so she wouldn't burn her tongue.

She glanced up and suddenly set her cup

down with a thump. Edward had materialized before her eyes. The young soldier sat opposite her in his red jacket and white cross straps.

"Hello, Cathy," Edward said, as if it were the most natural thing in the world for him to appear in this tiny cafe.

"Edward." She stared at him wide-eyed. "Is it really you? *Here?*"

The waitress laid the check on the tabletop. Cathy's panicky eyes swept from the waitress to Edward, but the woman was oblivious to his presence. How could this be? Couldn't she see Edward in his bright crimson coat?

Edward smiled at her. "Don't worry. No one can see or hear me. Except you, of course."

Cathy's astonishment faded away, changing to delight as she took in Edward's straight nose, firm chin, and steady blue eyes. "I was afraid I'd never see you again," she said in a low voice.

"I'll always come to you, Cathy," Edward replied softly, giving her a reassuring smile.

"I waited for you in the gazebo," she said.

"I'll come to you in different places. I'll take you to different places," he said, looking into her eyes.

She puzzled over his meaning, but she had too many questions on her mind to pursue it.

"I've been reading about the Revolutionary War, so I can feel closer to you," she said, leaning forward eagerly. "When did you leave London, Edward?"

"We sailed from Southhampton," he corrected. "Our ship had a rough crossing."

"Did you run into storms on the Atlantic?"

"Yes." His mouth twisted ruefully. "Our ship dove down to the depths of the sea, then crashed upward to the sky. I was seasick every day of the crossing."

"Poor Edward," Cathy murmured sympathetically, yearning to touch his cheek. "Was that in 1776?"

"It was. April 1776."

"King George the third sent you to fight." Cathy shook her head.

"Our royal monarch was a bit daft," Edward admitted. "He'd been seen talking to trees."

"To think a leader like that could send men to die!" Cathy said with annoyance.

Edward touched her hand. "It happened over two hundred years ago."

"I know," Cathy replied. "But I can't help thinking of all the blood that was shed."

For awhile the only sound was the groaning of the coffeemaker.

At last Cathy asked, "Were you one of the

British units at Princeton that was pursued by the Americans?"

"Yes. We were the Fortieth Regiment and the Continentals attacked us from every side. I saw the American general, George Washington, sitting astride a big white horse. Unafraid of artillery bombardment around him, Washington looked fierce and stubborn." Edward looked down at his tapered long fingers and said with a trace of bitterness, "When a group of our soldiers broke ranks and ran across the open field, I heard Washington shout, 'It will be a fine foxhunt, my boys!'

"Our unit fled into Nassau Hall where we were determined to stand fast." He paused. "However, before I could take cover in the hall, a Colonial marksman yelled, 'Rotten redcoat!' He aimed and shot. I crumpled and fell. The musket ball had penetrated my chest."

Cathy moaned. "Oh, Edward. How terrible!" She felt such pity for this strikingly handsome soldier.

"I bled a great deal," Edward said, his blue eyes clouding at the memory, "but I did manage to crawl inside Nassau Hall. The rooms were filled with smoke, but I was able to raise my head to see our troops firing from every smashed window. After several holes burst through the wall, our lieutenant waved a white flag from an upper window."

"Were you taken prisoner?" Cathy asked.

"No, I couldn't march out with my comrades. I was too weak. A cold wind blew over me. I knew my life was ebbing away."

"Dear Edward," she breathed. The image of Edward lying in a pool of blood, becoming colder and colder was almost more than she could bear. Tears stung her eyes. "How awful."

"A young American soldier rushed in with bayonet fixed, but when he saw me lying wounded, he came over to help. He lifted my head, so I could drink from his canteen. He bandaged me as best he could and said he'd be right back with a doctor." Edward shuddered, taking a breath. "I held up my hand in protest, not wanting him to leave me. You see, I knew I was finished. No doctor could save me."

"Did the American soldier return?"

"I don't know," Edward answered. "As soon as he left I leaned back on my knapsack and breathed my last."

"I'm sorry," Cathy said, blinking back tears that threatened to spill down her cheeks. "You had your whole life before you."

Edward rose, almost as if standing at attention. "I will see you tomorrow, dear Cathy," he said, his expression gentle.

"At the gazebo?" she asked.

But her question hung in the air, for Edward had gone.

Soon, Cathy followed, stopping at the cash register.

"Were you talking to someone?" the waitress asked, confusion written on her face.

"Ah — er — no," Cathy muttered, fumbling with her change.

The odd look on the woman's face, prompted Cathy to add, "I — ah, rehearsed lines for a play." She lied and didn't dare look at the waitress.

When she dashed outside, the brisk air hit her flushed face, giving her a sense of relief. As she walked along the shoveled sidewalk, admiring the sunlight on the snow-laden branches, her heart sang. For tomorrow she would see Edward again.

When she arrived home, Aunt Hannah peeked out from around the kitchen door. "Hi, Cathy." She smiled broadly. "You're just in time for sausage and pancakes."

"Sounds marvelous!" Cathy said, glancing at her watch. She was surprised it was only nine o'clock. It seemed as if she'd been gone all day.

She sat down and rubbed her hands together, smelling the sweet aroma of pancakes.

Uncle Frank lowered his paper halfway. "Did you have a good walk?"

"Oh, yes, but it's frigid!" she said, relishing the short stack of pancakes Aunt Hannah placed before her.

Cathy reached for the butter, a secret smile playing about her lips. Oh, Uncle Frank, she thought, shooting him a sidelong glance, you'd be so jealous if you knew I'd been talking to a British redcoat. She bit her smile back as she cut into her pancakes and took a mouthful, savoring the sweet maple syrup. She had such a strange secret and yet she couldn't share it with a soul.

"Cathy," Uncle Frank said, "I've discovered something you might be interested in."

Cathy gave him an inquiring look.

"It's about the Purple Heart," he said. "Do you know where it originated?"

She shook her head, giving him a half-smile. "No, but I'll bet it has something to do with the Revolutionary War. Am I right?"

Uncle Frank said, "Washington decreed that in instances of unusual gallantry, the common soldier should be entitled to wear on his left breast the figure of a heart in purple cloth or silk.

"It was a wonder they found purple cloth to reward any valiant soldiers. Washington's troops were so bad off that Washington said you could find your way from Trenton to Princeton by the bloody footprints of his barefoot men. Some had their feet wrapped in rags. And anything went for a uniform."

Cathy shuddered. "War is awful."

"I agree with you," Hannah said. "Such needless killing."

"Yes," Cathy said in a soft tone, thinking of Edward's terrible death.

She enjoyed discussing history and sitting in the kitchen with her aunt and uncle. They made her feel at home and loved.

Chapter 14

After their late breakfast, Cathy, Aunt Hannah, and Uncle Frank had a cup of coffee before the fireplace. Frank poked at the embers, but only stirred a few flying sparks. Cathy longed to tell them about her adventure with Edward only a short time ago, but of course, she couldn't.

"What's on your agenda today?" Hannah asked Cathy, stirring her coffee.

"Susan and I are going ice-skating down by Stony Brook Bridge. She'll stop for me about noon." Cathy looked at her rosy-cheeked aunt, feeling warm affection for her. "And, you, Aunt Hannah? Will you be at the shop?"

"I'm giving a talk on antique dolls this afternoon at the local library. I'm giving Susan the afternoon off." Hannah put down her cup and stooped down for the bellows. Working the handles back and forth, she stoked the fire.

Flames spurted from the dying embers.

"Antique dolls," Cathy mused. "Your talk sounds interesting, Aunt Hannah. I wish I could be there."

"Oh, your aunt is quite a spellbinder," Uncle Frank said proudly. His white teeth shone through his bark-colored beard.

Hannah reseated herself and wrinkled her nose. "Oh, Frank," she protested, but underneath her slight frown, she tried to hold back a pleased smile.

Frank leaned over and patted his wife's hand. "Hannah has a big following in these parts. When she lectures, the auditorium is packed."

Hannah chuckled. "Seems like folks never tire of hearing how people lived centuries before us."

"And I suppose you'll be working on your book today, Uncle Frank," Cathy said, placing her empty cup on the coffee table.

"Yes, I have to go to Firestone Library and research Hugh Mercer, one of Washington's trusted generals."

"He was killed at the Battle of Princeton, wasn't he?" Cathy said.

"You have a marvelous memory, Cathy," Uncle Frank said, standing.

Yes, Cathy thought. Uncle Frank, you'd

give a thousand dollars to meet with my secret Edward Marsh. He could give you an eye-witness account of the Revolutionary War. But, naturally, she remained silent.

"Before the library, I need to go to Copycats and Xerox what I've written to date." Frank held his cup, turning toward the kitchen. "I always keep a good copy in the trunk of my car in case my original manuscript should be destroyed." He turned back. "May I take your cup?"

"No, thanks, Uncle Frank," Cathy said. "I just want to sit here awhile before the fire."

When Frank left and Hannah went upstairs, Cathy continued to gaze into the fire, reliving her morning with Edward. The yellow flames danced, conjuring up Edward's features. She loved his long golden hair and steady eyes. When they met next, she must ask him about his home life. She was certain he'd never done any hard work, associating no doubt, only with his own class.

Not like Mike Novak, she thought. She smiled. Down-to-earth Mike as opposed to ethereal Edward. What a contrast! Neither would have the slightest idea of the other's life. But she could see how Edward had been shaped by his narrow upbringing.

She wished Mike were here now. He'd take

her in his arms and all her doubts about her feelings would evaporate. If only she were going ice-skating with Mike rather than Susan. Not that she wouldn't have fun with Susan, but now she longed for Mike!

Impulsively she jumped up. She'd phone him right this minute!

Dashing up the stairs, she reached for the phone, but before she could dial Mike's number, the phone rang. Bryan's voice greeted her. Even though she'd decided not to see him tonight, his persuasiveness caused her to change her mind. He had tickets for a concert in Trenton and would pick her up at seven. By the time she hung up, his jokes had left her laughing.

Remembering Mike, she immediately dialed his number. She was elated to find him at home!

"Hi, Mike," she said.

"Cathy! I'm glad you called. I've been thinking of you!" he said in his deep voice.

"And I've thought of you," she replied. "I received your letter, and I accept your invitation to the DePaul dance."

"Great!" he exclaimed. "Nothing will interfere with our plans that night!" He paused. "I've wondered what you've been doing."

"Oh," she replied evasively, "I'm helping

Hannah in the shop. I met Susan Gorman, who works part-time for my aunt. We're going ice-skating today." She couldn't tell Mike about Bryan and Edward yet, but if there was to be a foundation of honesty between them, she knew she had to later. He'd understand why she went out with Bryan. But would he ever understand her meetings with Edward?

"What have *you* been doing, Mike?" she questioned, attempting to keep her voice light.

"Going to the reading center, hitting the books," he responded, "the usual. I did have time to teach Johnny the finer points of hockey."

Cathy laughed. "I thought Zack was doing that."

"We're both helping him. Today Zack invited me to go along with Johnny and your mom to a Blackhawks game."

"I see," she said coolly. She'd only been away five days and already Zack had won over Mike, too!

Mike said, "I know you don't like Zack, Cathy, but he's an okay guy. Give him a chance."

Fortunately the doorbell rang and she didn't have to comment on that.

"Got to run, Mike. Susan's at the door."

" 'Bye, darling. See you next Sunday." Mike hung up.

Cathy, however, held the receiver for a few seconds longer before hurrying to open the door for Susan.

The tall girl entered like the wind, wearing black tights, a short green flared skirt, and a green leather jacket. Her hair, usually in a ponytail, fluffed around her pretty face. "Ready to go, Cathy?"

"Ready," Cathy said, slipping into her jacket and slinging her shoe skates over her shoulder. She, too, wore tights, except hers were white, and her short pleated skirt was navy.

All the way to Stony Bridge, they laughed and talked. When they arrived at the frozen pond, only a few skaters skimmed around the ice. As the day wore on, though, the pond filled up.

When Phil arrived, he raced to Susan and swept her away. Arm in arm they skated twice around the pond. Then the two of them sat on a nearby bench in deep conversation. In the meantime, Cathy practiced skating backward.

After an afternoon of skating the two girls went to Pete's Place for hot chocolate. Their faces, pinched red by the cold, were filled with enthusiasm.

"That was fun," Susan said. "Let's go tomorrow after I finish work."

"Sure," Cathy agreed, thinking this might be the perfect opportunity to confide in Susan. If she didn't tell *someone* about Edward, she would explode. She hesitated, biting her lower lip. I can trust Susan, she thought.

Susan gave Cathy a sly glance. "What about my brother? Have you fallen for him yet?"

"No!" Cathy replied. "But I can see why Bryan has girls lined up to go out with him."

"Maybe," Susan said thoughtfully, swirling the whipped cream into the hot chocolate. "But I think he misses — oh," she said, putting long fingers over her mouth.

"Bryan misses *what*?" Cathy asked.

"Oh, nothing," Susan said, waving her hand in dismissal.

Cathy didn't pursue the subject. Instead, she wet her lips and plunged ahead. "Susan, I-I have something I want to tell you."

Susan gazed at Cathy, waiting.

Cathy fidgeted with her spoon, then took a swallow of cooling chocolate. "I've been visiting Battlefield Park every morning."

"Yes?" Susan prompted.

"The first time I walked through the park I stood by a grave overgrown with weeds. The broken tombstone seemed so lonesome, being untended like that. The inscription was of a young British soldier killed during the Battle of Princeton."

Susan's eyebrows lifted, but she remained silent and expectant.

"Edward Marsh was the name on the tomb. He died on January 3, 1777." Cathy studied her fingertips. "I was drawn back to his grave as if it were a magnet. Susan . . . I *talked* to that soldier."

"Did he answer you?" Susan queried, an amused twinkle in her eye.

Cathy's steady gaze locked with Susan's. "Yes, he did," she said in a firm tone.

Susan's eyes widened. "The *dead* soldier actually talked to you?"

"Please believe me, Susan. I heard him!"

Cathy leaned forward. "Edward appeared to me in his British uniform. He's very handsome and tall and blond. He explained how he'd been shot in the battle. He died in Nassau Hall. He was just twenty years old." She continued breathlessly, "He grew up in London and when he was only fourteen he was sent to military school."

Stupefied, Susan stared at her.

"Susan, say something." Cathy felt her body grow tense, waiting for her friend to speak.

Susan was silent for a few seconds, then

said in slow, measured words, "Cathy, you've dreamed up this soldier." She stopped for effect. "There's *no* Edward Marsh. He's a figment of your imagination."

"He's real, Susan," Cathy said earnestly. "I saw him! We had conversations!"

Susan glanced around at customers and waitresses. "Let's get out of here." She picked up the check and slid out of the booth.

"All right," Cathy said in a small disappointed voice. Clearly, Susan didn't believe her.

Once outside they quietly walked side by side. Unable to say another word about Edward Marsh, Cathy plodded through a narrow snow path. She didn't look to the right or left.

"Cathy," Susan said sincerely, "you've got to admit your story is bizarre." She grabbed Cathy's hand. "I think you've fantasized a spirit to talk to. Maybe to *you* he's real."

Cathy still stared ahead of her, unable to look at Susan. She muttered dispiritedly, "I hoped you'd believe me, Susan. I guess that was stupid of me."

"I want to, Cathy, but I stopped believing in ghosts when I stopped believing in Santa Claus."

Cathy lashed out, "If you saw Edward like I saw him, you'd believe me!"

"Don't be angry with me," Susan said softly. "I guess I'm just too practical."

A horrible thought struck Cathy. "Susan," she begged, "please don't tell anyone about this."

"I won't," Susan said. "Honest."

"Promise?"

"I promise," Susan said solemnly.

But Cathy wished she hadn't told her. What if Edward never came to her again because she'd divulged his name!

Crushed, she parted from Susan slowly and went home. Oh, why did she ever tell her? She vowed she'd never breathe Edward's name to another living person.

That evening while waiting for Bryan, Cathy caught a glimpse of herself in the mirror as she fastened a silver necklace around her neck. She moved closer, not displeased with what she saw. She felt pretty tonight. Her short skirt flared around high boots and she straightened the collar on her crisp white blouse.

She had put her conversation with Susan out of her mind. She knew Susan would never reveal her secret. No matter how — what was the term Edward would use? oh, yes, "daft" — no matter how daft Susan thought she was.

At least, Cathy thought, I'm talking to a real person, not trees.

When Bryan arrived, she was determined to enjoy the concert and to forget this afternoon.

Bryan took her hand and said she looked wonderful. Cathy enjoyed the ride to Trenton and the string quartet concert.

After the concert they stopped for hot dogs and Cokes, then, on the return trip, drove along the Delaware River.

"You know, Cathy," Bryan said, pulling up before Aunt Hannah's, "you're gorgeous, you appreciate classical music, and you're happy eating a hot dog." He smiled down at her. "That's quite a combination of attributes."

Bryan held her hand, moving forward to kiss her cheek. "Ummm. You smell delicious." He smiled. "I don't know when I've had more fun with anyone."

She didn't know whether this was the time or not, but she had to know. She wasn't the type to trespass. Pulling away from him, she sat back against the leather and said, "More fun than with *anyone?*" she stressed the last word.

Bryan's eyes narrowed, but his tone was light. "More fun than *just* about anyone."

"Ah," she said with a knowing tilt of her

head. "You have a girlfriend, don't you?"

"You have a boyfriend," he stated in a bantering way.

"Yes," she said, "I do."

Bryan gave her a half-smile, then shrugged. "But he's in Chicago, right?"

"Yes, and you and I are only friends. Right, Bryan?"

He held out his hands in front of him, giving her a likable grin. "Only friends, Cathy." Then his grin vanished. "I did have a girl, Ann Bishop, but we broke up last month. We agreed to date others. So you see, you're not stepping on anyone's toes."

She was glad *he* had told her himself.

He lifted her chin with his thumb. "Your eyes sparkle in the dark like cats' eyes. Tell me, Cathy," he said reaching for her hand again, "are you serious about this Mike?"

Not answering him, she thoughtfully mulled over his question. When she left Chicago she was angry at Mike, but she loved him. Now sitting here with Bryan, she wasn't certain about Mike at all. Maybe she just wasn't ready for a real commitment. Maybe she was too young.

Chapter 15

Cathy waited for Edward at the gazebo. She gazed out over the glistening snow and wondered if he would be there.

But she didn't have to wonder long. Edward Marsh, in his splendid red and white uniform, appeared in the gazebo. She hadn't seen him coming. He had just seemed to materialize. "Good morning, Edward," she said, her heart fluttering.

"Good morning, Cathy." He bowed slightly, removing his tricornered hat.

"Sit beside me," Cathy urged.

With a smile, he seated himself. "Cathy," he said softly, "you are always in my thoughts." He took her gloved hand in his. The breeze ruffled his golden hair and he said, "Would you like to go dancing in London?"

Cathy stared at him in amazement, then laughed aloud. "Someday I hope I will."

"No, my dear Cathy, *now*." He waved his hand to the east. Two huge double doors with golden insets loomed before her. Edward got up and turned the ornate doorknob and a door swung open to dazzling light and beauty.

Cathy gasped. No longer was she surrounded by snow or cold, but there was warmth and loveliness. In wonder she stared at the yellow satin gown she wore. Lace panels trailed down the front with tiny roses embedded in the frills. The sleeves were elbow-length trimmed in several tiers of lace. A high frilled collar set off a low rounded neckline. She touched her high hairdo with a coil of curls draping over her shoulder. On the top of her head she wore a small yellow cap with ribbons and feathers, and on her right wrist, tied with a ribbon, a jeweled green fan.

Before her, Edward bowed, looking exceedingly handsome in a black waistcoat, a tight-fitting blue vest, and a shirt with a frilly lace shirtfront. Lacy cuffs peeked out from beneath his coat sleeves. His gray knee breeches and white silk stockings were accentuated by shiny black shoes with big buckles.

Edward swept off his tricornered hat, revealing a powdered wig tied by a black ribbon on the nape of his neck. "Miss O'Brien," he asked gallantly, "would you allow me to escort you into Vauxhall Gardens?"

"I'd be honored, sir," Cathy replied, placing her hand on his and moving forward. Lifting her skirt and displaying a lacy underskirt and embroidered shoes, she climbed the stairs into a ballroom.

Lilting music swirled about her as she stared transfixed at the glittering chandelier, the white walls with gold-trimmed mirrors, and the highly polished floors. Couples danced sedately to the minuet. The next dance, Edward encircled her waist and swept her onto the floor to enter the formal dance.

Edward smiled as they danced to the sweet music of violins and a spinet. "You look radiant tonight, Cathy," he said in a husky voice.

"And you also, Edward." Her words were light, but he fairly took her breath away. His height and grace dominated the ballroom.

But she was mistaken if she thought all eyes were on Edward, because every time she glanced around the room, gentlemen stared at her, their eyes moving from her head to her toes. They smiled in approval and slightly nodded their wigged heads in greeting. Coyly, she acknowledged them by lowering her eyelids and discreetly smiling.

Her heart soared and her slippers felt as if

they had wings. She smiled at Edward, stepping sedately to the rhythm of the music.

When the dance was over, Edward asked, "Would you like to see the gardens?"

"I'd love to," she answered, feeling as sparkling as the ballroom.

Outside they walked hand in hand along a graveled path, covered with awnings and lined with elm trees. "This is the Grand Walk," Edward said, then slowly steered her to a second walk or South Walk. As they strolled through its many archways, he dipped his head murmuring in her ear, "Now, we're walking into the Dark Walk, sometimes called the Lover's Walk. Do you dare?"

Her laughter rippled on the night air. "I'll dare, Edward." They entered a narrow path with blooming rosebushes and yew trees and hidden alcoves. The scent of honeysuckle filled the summer evening and benches dotted the path. Here and there couples sat side by side. She noticed a gentleman steal a kiss from a woman in a blue dress with white ribbons around her neckline. The woman giggled, playfully hitting the man's arm with her fan.

"Shall we?" Edward asked, dusting off a wooden bench with his handkerchief.

Cathy seated herself, unable to believe where she was, what was happening.

Edward touched her cheek, gently turning her toward him. "I love you, Cathy."

"Oh, Edward," she said breathlessly. "Don't! This isn't real. This is . . ."

"Do you think you could learn to love me?" He asked earnestly, ignoring her remarks.

For a swift moment a cloudlike face hovered above Cathy. As the features cleared she could see who it was — Mike Novak! He whispered, "Don't forget me, Cathy."

Impatiently she shook her head to rid herself of the troublesome image. She was in the eighteenth century with Edward. She wouldn't allow a disturbing twentieth-century Mike to intrude on this magical night.

Edward leaned over and kissed her cheek, then his lips found hers. Enjoying the delicious sensation of his kiss, she put her arms around him. He kissed her again. Feeling giddy, Cathy drew back. The image of Mike lingered around the edges of her mind.

All at once a bell clanged and Edward released her. "Nine o'clock and time for an extravaganza." He stood again, taking her hand.

"Now we'll witness magic, Cathy." He smiled, helping her to her feet.

They went out to the Cascades, where Cathy glimpsed a miller's house. What, she wondered, was an old miller's house doing in these elaborate gardens? Suddenly, a tumultuous waterfall cascaded over the miller's wheel. The wheel turned! A picturesque mill and foaming water were indeed a spectacle.

An organist played, pounding the chords until the notes rose to a crescendo. The crowd cheered and applauded.

Edward looked down at her, clearly pleased at her reaction. "Now we shall dine," he said. He threaded his way through the crowds, pulling Cathy behind him.

"We have a reserved supper box where my parents will join us," he explained.

Edward and Cathy were the first to arrive in the supper room, a comfortable, small chamber. Cathy examined two charming wall paintings, one, a country dance, hung on the east wall and the other, a game of leap frog, hung on the west.

"My father and mother should be here by now," Edward said, glancing about.

What would they think of her, Cathy wondered.

And just then the drape on the doorway was pulled aside and a middle-aged man and woman entered.

Edward introduced his mother, a tiny woman with a shy manner. Mrs. Regina Marsh said in a sweet quavery voice that she was pleased to meet Cathy. Her white muslin dress, decorated with blue and gold ribbons, rustled as she moved daintily to a chair. Once seated her eyes darted from one face to another causing her blonde curls to bob about her head.

When Edward's father, Colonel Nigel Marsh, was introduced to Cathy he bowed stiffly from the waist, then stood as if he were on dress parade. At least six feet in height, he looked splendid in his uniform of buckskin trousers and a red coat with brass buttons.

"How do you do, Miss O'Brien," Mr. Marsh said, smoothing his large handlebar moustache. Then, after kissing her hand, he marched to his chair.

As if a signal had been given, the waiters brought in steaming silver-covered dishes: ham, chicken, tongue, peas, and biscuits. These succulent foods were followed by pickled peaches, cherries, strawberries, plums, grapes, and cheese cakes. The last course consisted of mounds of ice cream.

Once finished, Cathy leaned back in her chair, touching her mouth with her napkin. "What a sumptuous feast! I don't know when I've eaten so much or so well!"

Colonel Marsh stared at Cathy with pale blue eyes. Finally, he spoke in clipped words.

"Where are you from, Miss O'Brien? I can tell by your speech you're neither Irish nor English."

Cathy felt intimidated by his cold look and before she could answer, Edward said, "Father, Cathy is from the American colonies."

"The American colonies! Those upstarts!" The colonel sputtered, his moustache twitching. "Damn rebels! We need to send over our troops and teach them a lesson! Throwing tea into Boston Harbor, my eye!"

"But England has taxed us more than any other colony," Cathy protested, feeling a warm flush of anger stain her cheeks. "It's not the Americans' fault and the more England taxes us, the more we should fight for our freedom! And we will!"

And we will win, she thought. But how could she say that? How could she explain knowing that?

Colonel Marsh reared back in his chair, surprised at Cathy's outburst. Then he leaped to his feet. "Come, Regina. We'll leave Edward with this little colonist!" He turned to his son. "Don't tarry long, Edward, you'll need to get up early in the morning to join your regiment!" With a parting glare at Cathy, he yanked open the curtain and stormed out.

Regina twittered after. "Now, Nigel, please,

let's be calm. Don't . . ." her words trailed off.

"I'm sorry I upset your father, Edward, but I must stand up for what my country did. Please understand," she pleaded.

Edward took her in his arms. "Of course, my dearest. I admire you." He chuckled. "Not many people dare stand up to Father."

She smiled at him, pleased that he could see her viewpoint.

"Let's go out to the Garden Walk." He took her arm and they left the supper room.

In the garden she delighted in the clusters of violets and sweet smelling lilacs. She bent to smell a dusky rose. "Oh, Edward, isn't this beautiful?"

But when she glanced around, Edward had disappeared. The garden, too, was gone. She looked down at her dress only to find the filmy yellow gown had been replaced by plaid pants and a ski jacket. Surrounding her were piles of snow and icicles dangling from the gazebo.

She gazed at the clear sunny sky. What a wonderland Edward had taken her to. A ball in London at the Vauxhall Gardens! She thought of the Garden Walk, the waterfall, and the delicious supper. But of all her memories the one she would never forget was Edward's kiss. She smiled, remembering. But there were tears in her eyes.

Now, however, she was back in Princeton. She left the gazebo, knowing Edward wouldn't return today, and she felt cold. He'd said he loved her. To be loved by such a handsome British soldier was a marvel. But it was all so strange and confusing. She was pleased he had shown her his life before he'd joined the army. She could be happy in London society. She might even win the colonel over. At this idea, she shivered.

How could she think these things? She was a twentieth-century girl. She couldn't go back. She didn't *want* to go back. Or did she?

Chapter 16

That afternoon at the shop, Cathy was silent as she unpacked toy soldiers and placed them on a shelf. Each soldier wore the uniform of an American in the Revolutionary War. How different they were from the colorful British redcoats.

Cathy examined one soldier, no taller than six inches. The private wore a brown coat, mustard-yellow vest and trousers with gray leggings fastened up to his knees. He carried a musket. Carefully she put him on the shelf.

She picked up a second soldier and discovered this was no mere private. This was a diminutive likeness of General George Washington. His striking uniform consisted of buckskin trousers, black boots, a blue jacket with gold buttons and epaulettes, and a white frilled shirt. A curved saber was strapped to his side. She remembered that Edward had seen Washington at the Battle of Princeton. The general sat on a white horse. What a sight he must have been. Here, in her hand, Washington was only a few inches high. In real life, though, he was over six feet tall and a forceful man. She put the little figure next to the private.

The third soldier who had fought in the Continental Army must have been a frontiersman. He wore a practical uniform consisting of a buckskin jacket reaching to his knees and cinched in the middle by a long red sash and buckskin trousers of the same soft yellow as the jacket. He carried a long Pennsylvania rifle with a powder horn at his side. And a jaunty fur cap completed his outfit.

She stood ten soldiers in a row, fascinated at the detail and accuracy of each one.

Susan, coming from the back room, wiped her hands on a towel. "Those soldiers are real antiques," she commented, plucking one off the shelf. "They're heavier than they look, aren't they?"

"They're made of lead," Cathy answered, glancing at Susan's red hands. "Did you and Aunt Hannah clean up that huge nineteenth-century urn that came from England?"

"Most of it," Susan said, dropping into a chair. "What a job! Right now, Hannah's finishing the polish. It's four feet tall and two feet in circumference. The gigantic vase was part of Lord Hadley's collection." She chuckled. "Those Victorians sure liked massive furniture."

"I can't wait to see it cleaned up," Cathy said.

"You're just interested in it because it came from England," Susan teased, "and because your ghostly Edward was an Englishman."

Cathy's face grew hot. What was she supposed to answer? She knew Susan didn't believe in Edward so she didn't mention the urn again.

"Oh! I almost forgot," Susan said, her eyes lighting up. "We're throwing a New Year's Eve gala tomorrow night. Will you come? Bryan will pick you up. He's dying for you to be there!"

"I'd love to," Cathy said, pleased to be invited, hoping she could forget Edward. She couldn't believe it was almost New Year's Eve.

"I'm going to buy a new dress," Susan said. "Will you come with me?" She squeezed Cathy's hand. "Please. I need some advice!"

Cathy smiled. "Sounds great. I might look for one myself. My mother gave me money and said I could buy something new as part of my Christmas present."

"I'll get my coat," Susan said, dashing to the back room.

Cathy stared out the window, seeing bundled up shoppers scurry by. Yet she didn't see them, either. She remembered last New Year's Eve. Her mom had gone out with a new man called Zack and Cathy had attended a party at Dana's. She'd enjoyed herself at Dana's, dancing with five different boys. Not one, though, really sparked her interest. How she'd longed to meet "Mr. Right." Last year she'd been a sophomore in high school and thought she'd never find someone to love. Then in the summer she'd met Mike! She'd fallen in love. But during this New Year's Eve, she found herself not only in love with Mike, but thinking of Edward and Bryan as well. Was she shallow? Fickle?

She traced a heart on the frosty windowpane. She had been so certain of Mike. What had happened? For one thing, Edward had entered her life.

"Ready?" Susan said, coming up behind her and looking at the heart on the window. "How about this?" And she drew two arrows through the heart. "One for Mike and one for my brother," she laughingly teased. "Cathy, you have two boys that love you and you're in a quandary. I should be so lucky."

Silently, Cathy thought, not just two boys, Susan — three! But Susan would never concede that Edward actually existed. Wistfully, she slipped into her jacket and walked with Susan to the dress shop. All the way, she wished she could tell her about her evening at the Vauxhall Gardens, but knew it was hopeless to ever mention Edward again.

Soon, though, she forgot her dilemma and lost herself in trying on dresses. Susan found a red taffeta. She stood before Cathy, then spun around, chestnut hair flying. "How do you like it?"

"That's the dress, Susan! You look terrific," Cathy exclaimed. "You'll have every boy swooning over you."

"Swooning?" Susan grinned. "Sounds like you're living in another century to me!"

Cathy turned, not wanting Susan to see her flaming cheeks. She went through more dresses on the rack. "Do you like this?" she asked, holding up a short white dress.

"Try it on," urged Susan.

When Cathy emerged from the dressing room, Susan nodded her head. "It's cool!" she exclaimed. "It shows off your great legs and that full skirt will be fabulous when you dance."

Again, Cathy checked herself in the three-way mirror. The satin belt made her waist look tiny. White also brought out the vibrancy of her red hair. Yes, it was perfect.

Both girls left the shop, pleased with their purchases. To celebrate they stopped for Cokes.

As Cathy waited for her drink, she drummed her fingers on the table, yearning to be able to talk to Susan about Edward. But she dare not. Instead, she asked, "What time is the party?"

Susan studied her. "Oh, anytime after eight o'clock." She sipped her drink, her large dark eyes never leaving Cathy's face. "There's something on your mind, isn't there, Cathy? Did you see Edward again?" she asked bluntly.

Cathy didn't know whether to shrug off her question or to answer her honestly. She decided to tell Susan all her wonderful adventures.

When she'd finished to the last detail, even mentioning Edward's stern father, she waited for Susan's reaction.

With her straw, Susan stirred the ice in her glass before replying, "I think Edward is as real to you as I am, but I'm afraid you're in for a letdown." Her eyes were compassionate.

"What will you do when he doesn't come to you again? Will you realize then that he's a fantasy?"

Cathy shook her head. "You don't understand, Susan."

Susan reached across the table and touched Cathy's arm. "No, I don't." She smiled. "It is hard for me to believe."

Cathy put her hand over Susan's. "At least you're not laughing."

And for a few minutes all that could be heard was the ringing of the cash register.

"Well, I suppose I'd better get home," Susan said, gathering up her gloves and scarf.

Cathy said, "Yes, I don't know what my aunt and uncle think of me." She chuckled. "I'm almost never home. Of course they have very busy lives, too, so I know they don't mind."

But before she could make a move to leave, Bryan flung open the door and spotted them. He sat down next to Cathy, a big grin on his face. "Did my sister ask you to our New Year's Eve party?"

Cathy nodded. "Yes, she did and the answer is yes."

"All right!" He banged his fist on the table. "This calls for a hot dog!" And he motioned the waitress over.

"You two can spoil your supper if you want

to, but I'm going home," Susan announced, pulling on a glove.

"See you later, Susan," Bryan said, giving her a two-fingered salute.

"I'll see you tomorrow, Susan," Cathy said, "but I'm not sure what time."

"I think I know why," Susan answered tightly. "You have business elsewhere."

Cathy gave Susan a warning look, but she knew it was unnecessary. Susan would never give away her secret.

After Susan left, Cathy glanced at Bryan but he was unsuspecting of any signals. He was too busy piling relish, mustard, ketchup, and onion on his hot dog.

"What's in the package?" he asked between mouthfuls.

"A new dress for tomorrow night."

"Ummm, may I see?"

"You'll have to wait," she said lightly.

"On you," Bryan said, licking his fingers, "anything would look good."

"There you go with that blarney talk again."

He gazed at her and slowly shook his head. "No, I mean it," he said softly.

"Thanks," she said, smiling. Then switching moods, she asked, "Who's going to be at your party?"

"Oh, a bunch of people you don't know. A

few of the Princeton guys that had to stay in town over the holidays. Oh, you know Phil Bronstein. He'll be there."

"Good, I like Phil."

"So does Susan." He winked at Cathy. "Maybe for once, Susan has not only found a boy she likes, but," he added, "one that's taller than she is."

Bryan grew serious. "Do you mind if I ask you a personal question?"

"Try me," she replied.

"Do you miss Mike?"

Startled by his inquiry, she wasn't certain how to reply. "In some ways," she answered. "But Princeton is new and exciting. I've met lots of people I like. I haven't had much time to think about Mike." She hoped her response would satisfy him. However, if he could ask a personal question, so could she. "And you, Bryan, do you miss Ann Bishop?"

He chewed on his straw. "Sometimes," he said noncommittally. "Ann is a lot like you, Cathy. She laughs a lot, she has a bubbling personality, and she's bright."

"But you decided to date other girls?"

"I didn't," he said gruffly. "It was Ann's idea. Then it became a mutual decision. We decided that we were too wrapped up with one another. Maybe we needed to have other experiences. No strings attached." He reached in his back pocket and pulled out his wallet, shuffling through cards and photos. "Here's Ann." He held out her picture to Cathy.

Cathy looked at the photo of a lively brunette who stood cradling a pair of skis. Laughing, she squinted into the sun, her sleek black hair held back by a ski band. Her green ski suit emphasized her slim figure.

"She's lovely, Bryan."

"She's a top student, too," he said with pride. "She's majoring in chemistry." He gave her a brilliant smile. "You two would get along fine." He took back Ann's photo. Slipping the picture back in its slot, he turned to Cathy. "Do you have a picture of Mike?"

"Yes," she said, almost shyly, not knowing whether to share Mike with Bryan or not.

"Let's see it," he prodded.

From her wallet, she removed a snapshot of Mike at the beach. She looked at it briefly before handing it to Bryan. Mike, wearing a swimsuit and casually leaning against a sailboat, brought a pang to her heart. His flashing white teeth against a tanned rugged face was so appealing. She'd almost forgotten how attractive he was.

"Where was this taken?"

"At Juneway Beach — last summer. That's

Lake Michigan in the background," she explained, remembering that day. They both loved the water and when they'd been exhausted from swimming and sailing, they fell onto a blanket where Mike had kissed her for the first time. The most wonderful kiss she'd ever received. At that moment she knew that Mike was the boy for her.

"I can see how he might impress a young girl, like you." Bryan's voice was light and mocking. "Does he have more brawn than brains?"

Cathy snatched Mike's photo from Bryan, irritated at his assessment. "He's the most intelligent boy I've ever known," she said, lifting her chin defiantly.

"More than a Princeton boy?" he bantered.

"Every bit!" she snapped, irked at his superior manner.

Bryan grasped her hand and rubbed it against his cheek. Obviously, he sensed her annoyance. "Please," he said, "don't be angry. I was only teasing you, Cathy. Where's your sense of humor?" When he saw she wasn't amused, he said, "I'm sorry, I didn't mean anything. Forgive me?"

He coaxed a smile from her and soon they were talking about movies and music. Bryan, she thought with a smile, could charm a cobra out of its basket and keep it swaying better than any Indian fakir.

"Will you go with me to a new French film at the Village Theater?" Bryan asked. "We'll grab a bite afterward."

Tonight stretched ahead of her rather bleakly for she knew her aunt and uncle were playing bridge. And she didn't want to be alone. "All right." She consented, giving him a weak smile.

Bryan was so pleased, he leaped up and hurriedly struggled into his jacket. "Then we'd better get going. I'll pick you up around six." He held her jacket for her. "Let me take you home first."

"No, I'd rather walk," she said. "It's not that far, and the fresh air will do me good."

He took her arm and walked her to the door. "See you in a little while," he said, pecking her on the cheek.

She broke into a run, then jogged most of the way home, the clear, exhilarating air cold on her face.

When she arrived home, she was pleased that a letter was propped up on the table for her. She hoped it was from Mike. No, this time it was from Johnny. She was happy, though, to hear from her little brother.

Tearing open the envelope, she read:

Dear Sis,

Vacation has been great. I've been skating on Lincoln Lagoon and playing lots of hockey. The other day I was over to Nick's and we went to the show and saw a new sci-fi movie, can't remember the name. My hockey game is improving. Zack gave me some pointers that really helped. He brought me a dog story to read, *Big Red*. It was good. Last night he took Mom and me to a jazz concert at DePaul. Saw Mike. Don't get excited. He wasn't with a girl. He was with a couple of guys. He said he missed you — don't know why. Ha!

Phineas misses you, though. That cat pokes his paw in a closet and sniffs all around. But you're not there. I play with him a lot. I hold up his mouse and he jumps six feet in the air. He's a real acrobat.

Hope you're having a good time in Princeton and say hello to Aunt Hannah and Uncle Frank for me. What do you do there all day long?

Nothing else to write about so goodbye.

Johnny

She folded the letter, glad Johnny was happy and Mike was taking time for a concert. Things seemed normal. She did miss everyone and would be glad to fly home on Sunday.

Gazing out the window, she thought of Bryan, Susan, and Edward. She'd miss them. And, of course, Aunt Hannah and Uncle Frank. But the two of them promised to come to Chicago this spring. With the others, she doubted if she'd ever see them again unless Susan came for a visit. But not Bryan or Edward. She'd probably never see them again.

She hurried to her room to dress. After showering, she put on jeans and a sweater. Bryan meant well, she mused, it was just that he could be brash. She'd never met anyone with quite so much self-confidence.

As she brushed on a faint pink blush, she abruptly stopped, hand in midair.

"Hello, Cathy."

Looking in the mirror, she saw Edward, who had appeared from nowhere. He sat gazing at her, his legs casually crossed. How handsome he looked in his shiny uniform and his golden hair curling about his ears.

"Edward!" she exclaimed. "I hadn't expected to find you *here*."

"I'll be where you least expect me," he said, tilting his head with an amused expression. "I see you're going out with Bryan again."

She swiveled about on her dressing-table stool and faced him, her eyes widening. "How did you know that?"

"I keep track of the girl I love," he said with a teasing grin.

"Oh, Edward," she came to him, holding out her two hands. "I care about you, too. What will become of us? How can we ever be together?"

"We'll find a way."

His positive attitude almost made her believe him.

"You'd better hurry," Edward said. "Bryan's at the door."

"I didn't hear anything," Cathy said, puzzled.

Just then the doorbell rang.

Cathy smiled at Edward as he rose and kissed her on the forehead. "Have a good time." And he walked through the door and was gone.

She pulled herself together, ready to face Bryan, but how could she? After seeing Edward?

Chapter 17

In the movie, Cathy sat rigidly beside Bryan, scarcely noticing the images on the screen. She relived her brief interlude with Edward. How amazed she'd been to see him in her bedroom. He'd looked so handsome in his British uniform and boots. She longed to spend more time with him. Hopefully tomorrow he'd be at her side.

Casually, Bryan threw his arm around the back of her seat, leaning close and whispering, "Did you see those scenes of Notre Dame? I've been there."

She shot him a wary look, but Bryan obviously was enjoying the scenes of Paris. He didn't realize how far away her thoughts were.

At last the movie was over and she hoped Bryan wouldn't expect her to comment on the plot. She didn't have the foggiest idea of what went on.

Fortunately, once they were seated in Pete's Place, Bryan was too excited about the party he and Susan were throwing to discuss the film. "Tomorrow afternoon Susan and I are decorating the house for the party. Want to help?"

"Sure, I'll help," she said. "It should be fun." The memory of the ball she'd attended with Edward crossed her mind. Nothing could compare to such a glittering evening.

"I said," Bryan repeated in a louder voice, "Is one o'clock okay?"

"Wh — what? Sorry, Bryan, I was thinking of something else." She cleared her throat nervously. "One o'clock is fine. How many are invited?"

"Twelve or fourteen, depending on the RSVP's we receive today."

After a light snack, Bryan drove around the park and headed for Carnegie Lake. "Thought you might like to relax and look at the lake in the frozen moonlight." He gave her a questioning glance. "You seem a little tense tonight. Everything all right?"

"Yes, I'm okay," she said, keeping her eyes on the sliver of road up ahead. Bryan probably thought she was dreaming of Mike. She prayed he'd never find out about Edward.

Bryan swung his sports car into a spot overlooking the frozen lake. "Beautiful, isn't it?" He put his arm around her and the two of them gazed at the moonlit ice.

Cathy was content to contemplate such a peaceful scene. Snow began, the large flakes falling like soft petals on the lake's surface.

Bryan seemed lost in thought, too. Was he thinking of Ann?

Bryan had been right. The restful spot and the comfort of his arms had erased the turmoil in her mind.

Cathy didn't know how long they sat together, but when the wind picked up, and snow swirled against the windshield, Bryan turned the ignition key and drove her home. It had been a quiet evening, Cathy thought. Quite unlike the usual laughing talkative Bryan.

Arriving at her aunt and uncle's, Bryan walked her to the door. He stroked her face and smiled down at her. "I guess we didn't have much to say this evening. It felt nice. You're an easy person to be with, Cathy." His smile widened into a grin. "We'll have a good stompin' time tomorrow, though!" He enfolded her in a big hug, then kissed the tip of her nose.

"Till tomorrow," he said in a low voice.

When Cathy entered the living room, Frank and Hannah sat in front of the fire, playing a game of cribbage.

"Fifteen, two, fifteen, four, and a pair is six," Uncle Frank said.

"Okay," Hannah said, marking down the score.

After removing her jacket, Cathy sat next to Uncle Frank as he moved the peg up two notches on the cribbage board.

"Hi, Cathy," Hannah said, keeping an eye on Frank's moves. "Have a good time?"

"Yes, Bryan and I went to a French film at the Village," she said. "I forgot the title." And, she thought, I forgot the scenario, too.

"There's chips and dip over on the coffee table," Frank said.

"No, thanks," Cathy replied. "We ate a bite after the movie."

"Oh," Hannah said, lightly slapping her forehead, "I almost forgot. A fax came for you. It's upstairs on Frank's machine."

"I'll run and get it."

She saw the fax addressed to her and read it. It was from Mike and his message was simple: I love you. Mike.

She laughed. Darling Mike. Everytime her thoughts strayed from him, he always reminded her of his love. She sank into Frank's big leather chair and twirled this way and that, thinking of Mike and their shared love.

She remembered the time when she didn't have swim practice and he had picked her up. They'd headed for the reading center. It was in a poor neighborhood near the el tracks, and the train often drowned out a reader who read aloud. The center had over twenty-five people who desired to learn to read. How their faces lit up when Mike appeared. She, too, felt pleased when she sounded out a word on the vocabulary list for someone. Good-natured Mike never tired.

She kissed his message and slipped it into her pocket.

Thoughtfully, she went back downstairs, picturing what Mike was doing this very minute. Knowing him, he was poring over a book, studying for his political science course. Or, maybe he and his father were discussing ideas to help the forty-ninth ward.

Frank and Hannah were having a cup of coffee, their game finished.

"Who won?" Cathy asked.

"Frank." Hannah said in a disgusted voice. "By two points!"

Frank guffawed. "Third time in a row, too!" He winked at Cathy. "Hannah is very competitive and hates to lose."

"I'm with you, Aunt Hannah," Cathy said, going toward the kitchen. "Be right back." She went to the refrigerator and popped open a can of soda, then rejoined them.

"You have a young man in Chicago that's very fond of you," Uncle Frank stated with a chuckle. When he noticed Cathy's surprise, he added, "I didn't mean to pry, but your fax couldn't be missed."

Cathy nodded. "That's okay. I guess you've heard of Mike Novak."

"Yes," Hannah said. "Your mother mentioned him."

"I was upset with Mike when I left," Cathy said ruefully. "Seems like he has no time for me. He's always working." She studied her rabbit slippers which she kept by the front door so she had something to put on when she pulled off her boots. "I'm feeling better about him now, though."

"I can see why," Uncle Frank said with a grin. His beard seemed to twitch when he added, "Be happy he's not just wasting his time."

Cathy knew he was right, but neither he nor Hannah understood her relationship with Mike. She took a swallow of soda and changed the subject, "Has Mother told you about Zack?"

Hannah chuckled. "Has she told us about Zack! Everytime Sara calls she raves about his sweetness and capability. This is the happiest she's been since your father died. I'm glad she's found someone." Hannah gave Cathy a penetrating look. "Do you like Zack?"

How could she answer without appearing totally selfish. "Zack is okay," she said in a less than enthusiastic tone. "Johnny is crazy about him."

Hannah leaned over and patted Cathy's knee. "A new stepfather would be an adjustment, wouldn't it?"

"A big one!" Cathy exclaimed. "No one can take the place of my dad."

"Of course not," Hannah said warmly. "Sean was the darlingest man I ever knew." She gave her husband an amused glance. "Outside of Frank, naturally."

Cathy smiled. "I miss him," she said in a small voice.

"I know," Hannah said sympathetically. "We all do."

"Yes, Sean was unique," Frank said, his eyes warm and caring. "I used to love to hear him sing."

"But, time goes on," Hannah said. "I think Zack is a fine man from what your mother tells me. I'm certain, Cathy, with your fairness and ability to get along with people that you will like Zack, too."

A log shifted on the fire, crackling and spitting.

Cathy jumped up, not wishing to talk about Zack any longer. Or even her father. It was too painful. "I think I'll get ready for bed," she said, giving her aunt and uncle each a kiss.

Uncle Frank smiled. "We like having you here, Cath. Come back often."

"Not," Cathy teased, shaking a finger under his nose, "until you visit us in Chicago."

"Sleep well, Cathy," Hannah said softly.

"I will," Cathy answered, climbing the steps.

But that night, she didn't sleep well at all. She tossed and turned, awakening frequently. What if Hannah was right about Zack? What if she was the only one that didn't want him in their lives?

She dreamed, too. Once, she walked in a garden filled with roses, but when she picked one, a thorn pricked her finger. Drops of blood fell to the ground. All at once an American soldier dressed in a Continental uniform rushed by. His bayonet drawn. "Where's he hiding?" he yelled.

Bewildered, she'd confronted him. "Who

are you hunting? There's no one is in this garden. Leave!"

Viciously, he'd shoved her to the ground, standing over her. "You know very well, Tory traitor," he sneered. "Where have you hidden the British scum?"

Trembling, she stumbled to her feet. She tried to flee but her legs wouldn't move. She stood, rooted to the path. Horrified, she watched the soldier plunge his bayonet into one rosebush after another.

"He's here!" yelled the American soldier. A shout, a groan! And a soldier with a red coat tumbled forward, lying motionless beneath the roses.

A moan awakened her. Cathy shivered. She was the one who had moaned. She sat up, arms clasped around her chest. What a terrible nightmare.

At last, she lay back, staring into the darkness. Pummeling her pillow, she tried to sleep. But if she had to risk another dream like that, she'd rather sit up all night. Eventually, she drifted into a fitful sleep.

Chapter 18

The next morning, Hannah came into her room, gently shaking Cathy's shoulder. "Your mother's on the phone, sleepyhead. She and I have been talking for thirty minutes. You can say hello on your phone."

Cathy squinted at her aunt. "What time is it?"

"Almost ten," Hannah answered. "Come down when you're finished. There are waffles for breakfast." She left, closing the door.

Rubbing her eyes, Cathy grappled for the phone. "Hi, Mom," she croaked.

"Cathy, you're sleeping late," Sara laughed. "Don't you know you're supposed to do that *after* New Year's Eve?"

"How's everything, Mom?" Cathy said, sleepily.

"Okay," Sara answered. "I've been busy, but I have today off and tomorrow."

"And Johnny?"

"Johnny's already left for Lincoln Park and hockey practice. Hannah tells me you've made friends in Princeton. I knew you wouldn't have any trouble. I hear you're going to a party tonight."

"Yes, at Susan and Bryan Gorman's," Cathy answered. "I work with Susan and I've been to a movie with Bryan." She didn't say how many times she'd seen him.

"Poor Mike."

"Why?" Cathy asked, her heart skipping a beat. "Is anything wrong?"

"No, not at all. But he'll be all alone. He's called several times and taken Johnny skating. He's a busy boy, but he misses you. He's asked a hundred questions. What are you doing? Who have you met? He really cares for you, Cathy."

Cathy felt a tingle of pleasure at these words, then she asked, "Do you have plans for New Year's Eve, Mom?"

She replied, "Yes, Zack and I are going to the Ritz-Carlton for dinner and dancing." A slight hesitation on the other end, then her slow words came on the line, "He's asked to marry me, Cathy."

Cathy felt as if someone had flung ice water in her face, but forced herself to remain calm.

"I hope your reply wasn't yes," she said, her voice cool. Fully awake now, she held her spine rigid as she waited for her mother's reply.

"I told him I'd think about it," Sara said. "We'll talk about it when you return."

"I'd better go, Mom. Aunt Hannah has a waffle waiting."

"Happy New Year, darling. And remember Zack wants to take us out to dinner when you get off the plane on Sunday."

"I know. Got to run. Happy New Year yourself! 'Bye." And Cathy slowly replaced the receiver. There was no escaping Zack. She'd been expecting his proposal to Mom, yet she'd always hoped it wouldn't happen.

Throwing back the covers, she got out of bed, and into the shower. She tipped her head under the water stream, soaping her hair. There must be ways, she thought, to discourage her mother about Zack. Surely other men could be found. Maybe Mike's dad could introduce her mother to an exciting man. She pressed her lips together. She'd think of something!

Stepping out of the shower and grabbing a towel, she thought of a more immediate worry. Rubbing herself dry, she prayed she hadn't missed her chance of seeing Edward.

She'd almost slept the morning away. And she still had to eat breakfast!

Wrapping a towel, turban-fashion, around her hair, she turned the doorknob. Then stopped! What if Edward were sitting in the chair, waiting for her. Opening the door a crack, she peeked around the corner. No, she surveyed an empty room.

Using her hair dryer, she blew dry her thick hair. Hastily, she pulled on her jeans and buttoned a plaid flannel shirt. She flew downstairs to the kitchen.

"Ready for your waffle?" Hannah said with a chuckle.

"You didn't wait for me, did you?" Cathy asked.

"No, Uncle Frank left a long time ago. He's already gone to his office." She reached for a bowl. "But I saved enough batter for yours." With these words, she poured the thick liquid onto the grill. When it turned golden brown, she put it on a plate before Cathy.

"I'm in a hurry," Cathy said, first smearing butter over her waffle, then drizzling syrup on it. With her fork, she speared a link sausage and quickly ate her breakfast.

"What's the rush, Cathy?" Hannah asked, using a brush to scour the waffle iron.

"Oh, I — I want to go for a long walk,"

Cathy said, floundering for an excuse.

"It's a lovely day for a walk," Hannah said. "A fresh snow fell last night, it's sunny, and not too cold."

Cathy pushed herself away from the table. "I'll see you later, Auntie." And she brushed her lips across Hannah's cheek.

Dashing outside, she jogged to Battlefield Park, seeing massive Greek columns encircled by pines in the distance. She neared the gazebo, surrounded by snowdrifts. What a beautiful sight!

Wading through the high fluffy snow, she was thankful she'd worn her knee-length boots.

"Hello, Cathy."

The voice she knew now! She glanced from one side to another, but Edward was behind her. How effortlessly he walked through the snow, almost as if he moved on top of it.

When they reached the gazebo, they sat together. Today Edward wore a heavy topcoat, reaching to his boot tops.

"I missed you," she said softly. "I always feel content and happy when I'm with you, Edward. But I know it isn't real."

"Cathy," Edward murmured, pulling her nearer, "it *is* real." For a while they didn't move, glad to be close to each other. At last,

Edward spoke, "Would you like a cup of tea?"

"Now? Where?" she asked in astonishment.

"At my home . . . in London."

She stared at him.

"Look around you," Edward stated, flinging his arms wide.

Cathy gazed at a green area that had once been covered by snow. Green hills, budding trees, and white sheep with black muzzles, dotted the English landscape.

"I want to show you my home," Edward said, taking long strides. Cathy hurried to keep up with him.

In the distance, she glimpsed a large columned house. As they drew near to it, Cathy halted in midstride, her pulse picking up a beat. The sun caught the coral-and-honey-colored bricks, reflecting a rosy-glow over the square-built house with a round tower on the west side. The stone-mullioned windows shot out myriad sunbeams over trimmed graceful curved iris beds.

"Ashcroft, my home," Edward explained.

Entering the house, Edward touched Cathy's elbow. "We'll have our tea in the garden." They walked through the Great Hall where tapestried chairs lined the wall and above them hung coats of arms.

Edward pointed to a high window embellished with heraldic designs. "The stag is my father's device and intertwined with it is a marten, my mother's device."

As they walked down the green marble corridor, Cathy peeked into the library, a warm room with a stone fireplace, shelves of books, and a claret-red Aubusson carpet. A ladder, placed against the books, gave easy access to the top shelves.

"What a beautiful home, Edward," Cathy said, marveling at the tall windows and burnished mahogany paneling.

"Yes, thanks to my mother, who inherited her wealth from her father, Sir Joshua Walford."

"How did Sir Joshua gain *his* wealth? He must have inherited lots of money," Cathy commented, looking up at the painted ceiling.

"It's a rather interesting story," Edward replied. "In the seventeenth century, Mother's ancestors aided the Stuart brothers, Charles and James, when they were fleeing from the forces of Oliver Cromwell. Mother's ancestors were of modest means, but when Charles the second returned from his exile in France, he awarded Ashcroft to the Walfords and a substantial money payment."

"What an exciting story," Cathy said.

"Let's go out to the garden," Edward said,

smiling at her. "I think you'll like it."

Stepping out into the flowers and oak trees, Cathy's hands flew to her cheeks. "Breathtaking!" she murmured.

"We'll sit over here, in the topiary garden," Edward said, indicating a private area by a vine-covered wall.

Cathy's laughter erupted and she clapped her hands in delight. "All the hedges are trimmed in the forms of animals!" She pointed to several. "An elephant. A camel! Oh, and there's a giraffe! I love every one of them!"

Edward chuckled. "I thought you might appreciate a bit of whimsy."

A small table covered with a pink cloth was set with a teapot, two delicate cups, and a silver plate of small pastries. Cathy fanned out her beige dress of gossamer muslin and sat down. Her gown was long but shortened some by the turquoise ribbon around her waist.

She thought Edward looked particularly handsome in a violet waistcoat, gray breeches, leggings, and a high-necked frilled shirt. He sat opposite her, putting aside the silver-knobbed cane he carried.

Cathy poured the jasmine tea and its pungent aroma almost rivaled the scent of the lilac bushes.

"With the sun catching the ruby highlights

of your hair," Edward said, admiringly, "and your green eyes shining like a mulberry leaf, it is a sight I wish I could paint." He shook his head. "I scarcely know," he said, smiling, "whether to drink my tea or come over and kiss you."

"Better yet," Cathy said with a light laugh, "why don't *I* come over and kiss you?"

Edward's eyebrows shot up and his eyes widened in disbelief.

"You mean English girls would never be so forward," she teased with a grin. Jumping to her feet, she bent over, kissed Edward's cheek, and returned to her chair, all in one fluid motion.

Edward brought his hand up to his cheek. "Girls today would *never* do anything like that. They would be considered . . . I don't know *what*."

Laughing, she stood and whirled around, her hair flying. "Even so, I love it here. I wish I could live near such beautiful gardens and own such a magnificent manor house!"

Edward rose and swept her into his arms. "You could. Cathy, you could! If I could keep you with me forever."

Cathy's knees weakened, when he gently took her face in his hands. She gazed into his blue eyes, loving his face and tenderness.

When she stepped back, Edward reluctantly let her go.

Her voice choked in her throat. "No, Edward, you know that is impossible." Then she changed the subject. "Are there more gardens?"

He dragged his eyes away from hers. "Yes, this way." They strolled down a path until they reached a lily pond. Aqua water, as still as glass, reflected their images. Cathy scooped up a pebble and tossed it in. Their distorted faces shimmered and disappeared. The pond was again undisturbed and placid.

"I painted this scene many times," Edward said, gazing thoughtfully at the lilies.

"Oh, Edward," Cathy replied. "If only you'd had the chance, you would have been a fine painter."

He breathed in the fragrant air. "If I had a palette, brush, and easel, I would never ask for anything else in this world."

A summer breeze stirred the leaves and Edward turned to her, "Shall we go in?"

As they walked down the path lined with roses and violets, Cathy felt at peace. Edward had shown her another side of his life before he became a soldier. A life he had to give up. What if he was right? What if she *could* stay with him? Would she?

Going into the mansion, he led her to the drawing room.

Cathy sat on one of the chintz chairs, glancing around the charming room, very different from the library. All the furniture was covered in blue and white material and even the drapes on the tall windows were of the same fabric. The blue rug and white marble fireplace finished the small room. She felt at home here. "Edward," she said, "this is the place where I'd spend my time." She turned around, but Edward was nowhere to be found.

The overstuffed chair became a bench and snow surrounded her. Her lovely dress became a winter jacket and jeans. She had returned to Princeton!

Chapter 19

Bewildered for a moment, Cathy stared at the gazebo. Awhile ago she'd been transported to Edward's mansion and now she was back in the snow and ice of Princeton. Pushing up her jacket sleeve, she checked her watch. Only twelve-thirty. She'd spent two hours in London, visited a mansion, and had tea in a topiary garden. It seemed like a whole day! Now, though, she must hurry and help Bryan and Susan at one o'clock. From being escorted by an eighteenth-century gentleman to decorating for a modern New Year's Eve party. Switching gears wasn't easy.

She jogged directly to Tarkington Road, which was a mile or so away. She veered onto a street of elaborate homes, and there, perched on a hill was a Georgian-style brick house with large columns in front.

Ringing the doorbell, Cathy stamped snow off her feet.

An angular statuesque woman answered. "You must be Cathy O'Brien," she said, opening the door wider. "Please come in. I'm Mrs. Gorman." A smile creased her face. "Let me take your jacket."

"Hi, glad to meet you, Mrs. Gorman," Cathy said, out of breath. "I jogged from Battlefield Park." She slipped off her jacket and handed it to Mrs. Gorman.

"Bryan and Susan are on the third floor decorating for the dance. Just go on up." She indicated a winding staircase to Cathy's left.

Cathy remembered Aunt Hannah's words that Beatrice Gorman was constantly written up in the society pages. With her flawless complexion and perfectly done short blonde hair that waved gently around her gold earrings, she certainly fit the type.

"Thanks," Cathy said, heading for the stairs.

"I'll be up shortly," Mrs. Gorman called after her.

Cathy walked into a huge room with an oak floor and streamers hanging from the high ceiling. The ballroom was empty except for chairs along the wall, a stage, and a table.

Bryan hurried to Cathy, giving her a welcome hug. "You're in time to help tie these bunches of balloons around the railing over there." He pointed to a wood trim across the back of the room.

"Hi, Cathy!" Susan turned and blew her a kiss. She was on her knees plugging in several ground lights.

"What a grand room. I've never seen anything like this in a home," Cathy said, taking a dozen tied balloons that Bryan handed her.

"At midnight," Brian said, "we'll release these balloons and they'll float up to the strobe lights."

Susan jumped up, wiped her hands on her khaki pants, and said, "That's done. Where's the confetti, Bryan?"

"In those sacks over there by the stage," he answered.

"The DJ will be up on the stage," he explained and grinned at Cathy. "You and I will be dancing fools." He put his hands around Cathy's waist. "I missed you."

"Since last night?" she gave him a teasing smile.

Bryan grinned, his arms tightening around her. "Since last night," he echoed.

"Hey, you two," Susan ordered, "we've still got tons of work to do."

Cathy glanced at every corner of the room. "It looks fine."

"This room is okay," Bryan said, "but now we need to tackle the dining room table."

"Oh," she said. "This is a fancier party than I'd imagined." She didn't say it, but she thought, I didn't know you had such an elaborate house with a third floor ballroom. But she should have realized that he would have.

Bryan's dark eyes twinkled. "Did you think we'd have a New Year's Eve party without pulling out all the stops?"

"You ain't seen nothing yet," Susan crowed. "Wait till you see the dining room."

Cathy trailed after them, down the stairs and into the dining room.

Bryan pushed open the sliding doors and Cathy sucked in her breath. Gold and silver streamers dangled over a long table set with fourteen gold-trimmed plates. Crystal goblets, silver, and gold candles in a row down the center of the long table.

At each place setting was a napkin, paper hat, horn, and a place card.

"Sorry, I didn't have time to come upstairs," Beatrice Gorman said, folding shut her cellular phone, "but I've been talking to the caterers."

"Everything okay, Mother?" Susan asked.

"Oh, yes! The food will be here promptly at seven."

"It looks as if the dining room is under control," Cathy said, wondering what else they could do.

Bryan winked. "Each guest will have a favor and we need to wrap them and put them at their place."

"I'll leave you, then," Mrs. Gorman said. "I know you'll have a marvelous time."

"Okay, Mother," Susan said, giving her mother a warm smile. "Thanks for all your help and ideas."

"You were great, Mother," Bryan said.

"Cathy, I'm glad you're here," Beatrice Gorman said. "Bryan and Susan have such nice things to say about you."

Cathy smiled. "They're both pretty terrific themselves."

Mrs. Gorman chuckled. "They have their days!"

"Let's go in the living room," Susan said, leading the way into a room with a fireplace. Cathy almost hated to walk on the black and rose Oriental rug.

Boxes were piled on a library table. Cathy picked up one. "Are these the favors?" she asked.

"Yes, go ahead and open it," Bryan urged.

She removed the lid and carefully took out a perfectly formed crystal pig. "How adorable!" She held it in the palm of her hand, admiring every angle.

Susan explained, "This is the Chinese Year of the Boar, but we thought a tiny pig would be more appropriate to celebrate our New Year."

"All we need to do," Bryan said, "is wrap these boxes and tie them with ribbons. Then we'll place them by each plate." He leaned over and whispered in her ear. "I wish I could give you something a little more personal."

Cathy smiled but didn't answer him. Instead, she said, "Hand me the gold ribbon, please." She sat down and began wrapping the square box with silver paper and tying it with a bow.

Bryan slumped in a chair, scooping back a swath of dark hair. "I think I'll watch the two of you. If you need help, I can hand you the ribbon."

When they were through, Cathy said, "I'd better leave. I want to spend some time with Aunt Hannah and Uncle Frank."

Bryan walked her to the hall and held her jacket. "Would you go skiing with me tomorrow? Susan and Phil are going," he said in his most persuasive tone.

"I don't have skis or ski clothes," she said. Ruefully, she thought of the new skis her mother had given her. But she wasn't sure she wanted to spend this much time with Bryan.

"No problem. The lodge will rent us whatever you need. Pick you up at eleven in the morning?"

She gave a low laugh. "Yes," she finally agreed. "I love to ski."

He tilted his head, grinning at her. "All the guys are going to envy me tonight," he said, putting her scarf around her neck and pulling her close. "Give me an early happy New Year's kiss." He rubbed his nose against hers.

"Bryan, you'll have to wait until midnight." And with these words, Cathy was out the door.

"I'll pick you up," Bryan called after her.

That evening Cathy filled the tub with bubble bath and soaked for a long time. She thought of carefree Bryan. What a lovely family life he had. And poor Edward, thwarted in his desire to be a painter. And Mike. He pursued exactly the career he wanted in politics. Three boys and each with such different backgrounds.

After slipping into her white dress and white sheer panty hose, Cathy felt like Cinderella going to the ball. She fluffed up her hair, which spilled over her shoulders, and ran downstairs. She had the empty house to herself, but she missed the voices of her aunt and uncle, who had gone next door to their neighbors for dinner and bridge.

Bryan pulled up in his sports car, running up the walk. He smiled at Cathy. "You're beautiful," he said.

He drove to his house up the circular drive, braked, and hurried to open Cathy's door.

"You spoil me, Bryan. I could have walked," Cathy said.

"In that dress? You would have been kidnapped!" he said with mock severity. "I wasn't about to take that chance."

Entering the Gormans' hall, soft music filled the air and voices buzzed from the living room.

Coming down the winding stairs, Beatrice and Bryan Gorman, Sr., greeted them.

When Cathy met Bryan's father, she was impressed with his thick white hair and Roman nose. She could see where Susan's height came from. Mr. Gorman towered over six feet. His tuxedo complemented Mrs. Gorman's strapless black gown.

The two left with a few admonishments, but

more concern that the party should be a hit.

In the living room everyone stood around talking, and Bryan introduced Cathy to each person present.

"And, here's Doug," Bryan said, "one of the poor slobs stuck here over the holidays. Cathy O'Brien, meet Doug Rayburn, a brave soul who is majoring in business."

"Sure, I'm going to get rich," Doug chortled, his pug nose wrinkling. Tugging at his vest circling his heavyset figure, the buttons seemed about to pop. At the sight of Cathy, he pretended to stumble backward. "Whoa! Where have you been hiding her, Bryan?" His eyes swept over Cathy in a way that made her uncomfortable.

"Hey! Keep your eyes in their sockets, Doug," Bryan chided, giving him a friendly poke on the shoulder. "Cathy's with me!"

The dining room doors swung open revealing a sparkling gold, silver, and crystal room.

Bryan called out, "Dinner is served, everyone!"

Immediately, the guests moved into the other room, checking place cards and waiting by their chairs.

Once Susan sat down, everyone else was seated.

Chicken piccata, asparagus, garlic mashed potatoes, and a Caesar salad were impeccably served by waiters and waitresses in their impeccable uniforms. Cathy couldn't get over the formality of everything. New Year's Eve parties at home were not like *this*. No parties were.

Doug, who sat across from Cathy, smiled at her, his small eyes glittering in the candle's glow. "Where are you from, Cathy?" he asked, leaning his bulk across the table.

"Chicago," she answered briefly, turning back to Bryan.

Doug said a few words to the girl next to him, but gave Cathy a sidelong glance and a half-smile.

After dinner everyone, wearing silly hats, walked up to the third floor where a DJ greeted them with thumping music. Soon the floor was crowded with dancers. Girls' shoes were tossed aside and boys' ties were loosened.

Sodas and dips were on a table and in between dances, the guests nibbled on more food. The night passed quickly and Cathy had to admit she enjoyed the luxury.

The last dance was a little softer, a little sweeter, and a little slower. Doug was at Cathy's side before she realized it. "May I have this dance? Bryan has monopolized you all night." Perspiration beaded his forehead.

"Sorry, Doug," Bryan said, suddenly materializing, "but Cathy's promised me this dance." He swept Cathy out on the floor and when she glimpsed Doug, he stood with his hands on his wide hips and mouth open.

"Saved," Cathy said with a smile as Bryan held her as they danced around the floor.

Bryan's dark eyes locked with Cathy's. "I'll always rescue you." His arms tightened about her.

Cathy felt as if she were floating. She didn't know when she'd had such an elegant evening. Except for the ball, she thought, with Edward. In the circle of Bryan's arms, she suddenly, guiltily, thought of Mike. For a moment she didn't like herself very much.

"Auld Lang Syne" came over the speakers and everyone broke into song, holding hands and swaying back and forth.

"Happy New Year, everybody!" Bryan yelled, releasing balloons to float up to the ceiling. Horns tooted and tossed confetti drifted over the laughing, shouting crowd.

"Happy New Year," Bryan said softly in Cathy's ear. His warm kiss wiped away thoughts of Mike . . . and Edward.

Bryan was *here*. Bryan was *now*. That was what she wanted on New Year's Eve.

Chapter 20

After such a glorious New Year's Eve party, Cathy was afraid she'd oversleep, but she awoke at seven. Before Bryan picked her up for their day of skiing at eleven, she had to go to the park.

She dressed and crept downstairs, not wanting to wake anyone. Going into the kitchen, Cathy was taken aback to see her aunt Hannah up this early.

"Good morning," Cathy said, pouring a glass of orange juice. "You're up early."

Hannah yawned and stretched. "I need to plug in the coffee," she explained, "then I'm going right back to bed."

"Did you have a good time last night?" Cathy asked.

Hannah nodded, pushing her disheveled bangs to one side. "Yes, Frank and I won at bridge."

"Good," Cathy said, draining her glass.

"And you?" Aunt Hannah asked, peering at her through sleepy eyes.

"It was wonderful. The Gormans live in such a posh house! I've never seen a party like that. I loved it, but it was a little stiff for me."

"That's the Gormans!" Hannah said. "I'm going upstairs," she continued, pausing to look over her shoulder. "Are you doing your morning walk thing?"

"Sure am," Cathy answered.

Hannah wagged her head. "Don't know how you do it this early. 'Specially on New Year's Day!" she said, in a throaty early morning voice.

Cathy chuckled. "Wouldn't miss it." But her aunt had disappeared upstairs. Little did her aunt know what awaited her on her walks.

Cathy pulled on her boots and jacket, lifting the parka over her head and tying it at the neck.

The cold air hit her, but she walked briskly and didn't mind. She prayed Edward would be waiting for her at Battlefield Park. As she half-walked and half-ran, she considered her week. It had been more than she had dreamed it could be.

As she approached a corner house, her heart skipped a beat. Edward leaned casually against the garage doors, waiting for her.

"Edward!" she cried, rushing into his open arms.

"Sweet Cathy! I knew you'd come." He bent down, kissing her deeply.

Edward smiled. "I thought the two of us might go horseback riding." He led her behind the house. "You do ride. Don't you?"

Cathy nodded. Now, though, she was confused. Turning to him, she asked, "What are we doing by this double garage?"

Amused, Edward said, "Look!" And he pointed proudly to a stable.

Cathy stared at what had once been the garage. It was now a long low stable. Beyond were green rolling hills and trees. She looked down, pleased at her clothes. She wore a mannish-style riding outfit, all in black, except for a white shirt and red tie. The tight-fitting short black jacket and long black skirt were the type of clothes Cathy loved. From her top hat, with a wispy white scarf trailing down the back, to her shiny black boots, she felt comfortable and stylish.

Edward, dressed in a long green jacket, breeches, and boots, brought out two horses from the stable. He handed her the reins of a black prancing steed and helped her into the saddle. Then, he easily lifted himself into the saddle of a white stallion.

Sitting sidesaddle, Cathy kept pace with Edward. They rode over the lush countryside toward the woodland. Galloping faster, Cathy took off her hat The ribbon which tied back her hair loosened and flew away. The summer wind caught her auburn hair and sent it streaming behind her. How refreshing the wind felt, cooling her flushed face.

Edward drummed his heels into the flanks of his stallion and he and Cathy, laughing with pleasure, flew together over the meadows.

At last they reined in their horses and stopped by a stream, its waters cascading over stones and pebbles.

Dismounting, they walked toward a giant oak, where they paused. Cathy leaned against the bark and Edward sat, looking up at her.

"You don't know what a lovely picture you make, Cathy," he said. "It's an image I want to hold in here for all time." He tapped his heart, and although he smiled, his eyes were sad.

Cathy sighed. "Oh, Edward, we don't *have* time."

He reached up, offering his hand. She slipped hers in his, and sank down beside him.

He smoothed back her hair, touched her brow and her lips. She closed her eyes, feeling his fingers straying over her face.

A hawk swooped and dived, then sailed away in the cloudless blue sky. A clover scent saturated the air. Cathy propped herself up on her elbows, gazing at Edward. His blond tousled hair appeared like molten gold in the sunlight and his blue eyes had never been bluer. His appealing mouth made him irresistible. She sat up, leaning close.

Their lips joined and Cathy's heart pounded in her ears.

"Cathy," Edward whispered, "if only you could live with me forever."

"Could I?" she murmured, the words choking in her throat. "Could I, Edward?"

He turned away, his eyes narrowing as he stared in the distance at grazing sheep.

Cathy clung to him. "I want to stay here."

A horse nickered. "Time to leave," Edward said, thoughtfully.

Once they had remounted, Cathy shouted, "Race you to the stable!"

And they rode full tilt over the hills. Edward pulled ahead and was waiting for her at the stables.

Cathy reined in and leaped lightly from her horse. The spirited mare neighed and lifted her head, as if enjoying the fast run. "You're a beauty," Cathy crooned, stroking the soft silky mane.

Then snow and biting cold assailed her and once again she had returned to Princeton.

She felt empty and alone. But what an exciting morning it had been. To ride through the English countryside with Edward had been like a wonderful dream. Had it been a dream? She *had* to talk to someone.

Reaching her aunt Hannah's, Cathy ran upstairs. She only had ten minutes before Bryan rang the doorbell. From horseback riding to skiing. It almost seemed like too much.

Bryan appeared in a black ski suit, and for a moment she stared at him. His suit was reminiscent of her black riding suit, still fresh in her mind.

"Hi, Cathy," Bryan said, an engaging grin on his face. "Ready to hit the slopes?"

"Yes," Cathy answered, still thinking of her ride. Then she said, "I love to ski. I just wish I'd brought my new skis that I received for Christmas."

"Not to worry," Bryan said, helping her in his car. He jumped in on the driver's side and started the car. "We're headed for White Top Mountain. It isn't Vail or Aspen but the runs are decent and there's a ski shop where you can rent all the equipment you need."

Cathy said, "This is a perfect way to spend New Year's Day." *If I can't be riding with Edward,* she thought.

"Better than watching the Rose Bowl game?" Bryan teased, squeezing her hand.

"I like football, but skiing is better," Cathy replied, slipping in a tape of Harry Connick, Jr. His New Orleans jazz fit her mood.

"Lots of my friends from the party will be here today," Bryan said. "I think there will be two more carloads.

"Fine," Cathy said, but she hoped Doug with the sleazy eyes wouldn't be there.

The drive to the ski run was only an hour and Bryan took her directly to the ski shop where she rented white ski pants and sweater. She also chose ski gloves, poles, bindings, and boots. Skis were another matter. She wanted a pair just the right height. She reached above her head, testing one pair after another. Finally she found skis that she could reach and touch the top.

"All right!" Bryan said. "Let's hit the hill!"

Before they could sit on the lift, however, someone called.

"Cathy!" Susan shouted, waving and running up to her.

"Susan! I'm glad to see you. You look great in that ski suit."

"Check it out!" Susan said, taking the goggles from the top of her visored ski hat and settling them on her nose. "Don't I look like a pro?"

"You do," Cathy said, admiring the easy confidence Susan had.

"Hey, where's the fire?" Wheezing, Phil slogged up a slight incline. His long nose dripped and he reached for his handkerchief. "I should have stayed in bed," he mumbled. "I'm sick!"

"Phil," Cathy said, "the fresh air will do you good."

Phil threw back his head and sneezed. He blew his cherry-red nose.

"Hellooo!" Another group from the party hurried toward them to huddle for a chat.

Cathy's heart sank when she noticed a bulging figure lumbering over the rise. Doug Rayburn! Just who she didn't want to see!

Puffing and huffing, Doug's eyes lit up when he saw Cathy. "Cathy! I didn't know I'd be so lucky as to be skiing with you all day." His dark suit didn't stretch well over his big stomach. "Let's go up on the lift," he said, taking her arm.

"I'm with Bryan," she said coolly, pulling free. Looking around, however, Bryan had disappeared into the lodge.

"Bryan's bindings weren't tight," Doug said, giving her his most charming smile, but to Cathy it was more like a leer. "He'll be gone awhile. Come on," Doug wheedled, grabbing her hand.

Resigned to being with Doug, she squeezed into the lift beside him. Hanging onto the T-bar, she glanced around at the skiers and the hill. She'd forget Doug and enjoy the sport. The hill wasn't too steep so it should be fun. If only she could be free of Doug.

"This is nice, isn't it?" Doug said in her ear and throwing his arm around her. "Just the two of us."

Cathy leaned forward away from his arm. "Please, Doug," she said, not hiding her irritation.

"Don't be so standoffish," he said. "I'm not such a bad guy once you get to know me."

The lift dumped them out on the hilltop and Cathy was thankful she was rid of Doug.

Cathy adjusted her ski poles and prepared to ski down the run.

"You know, Cathy, you're someone I'd like to know better," Doug breathed beside ear.

"Let's dump Bryan and sit in the lodge. We need to get better acquainted." His hand slid up and down her arm. "What do you say, Cathy?"

"No, Doug!" she said in a firm voice, confronting him. "I am with Bryan."

"So what?" Doug shrugged, gazing at her with a soft smile.

"*So* I'm with Bryan!" she repeated, emphasizing each word.

He grabbed her arm and pulled her against him, his close-set eyes boring into hers.

"Doug!" she protested angrily, giving him a push.

Laughing, he shoved her and she hit against another skier, almost upsetting the two of them.

"Watch it!" The other skier said, then pushed off the hill with his ski poles.

Before she could protest Doug's behavior, however, her eyes grew big with wonder. Edward was here on the slopes! He stood behind Doug, a frown on his face.

Suddenly, Edward grabbed Doug by the seat of his pants and sent him flying down the slopes, his ski poles flailing the air. He careened from one edge of the course to the other, struggling to keep his balance. Flinging his ski poles aside, he doubled forward, then with his arms whirling like a windmill, he bent backward. Racing and yelling all the way, he finally reached the bottom of the course.

His mouth working in and out like a goldfish, he glowered at Cathy up on the hill.

Cathy hid her grin behind her mitten. Covered with snow, Doug reminded her of a round, plump snowman.

Removing his skis, Doug retrieved his poles, then stomped into the lodge.

Cathy had a feeling that Doug wouldn't bother her anymore. She turned to thank Edward, but the only one beside her was Susan.

The rest of the skiing was exhilarating. Bryan joined her and the two practiced maneuvering faster turns. Laughing and falling in the snow, they thoroughly enjoyed each run.

Late in the afternoon everyone was ready for hot mulled cider and tacos. Sitting before the fire, Cathy and Bryan watched the flames. He asked her out again for the next night, and she couldn't refuse. He put his arm around her and she felt contented and happy . . . and puzzled as to *how* she could feel that way.

On the drive home, Bryan pushed in a tape of romantic music. She tingled with fatigue, but it was a good feeling. And a dreamy song about lost love put her in a thoughtful mood.

Only three more days in Princeton. What else could happen? How could she return home to Mike and his everyday routine? Not after Bryan. Not after Edward.

Chapter 21

The morning after New Year's Day, Cathy sat in the kitchen with Hannah and Uncle Frank. Uncle Frank didn't stay long, though. He folded his quarterly, and said, "Time to go to the office." He leaned over, kissing the top of Hannah's head. "See you for dinner."

She patted his hand. "I'll be home about five."

"Fine," Frank said. "And you have a good day, too, Cathy." He smiled warmly.

"Thanks, Uncle Frank. Every day has been great so far, and I know this one won't be any different," Cathy said, pouring milk over her cereal.

After Frank left, Hannah cautioned, "It's very icy and slick this morning, Cathy. If you go for your walk, be careful."

"I will," Cathy promised, taking a bite of her toast. She wouldn't miss her meeting with Edward no matter how cold and icy it was.

Hannah bent over, patting Cathy's shoulder. "Since I didn't advertise today's sale, I'm sure I won't have many customers. They'll all be lined up at the mall."

Cathy rinsed her dishes and put them in the dishwasher. "I'll see you later, Aunt Hannah. Susan and I are meeting at Pete's Place for lunch."

"Good. She's a delightful girl, very unaffected by her family's money. I've given her the day off. What's the point of sitting around with no one in the shop?"

A slight noise puzzled Cathy.

"It's the mailman," Hannah said, glancing at the kitchen clock. "He's early." She went into the hall and returned shuffling through letters and flyers that had been pushed through the mail slot. "Hmmm, this one is for you, Cathy." Hannah handed her an envelope.

"For me?" Cathy echoed in astonishment. She'd already heard from her mother, Johnny, and Mike. Who else would be writing to her? Looking at the letter, she frowned. The return address label said Zack Preston! Why would he be writing to her? He was the last person she wanted to hear from.

Hannah, dressed in a ski jacket and jeans, called out from the hall, " 'Bye, Cathy."

" 'Bye, Aunt Hannah," she said absently, opening Zack's letter.

December 30

Dear Cathy,

You must be surprised to hear from me, but I wanted to write and explain a few things before your arrival Sunday.

I know your mother informed you of my desire to marry her. We're both anxious for your reaction. I know how you feel about me, Cathy, and I'm sorry we couldn't at least be friends. I realize how much you loved your father, and rightfully so. I could never take his place, nor would I want to.

I love your mother and Johnny and I'm very fond of you, Cathy. But there's a barrier between us. I don't ask for your love, but I do ask for your understanding. Your mother and I are in love. Naturally, she wants your blessing. Even if you oppose our marriage, I must tell you that I don't intend to stop asking Sara to be my wife.

Sara and I want a home. I'd be a good

husband to her and a good father to Johnny —

Sunday I hope you and Mike will join us for a welcome home dinner at Joe Miller's Steak House in the Loop. Please think over what I've written. I want us to be friends.

My warmest wishes,

Zack

Cathy crumpled up the letter and stuck it in her pocket. Who did he think he was? Friends, indeed.

Angrily, she dressed for the cold weather and left.

Soon, though, she recovered her good humor. Eagerly, she slipped and slid her way to Battlefield Park. Icy sidewalks were a hazard, but even more so were cars that careened sideways around corners.

Her heart raced faster than her feet as she flew to the young man sitting in the gazebo.

"Edward!" she cried. "Have you been waiting long for me?"

"All my life," he answered, hurrying to meet her.

She went into his welcoming arms as easily

and naturally as if she belonged there for all time.

"I want to show you London as I remember it," Edward said, leading her across the snow. He halted and said, "Do you see the Thames?"

The snow opened up before her dazzled eyes. There was London's river. There was the Thames River with St. Paul's Cathedral in the background. She gazed at Edward in wonder.

Her hoop dress of blue cotton with a long sash, a butterfly cap of lace and ribbons, and silk slippers made her feel very beautiful. When she moved, her full skirts rustled about her feet.

She put her hand through Edward's arm, admiring his gray frock coat and black breeches. Atop his wig was perched a tricornered black hat. He looked down at her and a smile hovered about his mouth.

A young man, sitting on Blackfriars Bridge, had an easel propped up before him. He held a palette of many colors and he deftly used his brush to paint barges and ships on the river.

"We had a London townhouse," Edward said. "Often I'd steal down to the quays and paint. I'd sketch the same scene that artist is painting over there." Edward watched the painter, with pained eyes, slightly biting his underlip. Cathy hated to see the sad expression on his face.

"This river is never dull," he said, brightening, as he gazed over docks and warehouses.

Hundreds of ships were tied up to wharves. "Look," Edward said. "In the distance you can see a Portuguese man-of-war, Cathy. She's at least one hundred fifty feet off shore."

Cathy shaded her eyes. "Yes, I see it," she said in an excited voice. "How its red and green flag snaps in the wind." Her gaze shifted to small skiffs darting in and out like so many dragonflies. They made the whole river come alive.

As Edward and Cathy strolled along the bank, they stopped to watch an East India ship unload.

"See how low she sits in the water," Edward said, leaning on a piling. "The cargo must be a heavy one."

"Top of the morning to ye," an old seaman shouted at them from across the cobblestone street, a fishnet in one gnarled hand and a huge mending needle in the other.

"Hellooo," Cathy called back, waving and smiling.

Turning back to the large bales placed on

the dock, she moved closer for a better view.

"A rich cargo," Edward murmured. "Pepper, cloves, and cinnamon, plus silks and calico. Some merchant has earned a pretty profit today."

"It's thrilling," Cathy said, marveling at the bustling docks and workers.

Edward took Cathy's arm. "I want you to see more of London than the docks."

They walked in the direction of St. Paul's Cathedral's spire. A fishwife passed them with a basket of fish on her head. She yelled, "Fresh haddock! Buy fresh fish!"

Cathy held her breath, trying to escape the stench. Edward handed her his lace handkerchief which she immediately put over her nose. "The fish don't smell very fresh to me," she complained, grimacing.

Edward chuckled as they strolled on. Halting, he threw a pence to a ragged boy sitting in the gutter. The small dirty-faced child caught the coin with a flick of his hand. Leaping up, he dashed toward an old man standing guard over a barrow piled with oysters and oranges.

"Poor little thing," Cathy murmured. "He's hungry."

On they walked across London Bridge, dodging the many carts and carriages. When they reached Audley Street, they cut across Grosvenor Square.

"We owned our terrace house on the east side of this square," Edward said, pointing to the row of identical houses.

"You lived in a lovely house when you were in London," Cathy said.

"Yes, I longed to stay in London. I loved to paint the city. London has so much to offer. Once I even sketched George the third when his royal carriage rumbled by. The king glimpsed me and doffed his hat in my direction. I was in awe of my king."

Cathy hated to think of him becoming a soldier. His next words, however, took her mind off his tragedy.

"We've passed one coffeehouse after another," Edward said "but I'm looking for a cafe." He stopped, indicating a sign and smiling. "We're in luck. Here's Locket's Tavern of Charing Cross."

The sign creaked back and forth in the slight breeze. "This looks very nice," she said.

"It's one of the oldest cafes in London," Edward explained, escorting Cathy inside. "Merchants, shippers, and insurers come here and it's an eatery for the gentry. It's rather expensive." He chuckled at her look of alarm. "Don't fret. I have money."

Once seated, Cathy glanced at the walls which were plastered with advertisements, posters, and pictures of hunting scenes.

"Chocolate or coffee?" a man in a long apron asked.

"Chocolate," they both answered in unison.

"Today we have Westphalian ham, pigeon, or mutton steak."

"I'd just like bread," Cathy answered, since none of the choices appealed to her.

Edward ordered the mutton.

Cathy glanced around at the crowded cafe; both men and women apparently liked the huge slabs of mutton or ham put before them. Some even ordered pigeon to go along with the ham.

Cathy craned her neck. "I thought I might see a famous writer," she said in a disappointed voice.

Edward shook his head. "Most famous gentlemen stay in their own cities, whereas in France every well-known writer or painter resides in Paris."

Cathy drank her chocolate and broke off a piece of bread.

"Tell me," Edward said, taking her hands in his. "Do you think you could be happy here?"

"London is a wonderful city," she answered, gazing into Edward's blue eyes. "I — I don't know, though, if I could live here."

Edward's hands tightened over hers. "Even with me?" he solemnly asked.

She looked down at his tapered fingers. "Edward, I don't know where I belong anymore."

"Anything else?" the proprietor asked brusquely, hiking up his apron which reached to his buckled shoes.

"No, nothing," Edward answered.

"There's a couple of gents waiting for your table," the owner said, jerking his thumb toward the entrance.

"Then we'll leave," Edward said. "Ready, Cathy?"

"Yes," she said, picking up her fan.

"We'll take a hackney cab to a park," Edward said. "Would you like that?"

"I would," she said, smiling at him. She wanted to relax with Edward without these crowds.

Once in the street, however, she didn't relax. Cries of hawkers filled the air.

"Dumplins, Dumplins, Diddle, diddle dumplins ho!"

Another hawker stood alongside shouting, "Flag brooms, Flag brooms. Sweep, sweep."

"Cucumbers to pickle."

Cathy walked rapidly past. One hawker, though, thrust a knife in her face and, terrified, she clutched Edward's arm. "Knives to grind, Knives to grind," the man screeched. "Any knives to grind?"

They brushed by and walked through a square to a row of book stores. Each store had title pages of manuscripts hanging on posts. Edward and Cathy peered in one of the windows. "Look at all the loose manuscripts on the tables," Cathy said, a puzzled frown on her face.

"Patrons come in and read the top sheets and if they like the contents they have the book bound in red and gold calf or any color they like for their library," Edward explained.

"What a strange custom," Cathy said.

"Some buyers read the entire book at one of the reading tables or take the manuscript home, before they commit themselves."

Edward turned. "Time to move on," he said, hailing a cab.

The horseman quickly whisked them to a small public park near Westminister. The clop-clop of the horses over the cobblestones and her hand in Edward's was a reassuring feeling.

Arriving at the park, Edward helped her from the cab. She lifted her skirt and jumped lightly to the ground.

"Boats! Boats!" A hawker yelled. Cathy

smiled. There was no escaping hawkers selling their wares.

Edward approached the boatman, and rented a boat. He gave the man three pence and they clambered aboard a rowboat.

"What a wonderful idea, Edward," she said, tossing her cap on the seat beside her and lifting her long hair and letting it fall loosely about her shoulders. The sun, the water, and the weeping willow branches touching the water were soothing after the hubbub of the London streets.

As Edward dipped the oars in the rippling water, Cathy gazed at his clean-cut features. He'd removed his jacket and rolled up his shirtsleeves to his elbow. His aquiline nose, smiling mouth, blue eyes, bluer than the water, and ruffled golden hair, was an appealing picture. Cathy had never seen Edward quite so informal.

She trailed her hand in the water. Maybe, she mused, she could live in London. Especially with Edward's love. And then, startled, Cathy sat up. *What* are you thinking?

Chapter 22

After the excitement of London, Cathy once again found herself in the gazebo, alone. She shivered. She had come from the warmth of a summer's day in England to the chill of a winter's day in New Jersey.

On her way to meet Susan, Cathy relived her experiences with Edward. From a minuet to the topiary gardens to the Thames River and the tall ships. The fresh memory of the boat ride, though, danced in her head. How much she'd enjoyed the sunny day.

She had been with Edward today and tonight she'd be with Bryan. They were so different, yet each had his special charm. Edward's graciousness and propriety had an old-fashioned attractiveness. Bryan, on the other hand, was easy to be with. No complications. He viewed life with laughter and his grin was infectious.

As she walked past a book shop, she

stopped to check the titles. One caught her attention: *Imagin 'ion Vs. Reality*. Was she living in a real or make-believe world in Princeton? Maybe this week was an escape from problems in Chicago? Going on, she almost slipped on the ice and held out her arms to keep her balance.

Passing one quaint shop after another, she resolved that, yes, she must talk to Susan. If only Susan could see Edward like she could. Cathy slowed at a shoe store and broke off an icicle, hanging from a low sign. Susan believed Edward was a ghost, but he wasn't. He was as real as this icicle in her hand! She gave a bitter little smile, as the icicle melted into thin air.

When Cathy arrived at Pete's Place, Susan, already seated in a back booth, motioned to her.

Cathy smiled and slid into the booth opposite her new friend. But Susan no longer seemed new. It was as if she'd known her for years.

"Hello, Cathy," Susan said with a grin. "You look like the cat that swallowed the canary. What is going on?"

The girls paused long enough to order club sandwiches and sodas, then Cathy admitted seeing Edward.

"You mean he spirited you off to London?"

Susan threw back her head and laughed. "I didn't mean to use the term 'spirited.' "

"It's all right," Cathy said, smiling in spite of herself. She then began to relate the story of the horseback ride and the hustle and bustle of London. When she finished with the story of the boat ride, she breathlessly awaited Susan's reaction.

Susan ate the last of her sandwich before replying. "Do you want me to believe that you've been to London and back this morning? Cathy, you are fantasizing . . . you worry me."

The look on Susan's face hurt Cathy.

Desperately, Cathy said, "Come to the gazebo with me tomorrow and meet Edward for yourself."

"I thought you said Edward could only be seen by *you*," Susan answered.

"I'm sure he'll show himself to you. I know it!"

"All right," Susan said. "If I see Edward with my own eyes I'll grant that he exists. But, Cathy, I know I won't see him."

Seeing the pain in Cathy's eyes, Susan changed the subject. "Did you have fun skiing yesterday?"

"I had a great time," Cathy said. "Except for Doug Rayburn. What a gross guy. When he hit on me I didn't know quite what to do, but Edward came to the rescue."

"*Edward?*" Susan asked incredulously.

Cathy said firmly, "Yes, *Edward* took Doug by the seat of his pants and gave him a shove!"

Susan's eyes widened. "I saw Doug go flying down the hill! But he tripped on his skis."

When the girls finished eating, Cathy picked up the check, accepting Susan's share. "Will you meet me at ten at the gazebo?" she questioned.

"I'll be there," Susan replied, taking Cathy by the arm and leaving.

When Cathy returned home, she was surprised to see Aunt Hannah reading a book by the fire. "You're home early," she remarked.

"Yes, there's no point in keeping my empty shop open." Hannah closed her book. "It's so cozy by the fire. Did you and Susan have a good lunch?"

"The best," Cathy said, dropping into a wingback chair in front of the fireplace. And the best conversation, too, she thought. Tomorrow in the park should be interesting.

"You only have two more full days in Princeton." Hannah sighed. "The house has come alive with you here, Cathy."

Cathy laughed. "If you ask me, you and Uncle Frank don't need me to liven up your place."

"Our work may appear glamorous to someone outside our circle, but it's really fairly humdrum."

Cathy stared at the blaze, then bolstered up her courage and asked her aunt, "Did you ever have more than one boy who you were interested in?"

Hannah's mouth twitched with amusement. "I'll say. When I went to college I was in love with two fellows, each one with a personality as different as the moon and sun."

"Was one of them Uncle Frank?"

"No, this was before I met him." Hannah gazed at Cathy, a grin spreading across her face, as she remembered. "The first boy, Ralph, a bookish sort, loved movies. He wanted to marry me. Not even your mother knows, but we became engaged for a short time. Then Kit came along and we started seeing each other. He was a tall rangy fellow from Montana, who loved to go camping and hiking. One thing led to another and I fell in love with Kit. I broke off with Ralph. When I graduated and accepted a position teaching English in a small high school in Pennsylvania, Kit and I drifted apart. I realized neither Ralph nor Kit were right for me."

"When you met Uncle Frank, did you know immediately he was the one?"

"Nooo," Hannah said thoughtfully. "I vowed I'd never fall in love again. But Frank was persistent. He sent flowers and candy and books. He called me. We laughed at the same things. And cried at the same things."

"You do get along well," Cathy said. It was comforting to know, though, that Hannah didn't marry the first boy who came along. She had had doubts, too.

Hannah smiled at Cathy, tilting her head. "I think perhaps you're going through a few misgivings of your own."

Cathy nodded. "I was so sure of Mike, but since I met Bryan and . . ." she almost slipped and said "Edward," "I'm not so certain."

"Something will click in your mind, Cathy. And you'll know. You're only sixteen. You have plenty of time. When you're truly in love, you'll know in your heart and be ready to make a commitment."

Cathy stood and kissed her aunt's forehead. "Thanks, you've helped me a lot."

Then, before she could stop herself, Cathy asked, "Aunt Hannah — do you believe someone who lived in another time . . . hundreds of years ago . . . could come back?"

Hannah looked at Cathy carefully. "In your mind . . . in a book or a painting. That way, yes."

Cathy went to her room, thinking of the things ahead of her. She had to face the possibility of a stepfather turning her life upside down. Also, she had to reassess her relationship with Mike.

Chapter 23

Before eating dinner with Hannah and Frank, Cathy chose a book from her uncle's library. Sinking into his big leather chair, she read a chapter on Washington's victory at Princeton and what happened after. She was surprised to learn that the Americans dreaded the year 1777, for the numbers resembled a gallows. They felt that many of the rebels would hang.

After Washington's victories at Trenton and Princeton, he withdrew swiftly to the hills around Morristown. From this vantage point he could raid the British supply lines. The British General Howe vacated New Jersey. Cathy put down the book. Edward, killed at Princeton, knew nothing of the American victories, or that his death had been in vain.

She leaned back and closed her eyes, dozing.

"Cathy, Cathy," Uncle Frank said, gently

removing the book from her lap. "You've been asleep!"

Awakening, she saw her uncle's smiling face above her. A kind face. "Oh, Uncle Frank," she said, "I had a dream that was so real. I lived in Trenton and I was in a boat trying to reach shore and tell Washington about the Hessians, but the harder I rowed, the farther away the shore appeared."

"Well, Washington knew about the Hessians and saved Trenton," Uncle Frank reassured her. "Now, come downstairs. Hannah and I have prepared spaghetti and meatballs with French bread and a tossed salad. How does that sound?"

"Marvelous," she said, stretching her arms toward the ceiling. "What time is it?"

"Seven."

"Bryan is coming at eight and we're going out for a cappuccino." She took Uncle Frank's hand and he pulled her out of his deep chair.

"Do you ever doze in this chair?" she asked her uncle with a grin.

"Oh, once in a great while," he said gravely, but she didn't miss the impish twinkle in his eyes.

Entering the dining room, Cathy paused at the sight of candlelight, a steaming bowl of spaghetti, and a tomato and lettuce salad. "Oh, you two prepared all this, and I wasn't around to help! It looks wonderful and I'm starved."

Hannah beamed. "This is one of the few things Frank and I fix at home."

"Save room for a hot fudge sundae," Frank said.

"Ummhmmm," was all Cathy could say, holding her plate out for Hannah to dish up the spaghetti.

After dinner she helped clear the dishes, then ran upstairs where she brushed her teeth and her hair. She'd just finished when the doorbell rang.

Bryan stood before her, a single rose in his hand. "Oh, Bryan," she said, "you are sweet."

"A perfect rose for a perfect girl," he said, a lazy grin spreading across his face.

"Hello, Bryan," Hannah said.

"Hi, Mrs. Lambert," Bryan said, turning up his smile a notch.

"A rose," Hannah said. "How nice. This belongs in a bud vase. Shall I place it on your dressing table, Cathy?"

"Yes, please."

"You two have fun," Frank called from the kitchen.

Bryan drove to a small snug coffee shop near the campus and they went in, Cathy laughing with pleasure at Bryan's compliments.

Once seated, Bryan ordered two cappuccinos. His thick rumpled hair and dashing looks even had the waitress staring.

"I'm going to miss you, Cathy. I hate to think that you'll be leaving soon." His eyes never left her face.

"Chicago isn't that far," Cathy teased. "Susan is visiting."

"If I showed up, how would Mike like that?"

She shook her head, lifting the small cup to her lips. "Maybe it wouldn't be such a good idea," she admitted.

"Are you really serious about Mike?" He raised his thick brows inquiringly.

She turned the question over in her mind. "Yes, I think I am," she answered.

"You *think* you're serious?" Bryan teased. "In other words, you're not sure about Mike?" He gave her a slow smile. "Has someone else come into the picture?"

Cathy gazed at him over the rim of her cup. "Do you think that 'someone' is you?" she asked in a light tone.

"Well, isn't it?" Bryan said with a chuckle.

Not answering, she carefully set her cup down. If she told Bryan about Edward, she knew his smile would be mocking and unbelieving.

"Could I make you forget Mike?" he asked,

bending his head and gazing at her with a teasing light in his dark eyes.

"I don't think anyone could cause me to forget Mike," she answered truthfully. She didn't add, however, that someone might take his place. "You haven't forgotten about Ann, have you?"

"No, but I'm not seeing her any longer, either." He reached over, playing with Cathy's fingers. "I want to kiss you," he said in a low husky voice.

A rush of heat colored her cheeks and her skin tingled when she looked at Bryan's engaging smile. His compelling dark eyes held her.

"Let's get out of here," he said.

On the drive home, soft music played. She could feel his magnetism pulling her. And when they stopped and he took her in his arms, she didn't object.

"Cathy," he whispered against her hair. He kissed her throat, her eyes, her nose, and her mouth.

His kiss was warm and her arms automatically went around him.

"I've been looking for someone like you all my life," he said softly.

What was she doing? She'd soon be returning to Chicago? How could she love Bryan?

Edward? Mike? She began to doubt her senses. What was *wrong* with her?

Suddenly a siren screamed through the night. Red lights flashed as an ambulance screeched around a corner and swerved into the driveway.

"Something's wrong!" Cathy flung open her car door and dashed toward the front door of her aunt and uncle's house, Bryan racing behind.

Chapter 24

Her heart pounding, Cathy took the front steps two at a time, the red light of the ambulance flickering over her face.

Hannah threw open the door and the emergency crew rushed into the house.

Cathy ran behind the white-suited man and woman. "Aunt Hannah, what is it?" she cried.

"It's Frank," Hannah replied, pale and shaken. Holding the door wider for the crew, she stepped aside so they could wheel out the gurney.

"Oh, Uncle Frank," Cathy whispered, glimpsing his still face. Tears spilled down her cheeks. "Aunt Hannah, will he be all right?"

"I don't know," she replied. "He had severe pains. He doubled-over, then fainted." A worried look crossed her face. "Will you be all right? I'm going to St. Mary's Hospital and stay with Frank."

Cathy hugged Hannah. "I'll be fine."

"We'll follow you to the hospital," Bryan said, standing behind Cathy and rubbing her arms.

"I'll see you there," Hannah called, climbing into the back of the ambulance.

Bryan's cool and collected actions calmed Cathy, but her heart still fluttered rapidly and her every thought centered on Uncle Frank. She prayed he'd be all right.

"If Hannah stays all night, and she probably will," Bryan said, as they hurried to his car, "you'll be welcome to stay overnight at our house. Susan has twin beds in her room."

"Thanks, Bryan," Cathy said, tears trembling on her lashes. "I'm so scared right now, I don't know where I'll sleep. If Aunt Hannah wants me, I'll stay with her." She glanced at Bryan who stepped on the accelerator, but the ambulance was far ahead and soon out of sight.

Bryan's tires squealed, rolling into the hospital parking lot. Hitting the brakes, he had Cathy's door open before she could lift the door handle.

Together they ran into the emergency room. Hannah sat and waited. "The doctor is examining him, now," she explained. "Cathy, why don't you go home? Or are you afraid to stay by yourself?"

Cathy took her aunt's hand, stroking it. "I want to stay with you."

"I've invited her to our house to stay with Susan," Bryan spoke up, sitting on the other side of Hannah.

Soon a young man came out from behind a curtained alcove. "Your husband has been taken up to surgery, Mrs. Lambert."

Hannah bit her underlip and stood, her fingers nervously playing with a button on her sweater vest. "What is the operation for?"

The youthful intern smiled. "Appendicitis. He got here just in time. If his appendix had burst, it could have been serious. He'll be in surgery awhile." He checked his clipboard. "He'll be in room two-sixteen, if you want to go there and rest."

Hannah half-turned. "I need to be in Frank's room when they bring him in. Please, Cathy, get some sleep." She gave her a small smile. "I'll be okay."

Cathy's heart had slowed and a feeling of relief spread over her. "I'll go on with Bryan." She glanced at him. "And if you don't mind, I'll stay alone at Aunt Hannah's." Giving her aunt a kiss, she said, "Call me. I don't care if it's three in the morning!"

Hannah kept smiling, but her hands trembled when she gave the thumbs-up sign. "I promise." She moved toward the elevators.

Bryan and Cathy returned to the car. "Do you know we were only in the hospital thirty minutes?" Bryan said.

"Everything happened so fast," Cathy agreed.

On the ride home, she felt drained. "Appendicitis isn't serious, is it?"

"I don't think so," Bryan said, stopping before her house. "Like the doctor said, if it had burst then Frank would have had problems."

Walking to the front porch, Cathy gave Bryan a good night kiss. "You've been wonderful," she said. "Thanks for helping my aunt and me."

"Hey, I was glad to be able to," he said. "I hate to have you spend the night by yourself. Won't you reconsider and come home with me? Susan would love to have you."

"I know," she answered, touching his hand, "but I'd rather stay here. I'm not afraid to be alone."

"Then try not to worry," Bryan said. "I'll call you tomorrow." He blew her a kiss and left.

Going into the empty house, Cathy wished she could stop worrying. But if a person were operated on, anything could happen. Her only wish was for Aunt Hannah to call and tell her that Uncle Frank was fine.

She climbed the stairs and undressed. Once in her nightgown, she wondered if she should call her mother. No, she thought, why needlessly worry her? She'd wait to hear from Aunt Hannah.

Not turning on a light, she huddled in a chair by her window and stared at the snow-covered ground and the cold white moon. For the first time since she had arrived, she wished her mother were here!

She didn't know how long she sat, but when she rose, she felt stiff and achy.

She crawled beneath the covers on her bed and rigidly stretched out her legs. "Ring, phone, ring," she whispered between dry lips. She closed her eyes, trying to sleep. But all she saw was her uncle's drawn face.

When the phone shrilled, she sat bolt upright, grabbing for the receiver. "Yes?" she answered breathlessly.

"Frank is back in the room, sleeping. The doctor tells me he'll recover and be able to come home in a few days." Hannah's elated tone was transported to Cathy across the line. "Isn't that wonderful?"

"Oh, yes," Cathy exclaimed, happily. She

glanced at the clock. Two A.M. "It's the most wonderful news. Will you stay at the hospital? If Uncle Frank is asleep, you might want to come home."

"No, I'll stay here." Hannah chuckled. "The first thing I want him to see is my face."

"Shall I call Bryan and we'll come to the hospital and take you home?"

"No, dear, I don't know how long I'll be here. I'll take a taxi home when I'm ready."

"Is there anything I can do?"

"Would you tack up a Closed Until Further Notice sign on the shop?"

"Sure, Aunt Hannah, anything else?"

"No, I'll see you sometime tomorrow."

Cathy smiled with relief. Plumping up her pillow, she lay back and fell sound asleep.

The next morning, Cathy checked with Aunt Hannah and learned that Uncle Frank, aching and awake, grumbled at being in the hospital. A good sign, she thought. Next, she called Susan. She'd almost forgotten they were to meet in the park, but their appointment was still on.

Cathy showered, dressed, and ate breakfast. She wrote out a sign for the Blue Tiger, then jogged to the shop and tacked the sign to the door.

On the way to the park she wondered if Edward would be waiting. He had to be there. She had to make Susan believe everything she'd told her.

At Battlefield Park she glimpsed a tall figure in the gazebo. Edward was here! But as she moved nearer she discovered the person was Susan.

"Hi," Susan said. "I just arrived. I heard about your uncle. Is he okay?"

"Yes," Cathy answered, glancing around for Edward. "I called Aunt Hannah this morning and Uncle Frank is awake, minus one appendix."

Susan smiled. "Bryan said you were worried sick."

"I meant to call your brother this morning. He helped us so much last night," Cathy said.

Susan looked around. "Do you think Edward will show today?"

"I — I'm not sure," Cathy said. Maybe it hadn't been such a good idea to invite Susan.

The two girls chatted, stamping their feet as the cold crept around them.

"Edward isn't coming," Cathy announced after an hour. "Let's go to Pete's for a hot chocolate. I shouldn't have brought you."

Susan gazed at Cathy with sympathy. "I'm

sorry." She took Cathy's hand. "I know he's real to you."

"Maybe he'll be here later," Cathy said, her uncertainty evident in her quavering voice. She ached to see Edward today. She had such a short time left in Princeton. Added to her disappointment, was a feeling of guilt. If Susan hadn't been here, he would have come, Cathy thought.

At Pete's Place, the two girls drank their hot chocolates, but Susan sensed Cathy's reluctance to discuss Edward. Suddenly she brightened. She said, "I almost forgot. Today Bryan wants you to go with him to an ice-skating and pizza party. Phil and I will be there and a few others. Bryan would have called you, but he's helping Mom deliver used books for the library sale. Fourish, okay?"

"That sounds like fun," Cathy said. "I'll be ready." When the girls finished, they left, going in opposite directions.

Cathy went straight home, pleased to see Aunt Hannah descending the stairway.

"Hi, Cathy," Hannah said, rubbing her short hair dry with a towel, and with a terry cloth robe wrapped around her. "I just showered and washed my hair. After being at the hospital all night, a shower felt delicious. I feel like I've been renewed."

"How is Uncle Frank?"

"Getting sassier by the minute," Hannah replied with a wide smile. "He's already asking to come home."

"Already?" Cathy said, amused. "Uncle Frank is difficult to keep down."

"They won't keep him much longer. He'll either be home tomorrow or Sunday."

"If you can't take me to the airport Sunday," Cathy said, "I'll be glad to take the train."

"Nonsense!" Hannah said. "I'll get you to the airport, don't you worry about that!"

"Will you be going back to the hospital soon?" Cathy asked. "If it won't tire him, I'd like to visit Uncle Frank."

"Tire him?" Hannah snorted. "Never. He's tiring the nurses, though. He's already badgering them with questions like: When can I have more solid food? When can I go home? The nurses, however, adore him. He can be a teddy bear when he wants to."

Cathy laughed. "Then I guess I can ride with you?"

"Frank would love to see you. I'll be leaving about two," Hannah said. "I need to do a few things in the house and eat a bite of lunch."

Cathy said, "Shall I call Mother?"

"Why don't I do the phoning, then you can get on the line and give her the time you'll arrive at O'Hare? You'll need to make arrangements to be picked up."

"Fine, I'll be on the phone in my room."

When Hannah called Chicago, Cathy listened in. Details of the ambulance and Frank's emergency operation were discussed. When Hannah said good-bye to Sara, Cathy entered the conversation. She told her mother she'd be in at four o'clock, Chicago time.

"Wonderful!" Sara said. "It seems as if you've been gone months. We'll all come to the airport to meet you, then you and Mike can decide if you want to come to dinner with Zack, Johnny, and me."

Cathy paused, then said, "I'll think about it, Mom. I'm eager to see you, too."

"Give Frank my love, and I'll send him flowers."

Cathy laughed. "You'd better send them to his home address. I don't think they can keep him in the hospital much longer."

"I'll do that," Sara said. "See you Sunday." And she hung up.

Cathy stared at the phone. Soon she'd have to make up her mind. Should she go to dinner with Zack? She remembered his letter that she'd crumpled and stuffed in her pocket. She retrieved it, rereading parts of it. He really sounded sincere. And with or without her blessing, he intended to marry her mother. Well, she'd better at least give him a chance. Isn't that what Mike asked her to do? Should she go to dinner with everyone? It didn't mean Zack was her friend. But she was eager to see Mom, Johnny, and most of all Mike!

What would she tell Mike? How much about this week?

Chapter 25

Cathy had several hours before she went to the hospital. She was eager to visit Uncle Frank and hoped he was getting along as well as Hannah said. She remained in her room to read a book on English history. She wanted to learn as much as possible about Edward's background.

She had turned to the chapter on King George III, when she was interrupted by a light tapping.

Looking up, she was startled to see Edward tapping his foot and waiting for her to recognize his presence.

"Edward!" she cried, throwing her book aside. "I waited for you at the park today."

"I know," he said gravely, "but you brought a visitor along. I had planned to take you to the king's court."

"I thought you might enjoy Susan," Cathy

said, moving toward him. "It was my fault. I shouldn't have urged her to come, but," Cathy flung out her hands, "she didn't believe in you. I wanted her to see you as I do."

"Don't be alarmed." He took her in his arms. "Susan wouldn't have been able to see me. Now, however, we'll return to London to St. James's Palace, where the king and queen hold court. We'll attend a royal audience and you'll see what the feelings of the English were toward the American colonies."

Soon Cathy found herself walking down St. James's Street where people were carrying banners.

AMERICANS NOT PAYING FULL SHARE OF TAXES

TAX THE COLONIES

NO FAVORED TREATMENT FOR AMERICANS

A TAX ON STAMPS AND TEA

The angry crowd demanded that the upstart Americans be taxed. Many Englishmen said *their* taxes were too high. Time to tax the colonies and enforce past laws!

Cathy blinked. She'd never realized the British side of the war.

"To go to court means that you must be dressed for the royal audience," Edward said, "and I might add, you are beautiful! You'll take everyone's eyes away from Queen Charlotte."

"I will?" Cathy asked, looking at her low-cut gown of finest blue silk. The bodice was decorated with blue and silver beads. Pleased, she touched the white ruff around her neck, and almost skipped alongside Edward in her slippers of blue silk.

Edward, on the other hand, wore formal attire, a white vest and breeches, and a tailcoat of turquoise with satin trim of ecru lace. Around his neck he wore high stocks of white and a powdered short wig tied with a black ribbon. How tall and elegant he looked, thought Cathy. He would turn many a female head.

"Oh, Edward, I don't know what to say if I meet the king and queen."

"Just curtsy. No need to say anything," Edward answered, taking her by the arm. Going by the gatehouse of St. James's Palace, Edward said, "This was built by Henry the eighth." On a column, he traced two intertwining letters. "See, here are his initials and those of his second wife, Anne Boleyn."

"Yes," Cathy said. "One of his six wives, and one that was beheaded."

"You're right," Edward said.

Entering the palace, Cathy took a deep breath and tried to compose herself. She didn't meet a king and queen every day. The young girl stood beside Edward, not daring to let go of his arm.

"The doors to the throne room will be opened soon," Edward said, strolling with other onlookers down the vast hall. Portraits of past rulers lined the walls.

Cathy paused at the portrait of Elizabeth I. Her red frizzy hair was adorned with pearls and when you gazed into her determined steely eyes you knew she had great inner strength. The queen's magnificent gown with huge beribboned sleeves, lacy ruff, and rows upon rows of pearls made her look regal, indeed.

As they moved on, they examined more portraits, the Stuart kings and queens, then the beginning of the Hanoverian dynasty. George I and George II, until they reached the last painting of the current king. Edward peered closely at his monarch's features. "George the third was an honest king who appreciated hard work. In fact, he was known as 'Farmer George.' "

"I read he wasn't well liked," Cathy added, glancing at Edward. She was afraid he might take offense at her words. After all, he had given his life for this king.

But Edward chuckled. "Yes, when George the third came to the throne, he was a very religious man. He could be rigid and some even called him obstinate. They said he didn't know the meaning of compromise. He was always right and everyone else was wrong."

"That's one reason we went to war against him," Cathy said. "If King George had been more flexible, maybe we'd still belong to England." She laughed, brushing past a nobleman in a crimson suit with a frilly shirt. "In America George the third was called the 'tyrant king.' "

"But England needed money," Edward protested. "That's why the Stamp Act and Tea Tax were passed."

"Do you know what the New York Dutch called the Stamp Act?" Cathy asked.

Edward cocked his head, waiting.

"The Stomp Ack!" Cathy's chin jutted out defiantly. "Americans stopped drinking tea, too!"

"Cathy, not so loud. We're surrounded by English men and women," Edward said in hushed tones. "Remember we're at the king's court."

"Sorry," Cathy murmured, "but I wish they could comprehend the Americans' viewpoint, instead of calling us 'Rebels' or 'Sons of Violence.'"

"I do see the American side," Edward admitted. "A little. But it's difficult when the Americans in New York tore down the statue of King George on his horse, crushed it into little pieces, and turned it into forty-two thousand bullets."

A chamberlain dressed in a long red robe knocked on the floor three times with the long staff he carried. "The doors to the throne room are open," he announced in sonorous tones.

And the wide gilt doors instantly were flung open.

In awe, Cathy clutched Edward's arm as they entered the ornate room. The king and his wife, Charlotte, stood beside their thrones. How splendid they appeared.

The queen smiled and nodded, but the king appeared haughty and unsmiling. Cathy stared at Queen Charlotte, having read that she'd given birth to fifteen children. She was slim, not particularly pretty, but her gentle expression indicated she had a kind spirit.

When the doors were shut, the monarchs were seated. The royal seal hung above their heads. The royal arms in a flourish of gold, red, and blue depicted a white unicorn standing on the right side of the shield and a gold lion on the left.

Cathy couldn't take her eyes off Charlotte. Her gown of green brocade trimmed in white ermine and her ruffled sleeves coming to the elbow emphasized her slender figure. On her brown hair sat a tiara of blue stones and feathers.

George III, on the other hand, wore even finer clothes than his wife. His deep red velvet cape trimmed with ermine reached to his ankles. He wore ruffled breeches that came to the knee, white silk stockings, and shoes with satin bows.

Once the royal pair were ready to receive the court, the men bowed and the women curtsied, giving their obeisance. At times King George would utter a few words, at other times he only nodded at courtiers passing down the line.

Once the courtesies were over, people again conversed and roamed about freely.

"The king's downturned mouth shows how unhappy he is," Edward said, steering Cathy through the crowd. "He'd much rather be at Buckingham House or his country estate, Kew."

Cathy marveled at the richly dressed court.

She'd never seen anything this opulent in America.

"Many of these men and women are Loyalists," Edward said. "They left the United States to be with their king."

"We call them Tories," Cathy said, her eyes flashing.

Edward gave her a patient smile. "They fled the colonies when treasonous acts were performed against the crown."

Cathy bit her tongue, but she had her own opinion of people who shunned freedom, preferring an autocratic king.

"See, over there," Edward said. "That's Lord North, the king's prime minister."

Cathy observed the man's thick lips and prominent eyes. "He and the king could be brothers," she said. "They look so much alike."

"Lord North is a true ally of the king, one of the few men that George trusts," Edward continued. "He's well educated, and quite fit for his position."

"Well, he's heartily hated in America," Cathy said, not liking the appearance of either the prime minister or the king.

"Into the gardens!" the king said and the tall doors were opened onto delightful grounds of flowers and trees. An arbor of roses opened into a bed of violets and pansies. Underneath two large oaks romped six of the king's children. One of the boys had a pet macaw perched on his arm. Their nanny stood nearby seeing that the children didn't mix with the adults. Even the king and queen paid them little or no attention.

Edward and Cathy strolled down a path with irises and delphiniums planted on either side. The sweet scent of perfumed flowers filled the air. Cathy, entranced by the beautiful flowers, trees, and shrubs, listened to the trill of a canary. Walking on, she was especially taken with a shrubbery maze.

"Let's go into the maze, Edward."

Edward smiled at her, willing to indulge her every desire. "All right. But you go ahead, then I'll try to find you."

Cathy clapped her hands. "A game of hide-and-seek. I love it!" And she hurried toward the intricate maze. She turned to smile at Edward, but suddenly stopped. Her jarred senses reeled. In the midst of a group of courtiers who ambled into the maze was a tanned young man. He threw back his head, laughing at a jest. His dark hair was as shiny as his brown satin waistcoat. The handsome man disappearing into the maze was Mike Novak! Mike was here! Here in England! Her heart pounded in her ears. She must catch up to him.

Lifting her skirts, Cathy ran into the maze. She glanced to the right and left. Which direction did he take? "Mike! Mike!" she called, but no one answered. Hopelessly entangled in one turn after another, she wandered in and out of the myriad lanes. Finally, she gave up. She didn't even know if she could find her way back to the garden.

"Cathy!"

Who called her name? She whirled around, only to find Edward. "Edward," she said, caught off guard.

"Were you expecting someone else?" he questioned, a puzzled expression on his face.

"No, no," she answered, vaguely disoriented. As she followed Edward out into the open, she glanced into every pathway's entrance, hoping to glimpse Mike. Mike, whose darling face she knew so well.

Eating refreshments of strawberries and cream, Cathy kept searching for Mike, peering into one face, then another. Mike wasn't to be found.

"Shall we leave, Cathy?" Edward asked.

"Is it proper?"

"Anytime after the refreshments."

Reluctantly, Cathy, looking over her shoulder, left the palace.

Edward hailed a cab.

On the road to Piccadilly, Cathy tried to understand how Mike could be in eighteenth-century London.

"I heard several gentlemen ask about you, Cathy," Edward said warmly. "You do create a stir."

A smile hovered around her lips, but she scarcely heard Edward's words. Mike filled her mind.

"You have this gentleman friend in Chicago, Cathy. What is he like?"

She swallowed hard, too shocked to answer. Finally she said, "Mike is in college. He's going into politics."

"Is he a Whig or a Tory?"

Cathy laughed, regaining her composure. "Neither. He'll be an Independent, voting for whatever he thinks is right."

"He sounds like a good man. Hardworking and loyal. I know you think highly of him, Cathy," Edward said, taking her lace-covered fingers in his, kissing each one. "But I love you, too. I need you more than Mike does. Does he love you or his work more?"

Cathy thought of the fax Mike had sent. I love you, he'd said. "He loves me, above his work," she answered, hoping she hadn't hurt Edward's feelings. But she wondered if Mike really *did* love her above his work. She doubted if it were true even as she said the words.

"I see," Edward said, an amused sparkle in his eyes. "I think I'll be able to persuade you to love me above anyone else."

She said nothing, staring out the window. How should she respond to him?

On they rode, clattering over the cobblestones.

Cathy leaned down to flounce up her skirt. To her astonishment, however, she wasn't wearing a dress, at all. She gaped in disbelief at her faded jeans.

She stared at the familiar floral wallpaper of her bedroom, then her eyes shifted to the bud vase with the red rose Bryan had given her. Everything was just as she'd left it.

"Cathy," Aunt Hannah called. "It's almost two o'clock. Do you still want to come with me to the hospital?"

She answered, "Yes. I'll be right down." Her thoughts, though, were not of Uncle Frank and the hospital. They still belonged to Edward and Mike.

Chapter 26

As Cathy accompanied Aunt Hannah down the hospital corridor, the memory of London with Edward still lingered. And how could she forget her fleeting glimpse of Mike in the garden maze?

Two doctors passed them and Hannah said, "This is Frank's room. He'll be glad to see you, Cathy."

Frank was sitting up in a chair and eating a small serving of ice cream.

"Cathy!" he boomed. "Give your old uncle a kiss."

Laughing, she ran forward and kissed his cheek. "You're more chipper than I thought possible," she said.

"Did you think I'd be prone on my back?" he chuckled. "Don't you know you can't keep a good man down?"

Hannah leaned over and gave him a kiss.

He held her hand for an instant and love shone from his eyes.

"Tell me what you've been doing since my operation, Cathy," he asked.

"Nothing much," she replied. "Aunt Hannah closed the Blue Tiger for a few days, so I don't help out like I did before." She sat on the edge of the bed. "Today I had lunch with Susan." How she longed to add, and I was in London at the court of King George III, but smiled instead.

"You might be interested in that book I'm reading," Uncle Frank said. "On the pillow."

She picked up *Redcoats and Rebels*.

"I know you're interested in the Revolutionary War," Frank said, "and that book is a dilly."

Cathy scanned the contents. "This sounds good," she said. "I'll remember the title."

"What did the doctor say about your leaving the hospital, Frank?" Hannah asked.

"Sunday afternoon," he answered. "Gives you plenty of time to take Cathy to La Guardia Airport."

"I told Aunt Hannah that I could easily take the train. I know how eager you must be to come home, Uncle Frank."

"When the doctor says four o'clock, that's what he means.

"You and Hannah go ahead. As long as I have a book to read I won't be lonesome. Besides, the nurses come in every five minutes to check my pulse." He chuckled. "No, Hannah will be back in plenty of time to bring me home."

A nurse entered. "Hello, everyone." Then turning to her patient, she said, "And how's Frank doing? Ready to have your temperature taken?"

Frank grunted as the nurse poked a thermometer in his mouth. Holding his wrist, she timed his pulse, then removed the thermometer. "Normal," she said, "Ninety-eight point six."

"See what I mean?" Frank said, pulling on his beard. "How can I be lonely when I have people popping in every two seconds."

The nurse laughed. "I've never seen such a quick recovery. We're going to miss you when you're dismissed, Frank Lambert."

"Ha!" was all Frank said, smiling and watching her leave.

Hannah and Cathy stayed an hour, then Cathy kissed her uncle good-bye. "I'll see you tomorrow," she said.

"Good, I'll look forward to it," Uncle Frank said, yawning. "I'm tired all of a sudden."

"You take a nap," Hannah said, helping him into bed. "I'll be back tonight." And she kissed his forehead.

"I wish I could come with you, Aunt Hannah," Cathy said, as they walked out to the van.

"You go ahead and enjoy your ice-skating and pizza party. Susan told me she and Bryan invited you and I want you to go."

Cathy hugged her aunt. "Thank you," she said simply.

Hannah smiled. "I think Bryan and Susan will miss you almost as much as I will."

Once home from the hospital, Cathy dressed for the ice-skating party. Black tights, black-and-white striped short skirt, heavy white sweater, and a white knit cap. It seemed she was always getting ready to go someplace. She'd never been on such a social whirl, but it was fun. And her meetings with Edward gave her more excitement and pleasure. But she only had two more days to be with him. Only two days in her lifetime.

When Bryan picked her up, he gave her a big slow grin. "You look great as always, Cathy. Everyone's waiting at Carnegie Lake," he said, sliding his arm around her waist as they walked to his car.

When they arrived at the narrow long lake shimmering in the fading sun, Cathy gasped, "Isn't it beautiful?"

"Not as beautiful as in the summer when we have our boat races," Bryan answered.

Skaters of all descriptions skimmed over the lake's surface.

"That small girl is doing a perfect layback," Cathy said, lacing up her shoe skates.

"That's Jennie's six-year-old sister," Bryan chuckled. "Megan's determined to be an ice-skater and even in the summer she practices at an indoor rink."

"I wonder if she knows what a life of practice and dedication lies ahead of her," Cathy mused aloud, skating out on the ice.

"She knows," Bryan said, gliding toward Cathy and twirling her about.

On the other side of the lake, Jennie was helping Doug stand up. Obviously a novice, he wavered as he took a few steps. Jennie's giggles could be heard across the ice, and she skated circles around Doug. Cathy was glad to see she had the edge over Doug.

For the rest of the afternoon, until the sun dipped in the west, Cathy and Bryan skated. The brisk air flowed over them. When the wind began to blow, it grew colder and colder. Once

Bryan lost his cap, easily swooping down and retrieving it.

Cathy noticed Doug ignored her and she was happy he stayed far away.

"Anyone ready for pizza?" Susan shouted, shooting by and waving her hands over her head. "Pizza, anyone?"

"Yea!" Bryan cheered. "Let's have at it!" His nose and cheeks were nipped red by the cold.

Little Megan skated to the bank. Her blonde hair fell around her face as she sat down to unlace her skates.

"I admired your skating, Megan," Cathy said, sitting down beside the little girl. "You're tops."

"I'm going to be a star someday. Just like Kristi Yamaguchi," she said, her eyes big and mouth set. "She won the Olympic gold medal!"

Jennie skated up behind her sister, putting her arms around her. "Time to go home for supper, Megan."

"Hi, Jennie," Cathy said.

"Hi, Cathy. Bryan tells me you're leaving Sunday. I hope you come back."

"Me, too," Megan piped up. "I didn't know you, but you're pretty and nice and you like the way I skate."

Cathy laughed. "I like you, Megan, and I like the way you skate. And, Jennie," she said, turning to her, "I'll try to come back. I promise."

The two sisters waved, and climbed the bank to a waiting car.

"They're not eating pizza with us?" Cathy asked, watching them leave.

"No," Susan said. "Just the four of us."

"Phil, again?" Cathy asked, a mischievous smile playing about her lips.

"Phil, again," announced Susan with a happy expression. "And, speaking of Phil, here he comes!"

Phil skated over and removed his skates. His long face was as pink as the sunset. "I'm freezing," he said. "The sooner we get to Carmen's Pizza Parlor, the better." He grabbed Susan and gave her a squeeze. "Keep me warm."

Gleefully, Susan hugged him, too. "You keep *me* warm!"

"I'd love to," Phil said, nuzzling her neck.

"We'll meet you at Carmen's in fifteen minutes, buddy boy," Bryan said jovially.

And in a short time the four of them were seated at a round table covered with a red-and-white checkered tablecloth. Nearby a fireplace blazed, flames crackling.

"It's supposed to get down to zero degrees tonight," Phil said, his eyes never leaving Susan's face.

"Brrr, too cold for any more ice-skating. How about a movie tomorrow night?" Bryan asked.

"There's a new sci-fi movie in town," Phil said.

"How about a Western?" Susan said.

"I'd rather see a thriller," Bryan chimed in. He lifted his brows and gazed at Cathy. "What would you like to see?"

"Hmmm, something romantic," she answered.

"Everyone wants to see something different," Susan said with a slight frown. "How will we decide?"

"Flip a coin?" Phil asked.

"Good, Phil. You own a four-sided coin?" Bryan said, a twinkle in his dark eyes. All at once he snapped his fingers. "Cathy should call it. It's her last night with us."

When the pepperoni and cheese pizza arrived, Susan cut it into four parts, and dished it up on each plate. "Of course, Bryan, that's the perfect solution," she said, looking up and giving Cathy a warm smile. "You decide on the movie, Cathy."

"Then romance it is," Phil breathed in a soft

voice, his brows lifting up and down as he ogled Susan.

"Phil!" Susan said in a mocking reprimand.

Suddenly, Bryan stopped eating, staring out the window.

"What did you see, Bryan?" Susan asked.

"Oh, nothing," he mumbled. "Just a bright blue mustang drove by."

"I see," Susan said with a knowing look. "So Ann is back in town."

"It doesn't matter." Bryan shrugged his shoulders.

Cathy noticed, though, that he pushed his pizza away and didn't eat another bite.

Cathy turned to Phil. "Do you live near Susan, Phil?"

"Three blocks west," he answered.

Cathy knew that neighborhood was very elegant, so the Bronsteins must be well off, too. "Is your dad in any upcoming plays?"

Phil's face lit up. "Funny you should ask, Cathy. He just got a callback from an off-Broadway producer. It's the role of a con man and he says it's a juicy part." He grinned and pushed his glasses up on his nose. "Mother's not very excited about it, though. It means he'll be staying in New York some nights. But Dad vowed that he'd commute most of the time." He glanced at Susan. "It's difficult to

be an actor. Dad says it's either feast or fam-
ine. One year he only had one part and the
play closed in two months."

"That's fascinating," Susan said. "I love
your dad's acting. He has to be good to make
a career out of the stage."

Impatiently, Bryan tapped his straw on the
rim of his glass.

Ignoring her brother, Susan said, "Phil, I'm
surprised you don't have any ambitions to be
an actor."

"Me?" Phil gave a hearty laugh. "Forget it!
Science is my gig. Can't get enough of it."

"I'll bet you could be anything you wanted
to," Cathy said.

"He could," Susan said emphatically. "Phil's
brilliant. He gets A's in history as well as
physics," she said, smiling at him. "But, no,
he'd rather be in some stuffy old laboratory."

"Especially, if you were with me," Phil answered, touching Susan's nose with his finger.

"Are you ready to go, Cathy?" Bryan asked
abruptly.

Cathy shot Bryan a look of surprise. He was
usually the last one to want to leave. Besides,
she enjoyed hearing about Phil. But she picked
up her gloves. "Sure, Bryan. I'm ready."

"We'll stay awhile, okay, Susan?" Phil said.

"Fine with me," Susan answered.

On the way home Bryan didn't say much. The soft music had clearly put him in a quiet mood.

As he deftly maneuvered his car around the turns and bends of Witherspoon Street, he said gently, "Cathy, you've been great this vacation. I've had such good times with you." He pulled up before Hannah's, and his car purred to a stop. "I've fallen in love with you."

She smiled and tenderly placed her hand over his. "Bryan, I've loved every minute I've spent with you. I think, though, you're in love with Ann."

Bryan gave her his familiar slow grin. "What are you? A psychologist, Ms. O'Brien?"

"No way," she teased, "but I sensed your feelings toward Ann the day you showed me her picture." She gave a low chuckle. "Most breakups signify picture ripping, too."

"Maybe you're right," Bryan conceded, "but right now I'm not thinking about Ann. I have a new girl. And that girl is you, Cathy!" He leaned over and gave her a kiss on her cheek.

He held Cathy in his arms for a few minutes.

"I need to go in," she said, pulling herself free. "My aunt is all alone."

"If anyone could make me forget Ann, it

would be you, Cathy." Bryan smiled in her eyes.

She returned his smile. "You'll always have a bit of my heart, Bryan." She laughed softly. "I'll never forget your entrance at the Blue Tiger. You breezed in as if you owned the place. You looked very cocky in your western boots, leather jacket, and wide-brimmed hat."

He bent and kissed her again.

"Good night, Bryan," Cathy whispered.

"Good night, sweet Cathy," Bryan said in a thick voice. He had his arms around her, gazing longingly at her. "During spring break, I may have to hop a plane for Chicago."

She remained silent. Only the hoot of an owl could be heard. At last, she repeated firmly, "Good night, Bryan."

He opened her door and escorted her to the front porch. "Till tomorrow and our romance movie."

"Till tomorrow," she echoed, going inside.

"Hi, Cathy," Hannah said. "Come in by the fire."

Cathy hung up her jacket and joined her aunt. "How's Uncle Frank?" she inquired.

"Chomping at the bit to come home," Hannah replied. "He was sleeping when I left."

"I'm glad he's healing okay."

"I see Bryan brought you home fairly early," Hannah said, placing her book on an end table.

"He's very nice," Cathy sat at her aunt's feet and stared into the fire.

"Will you see him again?" Hannah asked.

"Yes, we're going to a movie tomorrow night." Tears welled up in Cathy's eyes. "Oh, Aunt Hannah, remember when you told me about two boys who you loved?"

"I'll never forget them," Hannah said, giving Cathy a thoughtful look. "Are you in love with two boys?"

Cathy nodded mutely. Actually, more than two, but she didn't mention Edward. "When I return home, I don't know how I can look Mike in the eyes. He loves me, but now I'm not sure I can return his love."

"Sure you can," Hannah answered. "Just because you've gone out with Bryan and maybe even kissed him once or twice, that doesn't mean you've fallen out of love with Mike. Bryan is fun, and charming and good-looking. He could sweep any girl off her feet. This might just be what we used to call a 'fling.' "

Cathy said, "Maybe, you're right, Aunt Hannah." She wiped her eyes and shook her head. "Maybe it's a fling for both of us."

"That could be," Hannah said. "Time will tell. If it's serious you can always meet again. How long is the flight from New York to Chicago?"

"Two hours or so."

"See?" Hannah said. "You or Bryan could see each other any time without any great inconvenience."

"I think that Bryan's in love with Ann Bishop. I may be someone who filled in his time as he tried to forget her."

"Yes, I think you've figured it out." Hannah leaned down and stroked Cathy's hair. "But didn't Bryan help pass the time while you were away from Mike?"

Cathy tipped her head, smiling up at her aunt. "Yes," she answered in a low voice.

Hannah made hot chocolate and they sat talking for another hour.

At last Cathy went to bed, but she didn't sleep. She didn't want to sleep. She closed her eyes, bringing the image of Mike into focus. "Mike, Mike," she whispered, seeing his brown eyes, his smooth tanned face, and thick black hair. She was afraid he was slipping away from her. And yet, she would never forget the memory of their time together. Whenever he had appeared, her heart skyrocketed.

She recalled the sweetness of his lips on hers. She had a great deal to think about before she got off the plane at O'Hare.

She thought of Edward, her dear British soldier. He said he could cause her to forget Mike. He loved her. And he needed her. She wasn't certain if Mike really needed her. Not in the sense that Edward needed her. But Edward wasn't part of her time, she reminded herself. It was so easy to forget.

What was it that she wanted? To be needed? Sure, but she didn't want to devote her life to waiting on a man. She had her own hopes and desires. With Mike, she knew she could pursue them.

Falling asleep, she murmured one last word, "Mike."

Chapter 27

On her last full day in Princeton, Cathy rose early. She dressed for the cold, wearing a red plaid sweater, snow pants, heavy socks, and ankle boots.

Aunt Hannah had already left, leaving her a note.

Dear Cathy,

I need to run to the shop and to the hospital. I'll be back around noon. Then it's to the hospital again around two. If you're here, and want to come with me, that will be fine.

Love,

Hannah

Quickly, Cathy ate a slice of toast and drank a glass of milk. She needed to hurry or Edward might not wait. Slipping on her jacket, she then tied a scarf around her neck, and pulled on her green knit cap. She was ready for the park. Each time she went, she feared Edward might not appear. He just had to be there this morning!

The sleet hit her face like so many tiny needles, but it didn't bother her. She would soon see Edward and that made her feel warm and happy inside. When he was beside her, weather didn't matter.

Edward had already arrived at Battlefield Park. He rushed to meet her. He was wearing his British uniform. The red jacket, white cross straps, and white breeches clearly were as fresh and clean as the day they'd been issued.

"Cathy," Edward said, a smile creasing his firm features and softening his compelling blue eyes.

Cathy ran into his arms. "I was afraid you wouldn't be waiting," she said breathlessly. "I have such a short time left in Princeton."

He held her at arm's length. "You can be with me forever, my dearest girl." He bent down and kissed her.

"How?" she said, closing her eyes and enjoying the touch of his lips. For a moment she stayed quiet in his arms.

His voice, deep and clear, broke in on her reverie. "Today, Cathy, our carriage awaits."

And suddenly a warm breeze wafted over her face and her mouth formed a large O at the sight of a shiny black coach.

"We could spend an eternity, exploring all the nooks and crannies in London." Edward took her hand and helped her into a stylish carriage pulled by two perfectly-matched gray spirited horses.

Cathy settled her long skirts about her. Her lovely ivory dress of a light silk had a scooped neckline and around her neck was a pretty ribbon. By her side leaned a matching parasol.

The carriage arrived at a huge park where couples promenaded on the grounds. "This is Hyde Park," Edward said, gazing at her with fondness. "I thought to spend a day of leisure with you. Do you approve?"

"I do approve," Cathy agreed. "The days I spend with you are precious and fascinating."

Edward knocked on the roof of the carriage and it stopped. He paid the cab driver and lifted out a picnic basket. Cathy's laugh tinkled. "I love picnics." She threaded her arm through his and they strolled among the richly dressed people as small children played tag. Here and there over this lush landscape were dotted great private palaces.

"Care to see a cock fight?" Edward asked drily, as if he already knew her answer.

Cathy shuddered. "No, please, let's go on."

They turned in the opposite direction and kept walking.

"That wide open space ahead is where duels are held," Edward said. "My uncle Jamison was killed in a pistol duel three years ago. They fought over a woman."

"How dreadful. If he was anything like my uncle Frank, you must miss him terribly," Cathy said in dismay.

"I barely knew him," Edward said in terse tones. "My father said his brother was a gambler and wastrel and he wanted nothing to do with him." He softened when he glanced at Cathy. "Though I was five, the one time I met him, I liked him. I remember he loved to jest and hoisted me onto his shoulders and paraded about. Uncle Jamison was very different from my father."

Arriving at a group of weeping willows, the pair sat on the grass. Several families picnicked in the area.

Edward spread out a cloth, then brought out smoked salmon, bread, cheese.

Between them they ate every scrap. "What

a lovely idea," Cathy said, leaning back against a tree. For a while they savored the sunny day and the buzz of happy voices.

"How blue the heavens are, only a few clouds." She shaded her eyes and pointed. "That one cloud is shaped like a ship. See how fast it skims across the sky."

"Perhaps it's a warship," Edward said, chewing on a blade of grass. "I'll soon be sailing to America."

"Let's not think about that," Cathy said, bending toward him. She smiled and lifted his chin with her finger. "Today is for us," she said softly.

Edward caressed her cheek. "If only there'd be no tomorrow."

Their eyes locked and Cathy was certain he could hear her heartbeat.

"Oh, Cathy," he choked. "I need you so. I'm lost without you."

"Darling Edward," she murmured, "come, put your head in my lap and we won't think about tomorrow."

Edward stretched out and Cathy gently ran her fingers through his hair. Edward closed his eyes, a peaceful smile of contentment on his face. Children's laughter and rolling carriage wheels all were blotted out in this one sweet moment.

When the sun lowered in the west, Edward folded the cloth and they walked toward the croquet field. "I'll play you a game and if you lose," teased Cathy, "you must bring me back here tomorrow."

Edward didn't respond. He grabbed a mallet and the game was on. He knocked his red-and-white striped ball through the wicket and Cathy followed with her green-and-white striped one.

Once Cathy suffered a penalty and Edward, with a CRACK! — sent her ball flying into the hedges. Laughing, Cathy said, "You play rough."

At the end of the game, Edward had won. "Well, Edward, since you're the victor, you may ask a favor of me," Cathy bantered with a smile. "What will it be?"

Edward said, "I'll have a kiss."

Laughing, Cathy said, "Then a kiss you shall have," and she kissed him lightly on his mouth.

Edward grabbed her, pulling her tight against him. "A kiss," he said hoarsely. And he tipped his head down and kissed her long and hard.

"Oh, Edward," she said, pushing away.

Still holding Cathy about the waist, Edward whispered, "I love you."

Cathy felt warm in his arms, but finally she

said, "We must leave before it gets dark."

"Yes, yes, you're right," Edward said, releasing her.

In the carriage they were silent, and the only sound was the jingle of the horses' harnesses and the clippety-clop of their hooves. Edward squeezed her hand and held it tight.

When the carriage stopped at the docks along the Thames River, Edward again helped her out.

A large warship, *The Royal George*, was being loaded with kegs of gunpowder, but what held Cathy's interest were four horses being lifted onboard. They were lowered below decks in large canvas slings.

"They will be hooked up with their feet dangling about six inches above the wooden planking," Edward said. "This is to avoid damage and distress in heavy seas."

The British flag, or Union Jack, snapped in the breeze. The blue background and red-and-white cross stripes against a darkening sky was a dramatic sight. White sails unfurled. And seamen shouted orders back and forth. A trumpet blared. Next red-coated British Regulars and green-coated Germans filed by twos onboard.

"*The Royal George*, a one-hundred-gun-ship, is the pride of the British Navy," Edward said.

"It was built in 1756 and like most ships it's made of oak."

"The figurehead," Cathy said, her eyes widening. "Beautiful! Those wooden horses with their manes flying look as if they're racing!"

Edward pressed his lips together in a tense line. "It won't be long before I'll be on such a ship." Cathy touched his hand in a reassuring gesture.

The sunset cast a rosy glow over the ship and a sailor in white cutoffs shinnied up the mainmast as fast as a monkey. "Will they sail at night?" Cathy asked.

"Just down the Thames River. They'll be ready to set sail into the Atlantic at dawn."

Cathy was thrilled at the magnificent ship, yet she felt a deep anxiety for these good men going to war. So many would never live to see their homeland again.

She reached for Edward's hand. He seemed so vulnerable despite his demeanor and fine uniform.

Just as they were to leave the docks a coach stopped and out stepped a bewigged naval officer.

"That's Admiral Richard Howe, Commander in Chief of the Navy," Edward said. "His brother is General William Howe, a commander of the British Army."

The sober-faced admiral flipped a coin to the driver and strode up the gangplank. His gold collar and gold epaulettes were striking against his navy coat. White pants and high black boots completed his uniform.

Soon the command was given to sail and the huge ship moved into the river. The men cheered.

But even as their cheer echoed over the water, a lump had grown in Cathy's throat and she was unable to speak.

Edward turned her to face him. "I have a gift for you, Cathy."

"You do?" Cathy gazed into his deep blue eyes. "Just being with you is gift enough."

Edward reached inside his uniform and pulled out a medallion on a gold chain. "This was Grandfather Marsh's," he said. "I want you to keep it to remember me."

In her two hands she cradled the beautiful medallion. The surface was etched with a lion's head. The gold caught the last rays of the sun and it glittered in her hand. She pressed the medallion against her chest. "I'll never part with this, Edward. It's the most precious heirloom you could have given me." She smiled. "Besides your heart, of course."

He took the medallion from Cathy and hung the chain over her head. The lion's crest shone against her ivory silk dress. Breathless with such a magnificent present, she constantly touched it to be certain it was there.

Edward, delighted with her reaction, said, "Let's go on."

As they walked, Cathy suddenly felt a numbing cold and put her hands around her flimsy sleeves. But the sleeves had turned into a jacket and she walked in snow. As quickly as she had been with Edward, just as quickly she was alone.

Their day together had been splendid and she loved every moment they spent in Hyde Park, but the scene at the H.M.S. *Royal George* was not only exciting, but poignant as well.

Thoughtfully, she headed for home, but she didn't really want to go into an empty house. Instead, she found herself walking to Susan's house. She needed to show her the medallion and to talk. Now Susan must believe in Edward.

Chapter 28

Cathy hurried along the snowy sidewalk. Was it only a short time ago she was picnicking and playing croquet with Edward in Hyde Park? And together they'd watched troops board the *Royal George* before the ship set sail for the New World. How smart Edward looked in his uniform and how pretty she felt in her silk ivory dress. But at the sailing of the warship, Edward had all at once turned melancholy. The medallion, though, was her most precious gift in the whole world. Frantically she felt about her throat, but the lion's crest had disappeared. Oh, no, had she lost it already? She prayed she would find it. Maybe the chain had been a fantasy. Maybe Edward had been a fantasy.

Feeling in her pockets, her fingers closed around an object nestled in the bottom. The medallion! She brought it out and examined it.

None of this had been a dream! She almost cried aloud with joy.

Snowflakes fell over the ice-covered branches. With the morning sun shining through the trees, Princeton became a crystalline fairyland. She lifted her face, letting the snow touch her nose and lips.

She hoped Susan would be home. She must talk to her.

When she turned the corner, the Gormans' large house loomed before her.

As Cathy rang the bell, she almost expected a butler to answer, but was pleased when Susan opened the door.

"Cathy! Come in!" She gave her a quick hug and hung up Cathy's jacket.

"Is Bryan home?" Cathy asked casually. She couldn't really talk to Susan if he came bounding in.

"No, he's playing basketball at the gym," Susan said. "How about a soda? Let's go to the kitchen." She turned and Cathy followed her. "I've been trying to call you all morning. Where have you been?" Susan asked, opening the refrigerator and setting two sodas on the table.

For some reason Cathy was reluctant to reveal her medallion just yet. She tried to smile, but the memory of Edward and the

Royal George was too much. It was as if he'd realized sailing to America would seal his doom.

Susan tucked one foot under her. Her hair fell in soft curls around her face. She stared at Cathy. "I can see you're upset. I think it would help to talk about it."

"That's why I'm here," Cathy said, managing a small smile.

"What happened today?" prodded Susan.

Cathy's smile faded and she had to bite back her tears. "Oh, Susan, I'm going home tomorrow and leaving everything in such a muddle. What can I do? There's such a knot in my stomach. I'm afraid I'll be gone and Edward will be searching for me." She held the cold soda can against her burning cheek. "Nothing is settled."

"Why do you have to 'settle' anything?" Susan asked in a soft voice, brimming with compassion.

"I'll have left a piece of my heart in Princeton," Cathy murmured.

"Things have a way of resolving themselves," Susan said, reassuring Cathy. "I know before you leave that everything will fall into place."

"I hope you're right, Susan," Cathy said, her tone quiet.

"Where were you this morning?" Susan asked again.

Cathy told Susan everything. She carefully related her day in London.

Susan asked few questions, but she was amazed at Cathy's knowledge of eighteenth-century London. Had her description come from actual experience? Susan wondered.

"If only you could have met him, Susan. If only you could have seen the Vauxhall Gardens and Hyde Park the way I saw them. It was all so wonderful and I was *there* amongst the flowers. The picnic, the croquet game, everything existed. I *know* it happened."

"Cathy, I know *you're* sure but . . ." Susan's eyes were doubtful.

"Maybe this will convince you," Cathy said, pulling out the medallion and handing it to Susan.

Susan's eyes widened. Her fingers lightly traced the lion's head.

"Edward gave me the medallion," Cathy said softly. "It was his grandfather's."

Amazed, Susan whispered, "This is from Edward? I don't know what to think."

Cathy searched Susan's face. "How can I leave without seeing him again?"

"Maybe you will," Susan said uncertainly.

Her brown eyes had tears in them as she returned the medallion. "Go to the park in the morning before you leave. Maybe there . . ."

"Oh, yes," Cathy said, with one last look at Edward's precious gift before slipping it into her pocket. She rose.

"You need to take your mind off Edward for a while," Susan said desperately. "How about a game of Scrabble?"

"I love Scrabble, but I planned on being home about two and going to the hospital with Aunt Hannah."

"So, call Hannah," Susan handed her the phone. "Bryan will be home soon and he'll run you over."

Susan always had a solution, Cathy thought. She even felt better about Edward. She dialed her aunt's number and told her she'd be going to the hospital with Bryan. Cathy sighed. She was depending a great deal on Bryan, but he clearly loved to help her, so she was sure he wouldn't mind.

In the game room with its large windows overlooking the snow-blanketed garden, Susan set up the board. They drew their tiles and started to play.

Before the game ended, Bryan strode in and looked over Cathy's shoulder.

"Bryan! If you say one word to help her, I'll murder you!" Susan said in an ominous tone, eyeing him suspiciously.

Bryan hunched up his shoulders. "Me? I'd never do such a thing. I know how serious you are about the game."

"You can see I'm losing," Cathy said ruefully. Before she played, she moved her letters about, trying to form the best word possible.

"Never you mind, Cathy," Bryan said cheerfully. "Want to go and get a burger, anyone?" he asked, shaking his head at Susan.

"Not me," Susan said. "I'm going over to Francine's."

"Looks like you and me, Cath." Carelessly Bryan threw his arm around Cathy. "Will you go with me?"

"Only if you'll run me by the hospital afterward."

"Done!" Bryan helped her on with her jacket.

"Thanks, Susan, for listening," Cathy said, giving her a kiss on the cheek.

"Anytime," Susan said lightly. "See you tonight for a romantic movie!"

As Bryan and Cathy went down the walk, he asked, "What was that all about?"

"What?" Cathy lifted her eyebrows.

"You were telling Susan something important, weren't you? What were you two talking about?"

"Bryan," Cathy asked, "can't Susan and I have any secrets from you? Do you have to know everything?"

"Yes! Bryan-the-All-Seeing must know everything," he said in his best Dracula accent.

Cathy laughed. It felt good to banter back and forth with Bryan. How unlike Edward he was.

After they ate, Bryan drove her straight to the hospital. He was eager to see her uncle, too, so Cathy was pleased she wasn't taking him out of his way.

Arriving at St. Mary's, they went to Frank's hospital room. When they entered Frank and Hannah were playing cribbage.

"Come on in, you two," Uncle Frank called, smiling broadly.

Hannah set the cribbage board aside. "Bryan," she said, "I'm glad to see my niece brought you along."

"I wanted to come," Bryan said, smiling at her. Then he turned to Frank. "Hi, Mr. Lambert. Looks like you're well enough to come home today."

"You do have a bloom in your cheeks," Cathy agreed, giving her uncle a kiss.

"I feel fit as a fiddle," Frank boomed. "Although I doubt if I could jump over the moon." He chuckled. "I don't know why they're keeping me captive in this antiseptic bird cage."

"Now, now," Hannah said, straightening his blanket, "you'll be home tomorrow in time for supper. I'm making your favorite, roast chicken, mashed potatoes and gravy, and peas."

Frank threw back his head, shaking with laughter. "That's an achievement for Hannah." He grimaced, touching his side. "Ouch, I must remember not to laugh after my operation!"

"Uncle Frank," Cathy said fondly. "I'm going to miss your sense of humor."

Frank gazed at her with affection, holding out his hand. "Here I am, trapped! I can't even take you to the airport tomorrow."

Cathy held his hand. "It's okay, Uncle Frank. Aunt Hannah and I will stop by before we drive to the airport." The very words gave her a pang. The airport and home! How could she leave?

"You'll come back soon, I hope," Frank said.

"Try and keep me away," she answered, a knot in her throat. What was the matter with her? She felt like crying again. Edward, though, filled her every thought. Even with Bryan at her side.

"Cathy had better return," Bryan said,

winking at her and giving her that old razzle-dazzle smile. "Since she breezed into town, Princeton hasn't been the same."

After their hospital visit, Bryan drove her home. "I'll pick you up at seven," he said, squeezing her hand with affection. "Our last night together." His voice was soft and a little sad.

"Yes," she said lightly, "but there's always the plane."

Bryan chuckled. "Right. Always the plane." But a stillness fell between them. It was as if they both realized their relationship was coming to an end.

As Bryan passed the Greek columns of Battlefield Park, Cathy put her hand on Bryan's arm. "Would you please stop here? I — I'd like to walk the rest of the way."

"You would?" He gave her a lopsided grin. "What's the attraction in this park? Susan tells me you walk here every morning."

"It's just a — a lovely place to walk," she stammered. Did her words have a false ring?

Bryan braked and pulled over to the curb. "Want me to walk with you?"

"I just want to enjoy a solitary walk, if you don't mind."

Bryan shifted his shoulders. "Sometimes I don't understand you, Cathy O'Brien."

She narrowed her eyes and put on an inscrutable expression. "I am a woman of mystery," she said in a breathy, sexy voice.

Bryan laughed.

She gave him a brilliant smile and opened the car door. "Tonight."

"Tonight," Bryan echoed and sped off.

Cathy zipped up her jacket and pulled her cap from her pocket. She walked briskly toward the gazebo.

Stopping at Edward's grave, she cleared away dead leaves and tangled weeds. She smoothed and cleaned until his tomb appeared just as well-kept as those of the American soldiers who were buried nearby. Suddenly the dead leaves swirled around her and the snow made small whirlpools on Edward's grave. Was he close by? She could almost feel his nearness.

She hurried to the gazebo. If he was here, this is where he'd come to her. "Edward," she whispered. "Edward. I have such a short time, please . . ." her words faded away on the frosty air.

Remaining in the gazebo, she gazed at a large oak. Was that a shadow she glimpsed? She rose, moving slowly forward. Did something or someone move?

A couple ambled along the path but that wasn't what she had seen. She dashed to the tree, searching in every direction, but all was silent. Edward wasn't coming. Her heart sank. Didn't he understand that she had only one more morning?

Head down, she left the park, stopping at the same cafe she'd previously been. She ordered a hot chocolate. Edward had joined her here once. Maybe he would again. Sipping the chocolate, the hot liquid trickled down her throat, warming her. The memory of Edward's sudden appearance came back to her. He'd sat opposite her in this same booth.

At last Cathy walked home, feeling a deep disappointment.

Hannah had stayed at the hospital. She had left a tuna salad in the refrigerator, but Cathy wasn't hungry. She plodded up the stairs to her room.

She flung herself on her bed. Tomorrow at this time she'd be getting off the plane. Mike would be there. Mom, Johnny, and Zack. She'd soon have to make many decisions. Would she accept Zack's invitation to go out to dinner? And how would she feel toward Mike? She couldn't deny she wanted to see him.

Mike had many of Edward's attributes:

steady, solemn, and straightforward. And many of Bryan's traits: fun-loving and charming.

"Oh, Mike," she whispered in an agony of indecision. "I miss you, but do I still love you as deeply as I did two weeks ago?!"

Chapter 29

Sitting at the dressing table, Cathy gazed at Edward's medallion and wished she could wear it tonight. But she knew she couldn't. She brushed her hair and as she did, she smiled, suddenly recalling driving with Mike to Six Flags Great America, the largest amusement park in Illinois. She hadn't expected him to give up a whole day, but what fun they had had.

It had been a September day when they drove north, out of Chicago. Mike had the top down on his red convertible, and they'd delighted in seeing the trees ablaze with red and gold leaves. And how the sun tingled on their warm faces.

Like two kids let out of school for the day, they had laughed and romped. They rode one roller coaster after another. But the American Eagle, the largest, had been the most thrilling. How she'd screamed, clinging to Mike as their car dipped and climbed, flew around loops, and careened around hairpin turns.

They'd shot the Roaring Rapids, done the Logger's Run, and gone down the Splash Waterfall. The boat ride on the Roaring Rapids had been the most exciting, simulating a whitewater rapids expedition. They'd been soaking wet when they disembarked from that one.

They tried out every ride available. They ate cotton candy and the froth had left a pink rim around her mouth. Laughingly, Mike had kissed off the sugar mixture. Nothing had tasted better than his sweet lips. As long as she was with Mike, she felt a bubbling joy. He, too, enjoyed the day. How handsome he looked, the sun sparkling over his face, reflecting a radiant inner happiness.

Slowly she put down the brush. She'd never forget that day. They'd played games in the arcade and Mike had won, presenting her with a stuffed panda. They finished the day by going on her favorite ride, even though it was the most tame. The two-story carousel with its beautiful animals, especially the wooden horses painted in white, black, and brown, trimmed in gold gilt and their reins in every color of the rainbow, was a breathtaking sight. She elected to ride on the swan and Mike chose a camel.

By two o'clock they were exhausted and stopped for hot dogs with all the trimmings. Mike had told her he loved her and she couldn't get enough of looking into his eyes. They'd held hands in the great screen entertainment center and every once in awhile he'd kiss her.

She put down her brush. Now she was going to the movies with Bryan, but she no longer felt guilty about seeing him. She was confident they were just friends and that when she was gone they'd both return to their former relationships.

She reached for her purse and slipped Mike's picture from her wallet. His dazzling white teeth against his dark skin and his old familiar wide smile were reassuring and she held the picture against her heart. "Darling Mike," she said softly, "I'll see you tomorrow and we'll be in love again."

But when Edward intruded on her thoughts, she could only hope she and Mike could resume their love.

When the doorbell rang, Cathy ran down to greet Bryan. When she opened the door, Bryan said in an approving voice, "Hello, there!" He stood in the doorway giving her his slow grin. "Ms. Cathy O'Brien, you're my dream come true."

She chuckled. "Hi, Bryan." Suddenly, she

was in a good mood, too. Bryan had that affect on people.

"We're meeting Phil and Susan at the theater," Bryan said, escorting her to his two-seater sports car.

"I hate to see you go," Bryan said, starting the car and wheeling out with one hand. His other arm was draped casually over her shoulder.

"Yes, this has been a fun-packed vacation," Cathy agreed. Fun, however, wasn't exactly the word she would use where Edward was concerned. There was too much sadness connected with her Revolutionary War soldier. He had loved life, too. Perhaps in a more sedate way. He'd shown her eighteenth-century London. What would he think if she could show him twentieth-century Chicago? The cars, skyscrapers, art museums, parks, food, homes, paved highways, phones, radios, television, VCRs, CDs, electric kitchens, electric everything, books, libraries. Oh, it would be so wonderful to show him her world.

"What's the first thing you'll do when you arrive home?" Bryan asked, glancing at her.

"Wh — what?" She returned to the present.

Bryan repeated his question.

"Everyone will meet me at the plane," Cathy said in a thoughtful voice. "Even Zack, my mother's friend. Sure, I've been busy every moment in Princeton, but I've still missed everyone in Chicago. Even my cat, Phineas!"

Bryan laughed. "I'll bet you have a lot of friends, besides Mike, I mean."

"Yes, I have two close friends, Liz and Dana." Just saying their names made her feel guilty. She hadn't given them a thought this entire vacation. She wondered how their Christmas holiday had turned out.

Bryan parked and Cathy noticed Phil and Susan by the poster of *Bittersweet Love*, the movie they were to see. Bittersweet. The word described Edward's love perfectly.

The sad film had Cathy fishing for her hanky, but before she could find it, Bryan handed her one. Smiling through her tears, she whispered her thanks.

After the film, they went to a Chinese restaurant around the corner.

"I could eat an order of Mongolian beef by myself," Bryan said.

Susan read the menu. "I know what I want. Moo shu pork and egg drop soup."

"Everything looks delicious," Cathy said. "But don't you think three dishes are enough for the four of us?"

With a flourish, Bryan closed his menu.

"Let's have four dishes. And I'll order."

Susan wagged her head at her brother. "You think you always know best, Bryan, but don't forget my preference when you order."

The waiter placed a big pot of tea before them and four tiny cups. By each place he put chopsticks encased in paper.

"Your order, please?" he asked with a bow.

Bryan cleared his throat and rattled off a feast. "We'll start with egg rolls and crab Rangoons, followed by egg drop soup, Mongolian beef, moo shu pork, hot and spicy shrimp, and cashew chicken." He stopped.

"Very good," the waiter said, pouring their tea.

When the food was brought, Cathy stared in amazement. "Who's able to eat all this?"

"Don't worry, we'll finish it," Bryan reassured her, using his chopsticks to spear a shrimp.

"Did you like the ending of the movie?" Susan asked.

Phil shook his head. "Too sad." He winked at Cathy. "I saw you shed a few tears."

"I did," Cathy admitted. "I like happy endings." Oh, she wished her own love life could have a happy ending.

"You're too sentimental," Bryan said. "The film had to end with Eddie's death."

Even the hero in the story was named Edward, although they called him Eddie. Was this a coincidence? A foreboding of what was in the future?

Suddenly Bryan put down his teacup and jumped up. He stared out the window. In distraction, he ran his fingers through his dark hair.

"Bryan!" Susan said. "Will you sit down? What did you see? Ann's blue car again?"

"No, it's Ann. She's standing across the street." His voice betrayed his emotions as he glanced at Cathy.

"Go to her, Bryan," she said softly. "Don't let Ann get away again."

Bryan squeezed Cathy's shoulder. And before their astonished eyes he bolted out the door.

Unabashedly, Cathy craned her neck. Bryan dashed across the street where Ann Bishop stood beneath the streetlight.

"She must have seen Bryan's car," Susan speculated. "He parked out front."

When Ann and Bryan embraced, then kissed, Cathy smiled. "Now there's a story with a happy ending."

"Don't you feel deserted?" Phil asked.

"Not at all. I understand perfectly," Cathy said in a low pleased voice. "I think Bryan has found his real love and I only hope he hangs on to her."

Susan gazed at Cathy with understanding eyes. "If anyone would understand, Cathy, it would be you."

Cathy lowered her eyes, not wanting any questions from Phil.

"We'll take you home," Phil offered.

"Thanks," Cathy said, still caught up in the drama across the street. The two lovers were talking, their heads together. Ann laughed. Then Bryan held up a finger to indicate he'd be right back. He rushed into the restaurant. "Would you . . ."

Cathy laughed. "Take Ann home, Bryan. Forget about me. I have a ride."

"Bryan," Phil said, grinning at him. "I think you should finish all this food first!"

"You're the one who insisted on four orders," Susan reminded him.

They all laughed at Bryan's look of dismay.

"Will you get out of here?" Phil growled. "Quit standing around."

"Good-bye, Cathy." Bryan's eyes sparkled with warmth. "Did anyone ever tell you, you're pretty special!" He leaned over, kissing her on the cheek.

"Begone, fair knight!" Cathy ordered in a

teasing voice, "afore thy fair damsel disappears."

"Thanks," Bryan shouted, waving his cap in the air and racing out to Ann.

Cathy watched as a smiling Ann climbed in Bryan's car. Then Bryan drove away. Devil-may-care Bryan was out of her life forever.

"We've got a lot of food to finish," Phil said. "Any more moo shoo pork?"

Both girls shook their head.

"Well, I'm going to take home a doggie bag," Phil said. "Who knows, I might want to have a midnight snack."

The waiter brought four fortune cookies. Phil cracked his open and read, "Straightforwardness without the rules of propriety, becomes rudeness." He cocked his head. "I'll buy that."

Next Susan broke open her cookie and read, "Recompense injury with justice and recompense kindness with kindness." Her gaze slid over to Cathy. "What does yours say?"

Cathy read hers silently, a feeling of dread stealing over her. Slowly she read, "To love a thing means wanting it to live." She put the cookie down without eating it, thinking of Edward. Oh, yes, she did want him to live!

"I'll save Bryan's," Susan said, sticking the

wrapped cookie in her pocket. "Shall we go?"

Cathy nodded, glad Susan didn't comment on her fortune.

Phil and Susan drove her home.

Cathy kissed Susan a tearful good-bye. "Promise you'll visit," she said.

"Look for me over spring vacation," Susan said.

" 'Bye, Cathy," Phil said. "Have a safe trip."

"Write!" Susan called.

"I will," Cathy promised, going up the walk.

Going inside, Cathy was pleased her aunt was still awake.

"Hi, Cathy." Aunt Hannah stood at the head of the stairs, wearing a terry robe. "How was your evening?"

"Bryan and Ann are back together," Cathy said, climbing the steps.

"Oh. Did that ruin your evening?"

"Not at all. I'm glad they found each other," Cathy said, smiling.

"Then I'm glad, too," Hannah yawned.

"Looks like you're ready for bed, Aunt Hannah."

"Yes, I just got home from the hospital." She chuckled. "I think Frank would have kept me there all night, if he could."

"I'm going to bed," Cathy said, giving her

aunt a good night kiss. "I'll take my usual walk in the morning."

"Fine. We'll leave for La Guardia at noon." Hannah tilted her head, giving Cathy a warm smile. "Sleep well."

"Good night, Aunt Hannah," Cathy said, entering her room. She should pack, but she'd wait until morning. It would only take a few minutes. She slipped on her nightgown and brushed her teeth. Hearing a slight scratching noise, she stopped to investigate. She glanced in every corner. Nothing.

Suddenly, the shade flew up.

She froze. The wind began to howl and branches scraped against her window pane. An insistent tap-tap on the glass startled her and she ran to see what it was.

Strangely, she felt calm and unfrightened. The snow-covered ground, shimmering in the moonlight, was empty. Or was it? She stared at what looked like a white wraith. The figure skimmed over the snow and vanished among the trees.

Cathy flung open the window. "Edward! Edward!" she called. But the only sound was the wind. And the only movement was curtains billowing out into the room and Cathy's hair streaming behind her. "Edward," she said softly, but there was no response.

For a long time Cathy sat in the window, straining her eyes, and waiting, waiting.

The wind stopped and it became quiet. As quickly as the wind had arisen, it just as quickly died down.

Cathy went to bed, wondering if Edward had tried to communicate with her. At last she fell asleep, but her dreams were troubled by images of a sorrowful Edward.

Chapter 30

At dawn Cathy dressed, then slipped Edward's medallion over her head. He would be pleased she wore it close to her heart. Glancing out the window, she saw the fog had rolled in. The thought ran through her head that if the airport were socked in, no planes would fly.

Her heart ached for Edward. Last night he'd been near, but hadn't appeared. It left her with an eerie feeling. Was Edward gone forever?

She went downstairs, and out the door. Breaking into a run she raced to the gazebo, praying Edward would be there. But nothing stirred in the early light. As she waited she felt alone, white mist enveloping her. She could no longer see the tombstones from here. "Edward," she called. "Please. I'm frightened. Where are you? Won't you come to me?"

As if Edward had heard her cry, he materialized out of the gloom, limping toward her.

She stared in disbelief. Edward not only limped, but his once beautiful uniform was now torn and bloody. His matted blond hair curled around his bandaged head. His sad state shattered her.

"Cathy," Edward said softly. "You see me as I appeared in my final day of the Battle of Princeton."

"Oh, my dearest," Cathy whispered, racing into his arms. "What did they do to you?" Her throat thickened, choked with pain.

"It's what happens in war," Edward said matter-of-factly, holding her in his arms and smoothing her hair.

She buried her head against his uniform, her eyes brimming with tears.

Edward tipped up her head up and kissed her teardrops. She closed her eyes as his head descended, his gray lips touching hers. His cold mouth and cheeks alarmed her. Her arms tightened around him. If only she could hold him this way, he'd never leave.

He smiled, gazing at the medal she wore. "I'm glad you're wearing the Marsh lion's crest."

"I'll wear it forever," she vowed, taking his hand and leading him to the gazebo. Although he limped and his bullet wound bloodied his uniform, he didn't complain.

"Sit, here, my darling," Cathy urged, her heart breaking. His face was white and his blue eyes dull, but he smiled at her and obediently sat beside her. In silence, they clung to each other, content to be in each other's arms.

"Edward," Cathy said, breaking the quiet, "did you tap on my window last night?"

He nodded, but didn't speak.

"I longed to see you," Cathy said, gazing into his blue eyes. "Where were you?"

"Don't you know I'm with you every moment?" Edward's words were slow and halting, but his square jaw and angular face had strength and a kind of serenity.

Cathy took his icy hand in hers. She laid her head on his chest. "I've never felt so close to you."

"If you desired, we could remain like this always," Edward said. But his brows drew together in an anguished frown, as if he guessed she wouldn't stay.

Words wouldn't come. She couldn't reply. The only sound was the drip, drip of water from the ice-covered branches.

"Promise you won't forget me," Edward said, a wistful smile touching his lips.

"How could I? You'll be engraved on my heart forever," Cathy said in a soft voice.

"I must be gone," Edward said, rising. "But

here is a little poem I want you to remember me by:

> All my past Life is mine no more,
>   The flying Hours are gone:
> Like Transitory Dreams giv'n o'er,
> Whose Images are kept in store
>   By Memory alone.

She nodded. "We'll have our memories." Cathy hugged him tighter. "Don't leave me."

"I must, darling Cathy." Gently, he pulled away. "You're my one love. I've dreamed of a girl like you all my life." He added, ironically, "Short as it was."

Tears sprang to her eyes. "Edward. Edward."

"Don't cry, my sweet." He rose. Then he said frantically, "You can accompany me, if you will." He walked a few steps away from the gazebo. Turning, he held out his hand and pleaded, "Hurry, Cathy. Come with me."

Her heart twisted in agony. She stepped forward, holding out her hand. As she moved toward him, however, she stumbled, then halted.

Edward's voice echoed through the mist.

"Cathy," he called. "Are you coming? I need you."

"I can't. I can't," she whispered. She watched as he slowly moved into the white fog, now swirling about him. Before Edward vanished forever, her last glimpse was of his red coat. Soon he was lost, swallowed up by the vaporous fog. It was as if he'd never been.

"Edward," she called, but she knew there would be no answer. Hopelessness washed over her. Edward Marsh was gone. Cathy touched the medallion, but to her astonishment, it was missing!

Frantically, she searched every inch of the pavilion, but the medallion had vanished. The lion's crest was the one treasure she had to remember Edward by. She sank to the floor of the gazebo, sobs racking her body.

She had been left without Edward and nothing remained but a void. It was as if he never existed. Tears streamed down her face.

After what seemed like hours, she got to her feet, exhausted. Miserably, she wiped her eyes, glancing about. Sun rays peeped through the lifting fog. With heavy steps she turned toward home.

But as she neared her aunt's, she paused. Edward had left her with wonderful memories.

He needed the medallion more than she. The thought was satisfying. Now, she was going home to Chicago. Back to her own world. Her own life. Back to Mike.

She entered the house and Aunt Hannah met her. "Cathy, would you like to stop at the hospital before we drive to New York?"

"Oh, yes, I don't want to go without saying good-bye to Uncle Frank," Cathy said with a positive nod.

"Have you been crying?" her aunt said with concern.

She supposed her tear-streaked face gave her away. "Yes," she replied honestly. "But I'm all right now." She was thankful Aunt Hannah didn't pry. "I'd better pack." She gave her aunt a reassuring smile. "We'll be leaving soon."

"Yes, we'll go to see Frank about eleven." Hannah chuckled. "You should see him. Pacing the floor, waiting for the doctor's final okay to go home."

"He's tough," Cathy said, climbing the stairs. "Be down in a minute."

In her room, she folded clothes and placed them in the bag, but every once in awhile she moved to the window. The bright sun danced on the melting ice. And the melting snow from the roof fell to the ground in a constant trickle.

She stared below at the patches of snow, hoping to glimpse Edward one last time, but in her heart she knew he'd never reappear. Her heart ached, not knowing what had happened to him. Did he go back to his grave? Did he walk the streets of London? She prayed he had started another life in another time. Maybe he'd find a new love who would adore and comfort him.

Finished packing, Cathy dressed for travel in Levi's and her oversized green sweater. She slipped into her sneakers and tied the laces.

Hurrying downstairs, she found her aunt waiting. "I need to look around," Cathy said. "It may be a long time before I return." She'd miss the fireplace and comfortable chairs where she and her aunt had their cozy chats.

Aunt Hannah observed her with a warm smile. "We did enjoy ourselves, didn't we?" She squeezed Cathy's hand affectionately. "I have a gift for you from my shop." She handed her niece a small gold-wrapped box. "Open it when you're on the plane, will you?"

"Oh, you're the nicest aunt anyone could have!" Cathy hugged Hannah.

As they were about to leave, the phone rang. "Will you get that, Cathy? I forgot my wallet." And Hannah hurried upstairs.

Cathy answered the phone, pleased to hear

Susan's voice. "I'm glad you called. We're almost ready to leave."

"Did you see Edward this morning?" Susan asked, her voice shaking.

"Oh, Susan, you should have seen him. He was wounded, his uniform bloody, his head bandaged." Cathy kept her voice low so Hannah wouldn't hear.

"How awful," Susan said.

"You can't know how awful, Susan. I felt so awful for him." Cathy's voice was low and sad. "But Edward is gone now. He won't return."

"I'm sorry," Susan said.

Cathy changed the subject. "Will I see you this spring?"

"I'll definitely be visiting in April," Susan promised.

"Great!" Cathy exclaimed. "Don't forget."

"Oh, one other thing. Now that Bryan and Ann are together again, he says this time it's for keeps." Susan laughed. "You should see him. He's walking on air!"

Hannah came downstairs.

Cathy nodded at her aunt. "We're off to the hospital and then the airport, Susan, so I must run. 'Bye. I'll write."

"I'll answer," Susan said, trying to keep her voice lighthearted. " 'Bye, Cathy."

Cathy threw her bag in the back of Hannah's

van and they drove to the hospital. Quickly, they ran up to Uncle Frank's room and found him eating lunch.

"Hello!" he said. "You look wonderful, Cathy. I see you're all set for your flight back."

"I am," Cathy said, smiling at him. "Go ahead with your lunch."

"Jell-O!" he snorted. "I can't wait to get home and have some real food!"

"Maybe your diet should be more bland than the menu I'd planned," Hannah said doubtfully, eyeing his tray.

"Nonsense!" Frank laughed heartily. "I feel I can eat anything." He grimaced, touching his side. "I'm a little sore is all."

They visited for thirty minutes, then Hannah said, "You know how bad traffic is. We'd better get started." She leaned down, giving Frank a kiss. "When I return, I'll come right to the hospital." She grinned. "Don't go away."

"Humph. As if I could." Frank glowered at her but his eyes twinkled.

" 'Bye, Uncle Frank," Cathy said, kissing his cheek. "I'll be back before you know it."

"You'd better!" Frank grinned and gave her a thumbs-up sign.

Cathy and Hannah left. Hannah backed out of the lot and drove along Nassau Street. As Cathy departed Princeton, she took her last look around. Driving by Battlefield Park, Cathy swallowed away the lump in her throat. Silently, she said, "Good-bye, Edward."

"When you return, Cathy," Hannah said, "we'll plan a day of shopping in New York and go to the theater."

Cathy thought a bit, then said, "When I come back, I'd like to stay right in Princeton. It's a marvelous town."

"I'm glad you feel that way," Hannah said, clearly pleased.

When they arrived at La Guardia Airport, Cathy gathered her things. "No need for you to go in with me, Aunt Hannah. Just drop me off at the United Airlines terminal. I'll be fine. And you don't want to get bogged down in parking."

"I wouldn't mind."

"No, Uncle Frank is waiting for you," Cathy said. "Thanks for everything."

So Aunt Hannah pulled up before United and kissed her niece good-bye. Her eyes were suspiciously moist. Cathy, too, swallowed back her tears. Not wanting to linger, she jumped out of the car. With a final wave, she hurried inside.

Chapter 31

Checking her bag at the United desk, Cathy glanced at her watch. Relieved she had plenty of time before takeoff, she bought a Coke and strolled to the waiting room. There, she found a seat and soon became engrossed in her mystery until her flight was called.

While Cathy waited, she glanced up to see a pilot in a smart uniform walking by. He gazed at her for a moment, and gave her a big smile. His dark hair and sparkling eyes resembled Bryan. For a moment she felt as if she were back in Princeton. Shaking her head, she smiled, too, and returned to her book.

"All passengers. Flight four-seven-three is ready for boarding." Cathy stuck her book in her tote bag and walked onto the plane. Finding her place, she was pleased she had the wide three seats to herself. She sat by the window as the plane lifted off and circled the skyscrapers of Manhattan. Then clouds closed in, obliterating her view. She was going home!

Once in the air, Cathy leaned back. Now she would forget Princeton and concentrate on her relationships in Chicago. She had many feelings to sort out.

When the flight attendant wheeled up a cart of drinks, he said, "What would you like?" Cathy looked over the assortment, opting for orange juice.

Sipping the tart juice, she reached into her pocket and took out Aunt Hannah's package. She almost hated to open the beautifully wrapped box, but her hesitation lasted only a moment. Untying the bow, she removed the tissue paper and lifted out a lovely porcelain box that fit into the palm of her hand. The little square box had gold fittings and a miniature painting on the lid. Looking more closely, her mouth dropped open and her breath caught in her throat. Her lips moved in disbelief, "Edward."

Just as surely as she was sitting here, the painting was of Edward Marsh! Blond hair, blue eyes, straight nose and fair skin were all his features! What an amazing likeness! And the uniform! She stared at the Revolutionary War uniform of the British Army. The red jacket and white cross straps were exactly what Edward had worn. The stern expression but warm eyes belonged to her British soldier. "Oh, Edward," she whispered, recalling his kindness and sweet manner. She may have lost the medallion, but she had a portrait of her eighteenth-century love!

"More orange juice?" the flight attendant asked, taking her cup.

Startled, Cathy looked up, closing her fingers over her precious box. "No, no, thank you."

She gazed at the miniature. This is the way she wanted to remember Edward, not as he had appeared to her this morning. Bloody and ghostlike. This was the Edward she had danced with, played croquet with, and picnicked with. This was the Edward she had embraced and kissed. Yes, he was her love from another time and another place. She'd never forget him. Never! She clasped the box to her heart. And now she owned a keepsake which would always preserve her memory of Edward. How strange that Aunt Hannah had chosen this particular gift. But her whole experience with Edward had been strange.

She slipped the box into her pocket and put her head back, closing her eyes. Her family would be waiting for her at the airport. She was eager to see her mother, Johnny, and

Mike, but she wasn't so sure about Zack. And he'd be there, too. How would she react to his presence? Oh, yes, she'd been taught her manners so she'd be civil to Zack, but could she ever be his friend?

She loved her mother very much. It hadn't been easy for her, either, when she had lost her husband. Cathy wasn't the only one who missed her father. Dylan did and so did Johnny.

And now Mom had found happiness with Zack. Was she going to be mean-spirited and stand in the way of her mother's new love?

Oh, she didn't know! She yanked the magazine from the seat's pouch in front of her and flipped through the pages, but she couldn't read a word. Soon, she shoved the magazine back in its place. What if her mother felt about Mike the way she felt about Zack? She couldn't bear to think of how wretched she'd be if her mother shunned Mike. And yet, wasn't that exactly the way she was treating Zack?

She remembered when Mike had brought her mother roses on her birthday. "Here, Sara," he had said, "these flowers aren't nearly as beautiful as you, but are a token of how I feel about one special lady."

Cathy bit her lip, remembering the silver earrings Zack had given her. Certainly, she didn't react the way her mother had when Mike had given her roses.

Sara had beamed and kissed Mike. It made Cathy feel warm and good, knowing they liked each other. Mom and Johnny loved Mike, too. They formed a circle of love. If Dylan were home from Oxford, she knew he'd like Mike. They had much in common. Mike, though, was more dedicated than anyone she'd ever known. Clearly he had a shining goal before him. How fortunate she had been to have found someone like Mike.

Remembering an incident last fall, Cathy laughed aloud. Guiltily, she glanced about, but no one paid any attention to her outburst. On an evening in late October, she and Mike had left the late movie and headed to the car. But as they neared his car, suddenly, out of an alley, a boy darted forward and snatched her purse.

"Stop, thief! Help!" she'd yelled. "Mike, he stole my purse!"

Immediately, Mike gave chase. When he caught up to the thief, he made a flying tackle and brought him to the sidewalk. Pinning his arms behind him, Mike retrieved her purse, but he refused to turn the scared boy over to the police. Instead he talked the young robber into attending his reading group and working for a high school diploma.

The boy agreed and even today Robert Bryant attended Mike's reading center.

Still smiling, Cathy's thoughts shifted to Bryan and Edward. How did Mike compare to each one? She'd thought of this before, but again she needed to go over Mike's attributes. She realized Mike Novak was just as straightforward and sensitive as Edward Marsh. And Mike was just as handsome, fun-loving and charismatic as Bryan Gorman. The more she realized this, the more she was certain of her love for Mike.

Mike had both of Bryan's and Edward's best characteristics. There was, however, one major difference. Mike was involved with other people's lives. He paid attention to their needs and gave assistance wherever he could. True, Edward appreciated beauty and longed to become a painter. Never once, however, had he given a thought to other people.

Bryan, too, planned to be a lawyer like his father. But not a lawyer who defended people who needed public assistance. No, he'd demand a big retainer and live in a mansion like his parents. He'd lead a lovely life. If Edward had lived, he would have led an aristocrat's life, too.

Mike was different. He was unique. He really needed to manage his reading center. Why was she angry when he called and said he needed to help José or someone else? If she truly wanted to be with him there were many things she could do at the reading center, too. She and Mike could be a team and still have time for fun and quiet times together. It was a once in a lifetime dream to be loved by someone like Mike.

All at once the pilot broke in on her thoughts. "We'll be landing at Chicago O'Hare in twenty minutes. Skies are clear at thirty-six degrees. Please fasten your seat belts."

Eagerly Cathy stared out the window. Large jets were taking off. At last the pilot landed and taxied to a stop at the United terminal.

The all-clear sign flashed on and passengers stood, taking down their luggage from the overhead compartments. They moved to the front. Oh, Cathy thought, standing on one foot then the other, please hurry.

After deplaning, Cathy walked quickly forward.

When she entered the United waiting room, she glanced around. At first she didn't locate anyone she knew.

"Cathy! Over here!"

She'd know Johnny's shrill shout anywhere.

Waving, Cathy saw Mike and dashed into his arms, smothering him with kisses.

"Cathy!" Johnny said in a loud peevish voice. "I'm over here!"

Chuckling, she turned and gave her little brother a big hug.

Next, she fell into her mother's open arms and embraced her. "It's good to be home," Cathy said, her heart full.

Sara said, "Cathy, I've missed you terribly. I'm glad you're back." She smiled, her eyes shining. "You look wonderful. Princeton must have agreed with you."

Cathy nodded. "Princeton was great. In more ways than one." Edward would remain locked in her heart forever. She added cheerfully, "I've got lots of news from Aunt Hannah and Uncle Frank."

"I want to hear all about it," Sara said.

Cathy eyed Zack. He was tall, tilting his head and giving her a questioning look. Although she couldn't bring herself to hug him, she did hold out her hand and smiled. "Hello, Zack," she said. "It's good to see you."

Pleased, Zack smiled, too, grasping her hand. "I hope you'll go to dinner with us, Cathy."

For an instant Cathy paused, glancing at Mike. Then she faced Zack and said warmly,

"I'd love to." The least she could do was give Zack a chance. She didn't even know him and this was her chance to become acquainted.

As they left the airport, Johnny danced around her, wanting to know all about Princeton and his aunt and uncle.

Laughing, Cathy threw one arm around Johnny and one arm around Mike. They threaded their way through crowds of travelers.

Once in the car, Zack drove into the city and to the steak house, smiling all the way.

Cathy leaned back in the car. It was good to be home.

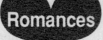

Romances

Dreamy Days...
Unforgettable
Nights

☐ BAK46313-6	First Comes Love #1: To Have and to Hold	$3.50
☐ BAK46314-4	First Comes Love #2: For Better or For Worse	$3.50
☐ BAK46315-2	First Comes Love #3: In Sickness and in Health	$3.50
☐ BAK46316-0	First Comes Love #4: Till Death Do Us Part	$3.50
☐ BAK46574-0	Forbidden	$3.50
☐ BAK45785-3	Last Dance	$3.25
☐ BAK45705-5	The Last Great Summer	$3.25
☐ BAK48323-4	Last Summer, First Love #1: A Time to Love	$3.95
☐ BAK48324-2	Last Summer, First Love #2: Good-bye to Love	$3.95
☐ BAK46967-3	Lifeguards: Summer's End	$3.50
☐ BAK46966-5	Lifeguards: Summer's Promise	$3.50
☐ BAK42553-6	The Party's Over	$3.25
☐ BAK45784-5	Saturday Night	$3.25
☐ BAK45786-1	Summer Nights	$3.25
☐ BAK44672-0	Winter Dreams, Christmas Love	$3.50
☐ BAK47610-6	Winter Love Story, A	$3.50
☐ BAK48152-5	Winter Love, Winter Wishes	$3.95

Available wherever you buy books, or use this order form.

**Scholastic Inc., P.O. Box 7502, 2931 East McCarty Street,
Jefferson City, MO 65102**

Please send me the books I have checked above. I am enclosing $_____
(please add $2.00 to cover shipping and handling). Send check or money
order — no cash or C.O.D.s please.

Name _____ Birthdate ___ / ___ / ___

Address _____

City _____ State/Zip _____ / _____

Please allow four to six weeks for delivery. Offer good in the U.S. only. Sorry, mail orders are not
available to residents of Canada. Prices subject to change.   R594